SHAD

G000147619

Marion Whybrow   o
   St Ives, Cornwa   ... husband,
Terry Whybrow, who is an artist. She began writing
for the local paper and these articles turned into
books on painters, potters and sculptors.
This is her first novel. It was shortlisted for the
Halsgrove/Western Morning News Peninsula Prize
in 2002.

Books by other publishers include:
St Ives 1883-1993 : Portrait of an Art Colony
The Leach Legacy : St Ives Pottery and its Influence
The Innocent Eye : Primitive & Naïve Painters in Cornwall
Bryan Pearce : A Private View
Virginia Woolf and Vanessa Bell : Remembering St Ives, *Marion
Dell & Marion Whybrow. Winner of a Holyer An Gof Gorseth
Kernow Award, 2003.*
Play
O.A.P. Rules OK
Smaller Books
Twenty Painters St Ives
Potters in Their Place
Forms & Faces : Sculptors in the South West
Twenty Two Painters who Happen to be Women
Studio : Artists in Their Workplace
Another View : Art in St Ives

SHADOW OVER SUMMER

Marion Whybrow

First published by Beach Books
Fauna Cottage, St Ives, Cornwall in 2004

ISBN 0 9522461 3 9

Designed by Kim Lynch
Riverside, Lelant, Cornwall

Printed by TJ I Digital
Padstow, Cornwall

Front Cover Photo – Porthminster Beach Café

'Cornubia'

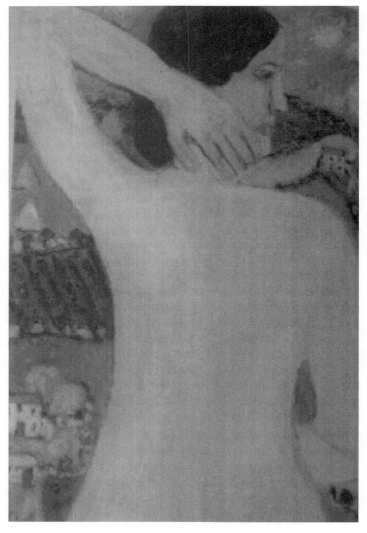

by Mary Jewels

1

The soft knocking of the yellow blind against the window was a reminder that they were here at last. Their house; their view of the sea; their riotous seagulls flying home to the cliffs; their small town, pricked with tiny beacons of light. The shush of waves gently lifting and falling on the beach below was their lullaby. The warm west wind, blowing across the bay, puffed through the open bedroom window and brought the scent of sea pinks and wet sand.

Standing on the balcony of her room at Talland House, Rosemary Knight thought of the woman who had stood on this same balcony one hundred years ago. Julia Stephen, a woman of some importance in the town, had stood looking out to sea, troubled by the poverty of the families of fisherfolk in St Ives. Her own daughters, and the rest of her family, had all the comforts they needed, and didn't require too much thought.

Julia's sympathies were with the obvious poor and needy, the women struggling to find food for their many children when the fishing was poor. And the men who sat on the wharf, anxious to launch their boats from the harbour; waiting for the cry of 'Hevva, Hevva,' from the watcher on the cliffs, to signal that a shoal of pilchard was swarming into the bay.

How different life in the town was today, Rosemary

mused. Now the pilchard never swarmed, and the fishermen had gone from the wharf. Very few boats put out to sea. Only the lone small boat, hoping to catch a few mackerel or empty their crab pots, left the harbour, and ventured round Smeaton's Pier. Now the Cornish Luggers were a quaint spectre of their working past. They ferried holiday makers to Seal Island, and trips round the Bay, their operators touting for custom outside the new lifeboat house.

In the adjoining balconied room Rosemary Knight's twin daughters, Demelza and Lamorna, were sleeping where the two Victorian girls of the same age had slept. They too were freed from the restrictions of city life and enjoyed their summers in Cornwall. They played cricket on the beach, and in the gardens surrounding Talland House. At that time the grounds were extensive. Now the grape house was demolished, the tennis lawn reduced to a car park and the rose garden a wilderness, with trees that had grown taller over a century.

Only the front garden, with its terrace was the same, shielded from the road by the escallonia hedge. The front gate and the steps, down which flowed an unstoppable natural spring, were never used as an entrance. At least the house remained, to be enjoyed by summer visitors.

'Some things never change,' Rosemary said aloud, looking at the stars. There too, was Godrevy lighthouse, reminding her that Virginia Woolf, one of the Victorian children, had become a famous author; her sister, Vanessa Bell, a noted artist. In their childhood, the beam from the lighthouse had flashed across the bay and lit up their nursery, night after night. Now it was a brief blip, winking every ten seconds. It would never disturb the darkness of the sky, or bounce off the surface of the ocean.

Rosemary Knight pulled the wrap round her shoulders, gave a small shudder, and closed the French doors. Tomorrow she would begin her novel. Tomorrow, the writing would flow with the release she felt in being in this house. It was Cornwall, and Talland House, that would bring about the ideas and inspiration for her work of fiction. She just knew it.

The house woke early. Rosemary and her daughters, Demelza and Lamorna flung open their doors to the morning and, at the same time, stepped out onto their balconies.

'It's going to be a fine day,' Rosemary said, looking out over that vast bowl of blue ocean.

'It's going to be a lovely day. Can't wait to get to the beach, Mum.' The girls hugged each other in the excitement of the expected sunshine and a golden day spent on Porthminster beach. Down Primrose Valley, three hundred metres below the house, the little coastal train that ran from the main line to St Ives, was already full of visitors taking their first breath of surprised delight at the harbour scene laid out before them.

'I'll make up a picnic for you,' Rosemary said. 'I want you out of the way while I get started on my writing. I shall sit in the garden under the sunshade, and I don't want to be disturbed for three or four hours.'

As far as the girls were concerned, this was the best

thing they could hope for, to be left on their own to explore the beach and wander into the town.

'Don't worry, Mum. We'll leave you entirely alone,' Demelza said, 'You'll probably have to send out a search party for us.'

'Or maybe even the lifeboat,' Lamorna laughed.

'Be sensible,' their mother said. 'I don't want to have to worry about you.'

'We're only joking Mum,' they assured her, softening the blow.

While the girls dressed and sorted out everything they would need for a whole day on the beach, Rosemary prepared the picnic.

'Give Joan my love, and tell her I'll be down at the café when I've got myself sorted out,' she called, waving them goodbye.

'We'll tell her to keep the kettle boiling,' Lamorna said.

'And the teapot warm,' Demelza joked.

The girls arrived at the beach clutching their bags of sun lotion, towels, drinks and sandwiches. They deposited their packages on a beach mat on a carefully chosen spot in front of the Porthminster beach café and made for a table on the terrace.

'Are you on your own Demelza?' Joan said, looking for Rosemary to appear.

'Yes. Mum said she'll see you later,' Lamorna answered.

'Oh well. Enjoy yourselves.' Joan introduced them to Brad and Dave, two of the young Australian waiters. 'Watch out for this precious pair,' she told the boys.

At twelve the twins considered themselves old enough to be moving into the cappuccino drinking crowd. In London they met their friends on Saturday mornings at Starbucks, in Finchley Road, thankful to be wearing proper clothes, having thrown their school uniforms to the back of the wardrobe.

They moved into fashion gear and away from white shirts, timetables and bundles of back-breaking books and homework. At the moment they were apeing the bare midriff of the older girls. Rosemary called it their 'never the twain shall meet' style. They were quite happy supporting tee-shirts, trainers and sweat-shirts advertising fashion shops, but not a modest logo for their school.

'It's gross Mum,' they moaned. Their complaint was of the white lettering on blue contained within a biscuit sized circle. The advert for their favourite shop spread itself hugely across their chests in six-inch tall letters.

'I think you've misunderstood the word gross,' their mother said. Nevertheless, she retrieved their uniforms from their hiding place at the back of the wardrobe, washing and ironing where necessary, and hanging the refreshed clothing in readiness for Monday's return to school. The girls accepted this with nonchalant grace. It was understood that they discarded and their mother retrieved.

'I think,' said Lamorna, licking the cappuccino foam from her top lip, 'that I shall call myself something

5

simple, like Ann.'

'How would you like to be called Demelza? I sound like a pudding. "Would you like Cornish cream, or ice cream, with your Demelza?" I bet it's not a Cornish name.'

'Oh, hang on,' Lamorna said. 'I've just seen the name on that boat.'

'Which boat?'

'The one unloading the fish.'

Down on the beach, the chef from the Porthminster café was hauling in a basket from a small fishing boat hovering in the shallows off-shore which, but for the skill of its skipper, was in danger every second of being beached. With the catch safely in the hands of the chef, he gave the thumbs up for mission accomplished, released the line, and the boat backed off churning up sand. The crew shouted a raucous farewell, and the boat turned and sped away. On its side was clearly marked 'Demelza.'

'See, you're OK. That proves your name is Cornish.'

'Maybe there's a boat in the harbour with your name on it. Let's go and look '

The girls were temporarily diverted from this discussion as they watched the chef, accompanied by a posse of small children, making his way to the café. Staff from the kitchen brought out some weighing scales. Looking down from their table on the terrace to the path beneath them, they watched as the chef took his catch of lobster out of the basket, weighing each one. They were alive, but handicapped by having their claws firmly bound with twine. The children on the beach were at once excited and repulsed by the fearful struggling creatures. The chef held up one of the lobsters and thrust it towards the curious children. They stepped back and screamed.

'Ugh! What is it?' shrieked the city children.

Sitting on the beach in their sun tops and wrap around skirts, and liberally stroking sun lotion onto their perfect young skins, the twins, unaware of anything save themselves, were watched by a man close by. They were so self-absorbed that he had no trouble concealing the fact that he was interested in them. George Tatum occasionally looked around to see that no one was observing him. The beach was gradually filling up and people were busy staking out their area and erecting their windbreaks and tents.

Feeling confident, George opened up his rucksack and pulled out a video camera. He stood up, climbed high up on the steps leading to the beach, and began filming the activity of the Carbis Bay Women's Gig boat rowing just off shore but, eventually, he trained his lens onto the unsuspecting girls as they lay side by side, eyes closed, wrap around skirts exposing their legs. Their lean, young, bodies stretched out to absorb the sun safely through their 20 factor sun cream. 'Ah!' he murmured, licking his lips. 'Mine.'

Although they visited St Ives, every year, it was five years since the family last stayed at Talland House. Then the twins were seven years old. It was where

Rosemary had written most of her first novel. It was a success. The second was a failure by comparison and, desperate that this third novel should succeed, she had chosen to write it at St Ives, believing that she had gained inspiration and a certain ease of writing in this lovely place.

After all, she argued, Virginia Woolf based much of her writing on Cornwall. Her letters and diaries were full of references to times past and her love of the place. Certainly, her novel *To The Lighthouse* revolved around her family's stay at Talland House, recreating a picture of her childhood. Why shouldn't Rosemary be equally stimulated and motivated in this very spot?

Rosemary had intended renting only the lower flat but her three sisters, on hearing she was going to Cornwall, insisted that they should also have a holiday. 'You can write your novel in the first week,' they laughed, not caring or understanding the difficulties of a writer, the sheer dogged labour, and the necessity of being alone with your thoughts. 'You can come out and about with us when we come down in the second week, and in the third and fourth week you can write two more novels.' It was hilarious to her sisters that Rosemary had turned to writing novels, after a fairly successful career as a writer and researcher on art and artists.

'I think you're clutching at straws,' Patsy her agent had said when Rosemary voiced her anxieties about her lack of ability to begin writing. 'Going away is not going to solve the problem. You just write anything to get you going,' she advised. 'I've known this happen to many writers. You have to overcome your fear. Put your pen on the paper and away it'll go.'

'It's not self-propelling,' Rosemary remarked drily.

She was disheartened by Patsy's attitude. She had expected support and sympathy. Her husband, Lewis, had given his opinion in very much the same manner. She felt totally isolated.

'I don't understand the problem, but I know what Cornwall means to you. Me too, you know,' he said grudgingly, 'but if you think it will help, do go. I'll manage. I'll pop down for a few weekends.'

Only the girls had championed her going off to the seaside, and their support had been self-interested. They were looking forward to welcoming three aunts about to arrive in St Ives, being treated by them, and keeping their own money safely in their pockets.

Rosemary wanted to see her friend Joan at the Porthminster café. It would be a good start to the day to be greeted by a friendly smile, but she willed herself to begin work and immediately set about establishing her base on the lawn, setting up the table in front of the escallonia hedge. Her chair was stuffed with cushions. Now there was the ritual of placing her writing pad at the centre, with pencils, rubber and pencil sharpener along the top. On the right, she placed her pens, one black and one blue. She couldn't use her laptop computer out in the open; it belonged on a desk with her printer and scanner.

It was a perfect day, with no wind, but sunscreen would be needed and was liberally applied. She picked up a pencil, examining its finely sharpened point. She emptied the pencil sharpener and rearranged the pens, checked her watch. She would just have to try and relax, Rosemary told herself. By her side she noticed the pinky red flowers on the hedge. She thought about Virginia and Vanessa. They would have had difficulty trying to see through a hedge that thick.

Rosemary remembered Virginia Woolf's description of the four young Stephens' trip to Cornwall in 1905. She, with her sister, Vanessa, and brothers Thoby and Adrian, returned to this beloved house, ten years after the death of their mother and their last holiday here. They visited the place in the dusk, peering through the escallonia hedge and watching a new family occupying the rooms that had once provided them with so much happiness, and so many memories.

Virginia was only a few months old when she was first carried over the threshold, and thirteen when the family relinquished the lease on the house. Vanessa was three when she toddled forth into the garden and fifteen when she left.

Rosemary recalled that during that memorable visit to St Ives the Stephen children witnessed a shoal of pilchards in the bay. Virginia Woolf wrote of it years later.

"It was only in 1905 when, after father's death, we four took a little lodging house at Carbis Bay, that the pilchards came; and we rowed out early one morning and the sea bubbled and spat with silver. I remember some stranger in the next boat shovelling an armful out of that bubbling mass into our boat."

10

Like Virginia Woolf, Rosemary was no stranger to Cornwall. She and Lewis had been visiting when she was pregnant with the twins. They were staying for the weekend at the Lamorna hotel to be near the Minack open-air Theatre. Lewis had booked tickets for the last performance of *A Midsummer Night's Dream.* Rosemary's childhood friend, Leah Carmichael, was one of Titania's fairies. The night was truly magical. A full moon rode in the sky and almost obliterated the stage lights. Into the ocean backdrop sailed a flotilla of fishing boats returning with their catch to Newlyn Harbour.

'There's nothing quite like flitting across the stage in a diaphanous, flimsy costume and being upstaged by a natural spectacular.' Leah said, greeting her friends after the show. 'But at least I had no words to learn.'

They treated Leah to dinner at the hotel, and an overnight stay. In the morning the three of them followed the stream and woods walking down to Lamorna Cove, noting the studios and houses occupied by the Lamorna artists at the turn of the nineteenth century, then drove to St Ives to stay a couple of days with Leah.

On the last day of that visit Rosemary persuaded Lewis to take a trip to Zennor. They lunched at the Tinners' Arms and visited the village church. During a wander round the churchyard they had come across the name Demelza on an ancient tombstone.

'If the twins were born in Cornwall, they could have Cornish names.' Rosemary said. And so it happened.

Rosemary was anxious to see the bench end in the

church, carved in the shape of a mermaid. 'I believe it's got magical powers,' she said, laughing and sitting on the worn wooden bench, not believing in those powers. She sat there quietly while Lewis looked round the church.

'Right,' he said, returning to the seat, and then he was alarmed to see her bent over, holding her back and breathing heavily.

'What's happening? Rosemary, are you OK? Has it started? Shall we call an ambulance? Tell me what to do.'

'I feel as if I've just been kicked,' she said, 'but no ambulance needed.'

'Stay awhile,' Lewis advised, as she attempted to get to her feet.

'It was just a spasm. I've been having them on and off the past couple of hours; but that was a big one.'

'You should have told me,' Lewis protested.

On the way back to St Ives Rosemary went into labour. Lewis made straight for the small maternity unit in Penzance. Within a few hours their premature babies were born and because of their safe arrival and their debt to the local hospital, (and especially the Mermaid, who had made it happen) they adopted the Cornish names of Lamorna and Demelza.

A few months later the family returned to Zennor to have the babies christened. Rosemary wrote to the vicar seeking permission, giving as her reason that she had gone into labour sitting on the Mermaid bench, implying that the church owed some responsibility for the early arrival of the girls. 'I hope this fits the description of divine intervention, through the medium of your mermaid.'

In writing his reply, the vicar agreed, entering into the humour of the request. 'I fully accept liability for the deviant behaviour of our incumbent mermaid. And I will be delighted to christen the Cornish twins.'

'Does it mean he accepts the Pagan story of the mermaid luring the vicar's son to her cave under the sea?' Rosemary asked Lewis.

'I would say he doesn't give a fig for the story of the mermaid. If it gets people into his church, then his prayers are answered.'

'He might also believe in fairies,' Leah said. 'I'm sure my moonlit performance on the Minack stage had something to do with the birth too. I claim my right to name one of the twins. Call the younger one Lamorna.'

The Knights wanted Cornish godparents for their Cornish twins. Over the years Rosemary had struck up a friendship with the owner of a local bookshop. Rachel had helped with many aspects of research for Rosemary's articles on the art colony of St Ives and Newlyn. They met on every visit to St Ives for lunch in the town, or at Rachel and Desmond Penhaligan's farmhouse on the outskirts of Penzance.

'I've never been a godparent, but I think Desmond and I would be good at it. Yes. We'd be delighted,' Rachel said. And so it proved. On every visit the twins spent days in the fields with their horses, or grooming them in the stables in wet weather. They had learnt to ride and handle the horses, sitting between Rachel and Desmond from the age of two, whereas Rosemary had barely patted a flank, being rather in awe of the animals' size and strength.

For the christening the family lodged with the Penhaligans. It was spring, the Knight's favourite time for visiting. They walked through the woods and laid the babies among the vibrant bluebells growing in clumps beneath the trees with their delicate spring greenery. The entrance to the small estate was through hedges of rhododendrons, hydrangeas, camellias, escallonia and fuscia, growing in wild abundance in Cornwall. The lane then turned and the house was suddenly there, a Georgian manor, like something out of Jane Austen. The house was full of antique furniture, inherited from previous generations, whose portraits lined the generous staircase.

Rosemary, dreaming by the hedge, roused herself from her writing space in the garden to make coffee. She had yet to write her first sentence, but she was thirsty. Entering the house through the front door and temporarily blinded by the sunlight in the garden, she thought she saw a staircase going up from the wide hall. She was startled, but on blinking her eyes, realised it was a trick of the light. There may well have been a staircase in the Stephen's time, but now the whole house was given over to holiday apartments and the ground floor was completely cut off from the flats above. The entrance to those apartments was by outside staircases built on the back of the house.

Rosemary and the girls occupied the first floor

14

apartments because of the balconies, where the doors could be left open on hot June nights. The view out to the bay and the lighthouse was delightful, day or night. During the day, Rosemary made use of the downstairs apartment because of the proximity to the garden. The sisters would sleep here when they arrived, and they would all use the big kitchen and dining room.

Next week, Rosemary told herself, I shall be able to do nothing. Lewis will be here and my sisters. I really must get started. She left the dark kitchen with her mug of coffee and thought she caught a glimpse of herself in a mirror in the hall as she passed a particular spot. She was so surprised, that she stopped, and walked back. She was looking at was a blank wall. 'How odd,' she said aloud, and continued walking to the garden, thinking no more about it.

The first sentence turned into a paragraph, and the paragraph into several, and then the first page was completed. Rosemary began to feel the weight of anxiety falling away. She took several sips of coffee and then forgot about her thirst, her worries, the garden, the hedge, and even the twins, flaunting their long limbs on the beach.

Time stretched into the afternoon, and still Rosemary wrote in a headlong rush, not allowing her surroundings to disturb her concentration. Bird song went unheeded and unheard. Cars arrived and departed in the nearby car park. Guests at the local hotels left the beach to dress for dinner. People toiled up Primrose Valley with their sandy belongings, leaving the beach fractured with a thousand footprints. The scavengers, with their metal detectors, moved in to sweep up the odd coins fallen from trouser pockets and purses.

Finally, the spell of writing was broken. Rosemary put down her pen and massaged her aching wrist. What had disturbed her so abruptly? Distinctly, from a short distance away, she heard the thud of bat and ball and the excited sound of children's laughter.

'Make way for the demon bowler,' a boy's voice called.

'Oh well played, Ginia!' called another.

'Howzat?' There was clapping.

'Yours, Nessa – Oh well caught.'

'Out!' a triumphant girl yelled.

There was certainly a fierce game being played somewhere over the hedge towards the car park. The girls must have found some friends to play with; but surely not among the cars? It used to be a lawn, long ago. Virginia Woolf's description of the garden came to mind, "the coffee garden; the fountain; the cricket ground; the love corner; the strawberry bed; the kitchen garden; the pond; and the big tree." There was certainly less garden now than the two or three acres of Virginia's time.

The sounds of the children's voices and a game of cricket continued. Rosemary rose stiffly to investigate; as she opened the gate on the pathway to the house, she saw Lamorna and Demelza, loaded with their beach gear, wearily toiling up towards her.

Immediately the girls came into view, the voices ceased. Rosemary knew they had not been involved in a game. There was no group of friends with them and they were sulky, as so often these days. No point questioning them. She would only get a curt reply. No use telling them of her experience. They would look at each other and raise their eyes to heaven, agreeing in unspoken gestures, 'She's mad. She's definitely off her rocker.'

'Mum, we're absolutely starving,' they said in one accusing voice.

'So am I,' agreed Rosemary. 'Would you go into town for fish and chips?'

'We've just trudged all the way up that hill. We're exhausted.'

No point asking if one of them felt she had enough strength to walk into town. They thought and spoke as one, usually after some agreed plan of action, or Demelza made a decision and Lamorna caught on and followed her sister's direction.

'I'll get the car out. We'll all go. Have fish and chips at the Balancing Eel.'

'Don't you want us to shower first?' Lamorna asked. 'We're a bit sandy.'

'I think you'll do.'

Thankfully, there was a space in the Sloop Car Park. The café upstairs in the fish shop was already serving. There were others, like them, leaking trickles of sand from shoes and clothing, and showing signs of having caught too much sun. Now that food was provided, the twins seemed willing to be friendly and uncritical and asked how the writing had progressed. Rosemary, having had a successful day, was also prepared to listen sympathetically to complaints of cellulite appearing on thighs, chapped lips, spots pustulating on chins, split ends and a host of teenage trivia.

On the drive back, Rosemary looked out to the bay and Godrevy lighthouse. The sun was still high. It was shining on Smeatons Pier and the last strolling holiday makers, but as she passed the Malakoff and looked down on Porthminster beach, the patch of sand, where her girls had dreamed away the day, was in deep shadow. Over at Hayle, the sand dunes, the beach huts, and the three miles of golden beach glowed in the evening sun. Small fishing boats found their way through the narrow silted channel of sand bars into Hayle harbour.

'This used to be the grape house,' Rosemary said, as she parked the car by the white painted wall separating the house and garden from the commercial car park.

'When was that?' asked Lamorna.

'When Leslie and Julia Stephen and the family lived at Talland House a hundred years ago.'

'Mum, she's teasing,' Demelza said. 'We've been weaned on those kids, especially Virginia and Vanessa. We could write a book on them.'

'Well, you seem to have listened. But after them came Thomas Millie Dow, the painter, and family of three children. He had that small extension built.'

'Mum. You've already told us that, too,' Demelza laughed.

The girls, still in their forgiving mood, grabbed Rosemary's arms and propelled her towards the house. 'And the daughter of the boy, Hope, of that family wrote *The Shell Seekers*,' Rosemary continued.

'We know. We know. We're going to read it one day, when we've grown out of Harry Potter,' Lamorna said.

'Come on. Let's go and stand on the balcony, and you can dream about Virginia Woolf and the lighthouse.'

'As long as you don't ask us to read the book,' Demelza warned.

The days passed at frightening speed, and still Rosemary wrote furiously in her chair in the garden. When the ideas were flowing like this she wrote in shorthand, so that she could capture her thoughts before they melted away. On other days she wrote in longhand, laboriously ferreting out ideas that were coming slowly. Each evening she committed her writing to the laptop and filed away the written pages. Later, she would print out and work on the hard copy, deleting and adding to the script.

Every day at their spot on the beach the twins placed their towels and deposited their bags and took their place on the terrace to drink their cappuccino. They were now regular customers and treated with friendliness and given special attention by the young Australians Brad and Dave.

'Gd –day girls. How's the suntan coming along?'

They laughed and displayed their long arms and legs and were duly admired.

'So, when's the great day you'll be going in for a dip?' they teased.

'Never,' they shuddered. 'Too cold.'

'The sea at Oz is warm. You'd like that. There's great surf there. Bigger than this. And great barbies on the beach. Christmas time, all the families are down on the beach,' Brad told them.

'So, will you be home for Christmas?' the girls wanted to know.

'Me and Brad will be travelling round Europe, when we've earned our money. Won't be home for another few months,' Dave told them.

It was good being noticed by older boys and being treated with respect, instead of being punched or tripped up by silly boys their own age. They basked in being talked to properly. Being told about Australia and how working at the café on the beach was the nearest the boys could get to being home.

Over on the steps leading to the beach, George glowered his disapproval at the flirtatious nature of these encounters. He was waiting for them to strip off their beach wraps and lie down where he could continue to look at them. He liked their assortment of bathing costumes, especially the bikini type, with the brief knickers, and the top which they hardly needed, barely covering a nipple. Fully developed, they would be beneath his contempt. Women were disgusting. These were fresh young buds to be played with. He would like to play with both of them.

Last night he watched the video he'd made of them. It increased his appetite. Today, he must get to talk to them, think how he could start an easy conversation, like they enjoyed with those idiot boy waiters. He couldn't just go up and start talking. He'd have to think of a scheme to get to know them. They were moving away from the café now. Coming down the steps to the beach, calling and waving their goodbyes. As they moved, their legs were revealed beneath their wraps. He liked those tempting glimpses.

Now they were lying on the beach, stretched out, tantalising him. Really they deserved a good smacking. He could delay no longer. Picking up his bag, he walked over and stood close. They both had their eyes shut. He took out his cigarette case, very sophisticated he thought, a cigarette case, nothing common like the flip tops they all liked at the Tax office where he worked, putting them on the table with their lighters on top.

Trying to manoeuvre the cigarette case, he caused himself to trip and the cigarettes splayed out over the two girls. He saw them open their eyes, startled, and gaze up at his face in shadow against the brightness of the sun. He loved blue eyes. 'Oops. Sorry girls. May I retrieve my cigarettes, which I've just littered all over you?' He laughed in a friendly way and knelt down beside them, leaning over to get the cigarettes, which had fallen between their two bodies.

Lamorna raised herself on her elbows. This stranger was bending over her picking up his cigarettes. She was trapped beneath him, uncomfortable at his invasion of her space, but too shy to protest. She lay cringing away from him and could smell his slightly sweaty odour and did not like the maleness of it. It made her nervous and helplessly angry. Lamorna, at a disadvantage, didn't know how to deal with the situation. Finally, when the man moved further down to pick up the cigarettes between her legs, she was able to sit up and scramble swiftly out of the way.

Demelza was kneeling up. She rolled away from his reaching hands and was quickly gathering the cigarettes on her side, handing them to him, to make him move away from her sister. It would be embarrassing and sound childish to tell him he was too close. The job was done at last.

'Sorry girls.' George chuckled, smiling broadly. 'Clumsy me. My mother always said I was like a bull in a china shop.' He sat back on his heels, close to them and continued smiling. 'Well, now we've become acquainted, shall we say, I must introduce myself. George Tatum. Down here for two weeks' holiday.' He held out his hand in a bluff, frank way. The girls took it gingerly and gave their names.

'Demelza and Lamorna. Beautiful. Hey, are you twins?' he said ingenuously.

'Yes.'

'I'm doing a study on twins at college, with a fellow student; friend of mine, and with my mother's approval. Lucky meeting you. At least, well … would you mind if I asked you a few questions?' George looked eagerly and openly at each of them.

If a man talked about his mother, the girls would reason, he must be all right. George knew from experience it would allay any anxiety they might feel. He watched them look at one another and shrug. He settled himself comfortably near them and took out a notebook, waiting for them to begin to talk about themselves. The silence made them slightly self-conscious. He'd made a mistake. They began putting on their wrap around skirts, covering themselves up in a protective way.

'I'm sorry,' he said, realising his blunder in not carrying on with his chatter. 'I should make a start. Now what were our set questions? Meeting you and being on holiday has made me forget.'

The girls gave him a slightly reassuring grin.

'First question. Where do you live? I don't mean specifically, general area. Manchester, Cardiff, you know,' he asked, with a careless gesture.

'London,' Demelza replied.

'North West London,' Lamorna added.

'That's where my friend and I live. The one I'm doing the study with. We share a flat. Do you know Camden Town?'

'We live not far from there. West Hampstead.'

They laughed, like old friends.

'Perhaps you could call on us. He's much better at questions than I am. I'm really the photographer. We're doing twins up to the age of twelve.'

'We're just twelve,' Demelza said.

'That's lucky. Can I make a test video of you?'

The girls shrugged again. They didn't see any reason why not. They had practised having their photos taken by looking in the mirror and apeing models. They had practised walking, swinging their hips in exaggerated fashion. They had draped themselves in swathes of material and looked provocatively at an imagined camera. It was easy.

George took a close up shot of their heads; sitting together; hugging their knees to their chests; lying facing each other. 'OK, now stand up. Bend down and touch your toes. Look at me between your legs. Smile.'

He was enjoying himself. 'Now lie flat on your backs.' He stood straddling them, his legs between theirs so they had to keep them apart. He bent down, panning in close, and saw the uncertain look on their faces. He'd better get in a few more shots before his pigeons were frightened off.

The girls were beginning to feel uncomfortable, and didn't know how to deal with the way he was taking more intimate shots of them; telling them what to do; coming in close. They obeyed everything he said, but were unhappy. They looked at one another, appealing for guidance. There was none.

'Hey! Twins!' a voice called from the terrace cafe.

It was their mother's friend, Joan, smiling down at them. 'Come up here. I've got a message for your mother and I'll treat you to a coffee.' She gave George a challenging look. 'Come on girls, make it quick!' she demanded.

The girls turned with relief to the voice which offered them a get-away from their embarrassing ordeal. They jumped up immediately, grabbed their things together and stuffed them in their bags. 'See you, George,' they said and ran up the steps to the café, grateful to be able to escape.

'See you tomorrow,' he called after them.

'Who's the creep?' Brad asked.

'Oh some bloke doing research on twins,' Demelza said.

'Oh yeah. And I'm a champion sky diver. We thought he was getting a bit close, wasn't he? That's why Joan called you up here. She's gone to get the coffee. It's none of my business, but I could see you getting a bit edgy.'

'Well, we did want to get away, but it was difficult,' Lamorna said.

'How long have you known him?'

'We just met him on the beach today.'

'Today! Looked as if he was a favourite uncle. What's his name?'

'George Tatum.'

'What do you think, Brad?' Demelza asked.

'I think you ought to be a bit careful. Don't let him take any more videos. If he suggests it, tell him you'll have to ask your mum and dad. From what I know of these characters, that usually freezes them off. If he bothers you, and you don't like it, you can call on Dave or me. We'll be watching out for you.'

'Thanks, Brad,' the girls said, feeling at once embarrassed and protected.

'Now if you were eighteen, you could say I was jealous,' Brad said, laughing to make them feel better, 'But as you're so young, well I only want to be sure you're OK. OK?'

2

Rosemary jumped, as the mobile phone on the table beside her rang. 'Bother,' she said. The words which had been forming in her head completely disappeared. The pictures of her characters faded from her mind's eye, and all the sounds of the garden intruded into her consciousness.

'Oh, it's you, Lewis.' She greeted her husband in a not too friendly voice.

'Who were you expecting? You sound disappointed.'

'Not expecting anyone. Just annoyed at being disturbed.'

'Perhaps I should ring back at a more convenient time.'

'No. Don't be silly. I thought I'd turned it off, that's all.'

'OK. I forgive you.'

'How kind. Now, what's the matter?'

'Nothing. I wanted to remind you that I'm coming for the weekend. Ring Joan and see if you can book a table for dinner at the Porthminster beach café. The girls can stay with your sisters. They're coming Friday, aren't they?'

After the interruption, Rosemary couldn't settle. She booked a window table at the café for Saturday, gathered up her shopping bag and walked into town along the Terrace, overlooking Porthminster beach. She thought she might see the twins on the sands, but it was too crowded to pick anyone out. She sat on a bench at the Malakoff, a high point overlooking the town and harbour, watching the small yachts setting out, rounding the buoys and lining up for their races.

Children were diving, tumbling, jumping and falling into the sea off the end of Smeaton's Pier; a dangerous game to play, but a traditional past time. The sea had barely warmed up but today's girls and boys, wouldn't venture into the sea without a sleek, black, wet suit to protect them from the cold. She watched now as a group of them showed off for the holiday crowd.

The Stephen children had watched the Regattas from this point a century earlier, the swimming races, gig races, and fun races. They were local boys, no girls, and young men of fisher families taking part, making rafts from barrels with planks tied on, shivering in their knitted woollen bathing trunks. Rosemary recalled Virginia Woolf's description of the scene.

"There was the Judges' boat, with lines of little flags going from mast to mast. The St Ives notables went on board. Then all the little boats came out. A band played. We went onto the Malakoff and stood in the crowd and listened to the blare of music wafted across the water; and then a gun was fired and off went the boats, racing round the bay; or the swimmers plunged."

As Rosemary left the Co-op with her shopping, she noted that *Harry Potter and the Philosopher's Stone* was showing at the Royal cinema. She thought the girls might like to go to the pictures with her sisters, while she and Lewis dined out.

At the Harbour Bookshop she bought an audiotape of *Three Men In a Boat* for Lewis, realising that, of course, it was his birthday, that's why he'd suggested going out for dinner. Really, she was hopeless, but she'd pretend she hadn't forgotten. He hadn't given her a chance to get round to it.

Rosemary's agent rang that evening. 'Listen. I talked to the publisher today. He said as you're in Cornwall, and he knows it's the home of millions of artists, you should try and find a woman painter's work, which could be used for the cover of your novel. Nothing too modern. I suggest someone from the early period. What do you think?'

'Well, first of all, thanks for volunteering me.'

'You are after all an expert, and in a three book deal, Rosemary, you have to make some conciliatory noises. I think their creative department's folded, and this could be the shape of things to come. OK? If you hope they'll sign you up again, you'd better agree. It took quite an effort setting this up. I hope you appreciate it. How's the writing coming along?'

'Actually, it's going really well. Absolutely great. No problem. So I'll be able to do some research on an artist for the cover of the book. Actually, I'm looking forward to finding someone different.'

'Good. I knew you were making all that fuss over nothing with your writing. Anyway, I have to go and see another of my authors tomorrow. He says he's having writing problems. I'll just give him a quick clip round the ear. That should sort him out. Cheers for now dear.'

'What a great comforter you are Patsy,' Rosemary said, hearing the raucous laughter that accompanied her remarks.

'I know. Where would you be without me! Bye.'

Rosemary emailed Leah. She outlined the theme of her novel, and the request to find a suitable image to illustrate the cover. Leah would know of several artists, maybe even contempories, whose images would fit in with the idea. Her world revolved around the art colony where she produced her own particular style of prints of St Ives. She could trust Leah's judgement – their thoughts travelled the same lines. 'I'll send you the first chapter so you'll get the gist of the book. Suggestions, please!'

Rosemary observed the performance of the girls as they arrived back from the beach and draped themselves helplessly on the sofa, hoping she would offer them sympathy.

She declined to notice their practised routine of 'look at us, we need help,' until, in desperation, they voiced their complaints.

'Mum, have you got any tea and cakes? We're absolutely starving,' Lamorna said.

'And we're exhausted. It's so hot, and that hill's so steep and ...' Demelza began.

Instead of enlisting Rosemary's sympathy, their whining merely had the opposite effect.

'You have the choice of making dinner this evening, or a cup of tea now, while I put my notes on the computer.'

Realising the option with the least effort, the girls hoisted themselves to their feet and went to put the kettle on.

'You're lucky. You've got two of you to share your jobs. There's only me,' she called after their resentful-looking backs.

By the end of the week, the twins were slightly bored with their daily routine. Rosemary was looking forward to the arrival of her three younger sisters. She would discharge the twins into their care. Their presence would provide a welcome release from her daily writing habit. She was, after all, the host and couldn't expect them to entertain themselves for the entire length of their stay. They arrived full of laughter and ideas about what they wanted to do.

'I'm taking you all out to dinner, for a start,' Sylvia informed her.

'I want to walk across the Causeway to St Michael's Mount, and come back in a boat,' Miranda said.

'And I want to lie on the beach, eat ice cream, and get a sun tan, like the twins. Just look at you – gorgeous. And your mother pale as a lily,' Penelope said.

'I'll sunbathe after I've been to the auction of paintings at Marazion,' Rosemary said, 'I'm looking for a turn of the century picture to illustrate the cover of my new novel. Hope to find something that's been buried in an attic for years, like an early Laura Knight, or Elizabeth Forbes.'

Lewis arrived at St Ives station, where Lamorna and Demelza were waiting for him. He put down his bags and encircled them both, kissing the tops of their heads. They picked up his laptop computer and weekend case, and urged him up the hill.

'The house is full of aunts,' Demelza said.

'It's just as well I'm only here for the weekend, otherwise I'm afraid I should have to throw them off the end of the pier.'

'I wish you would, Dad,' Lamorna said wickedly.

'Why? Aren't they spending enough money on you?' Lewis teased.

'No,' they replied, in one voice.

'You'll be able to make up for it, Dad. We want to see *Harry Potter and the Philosopher's Stone* and they want to see something different,' Lamorna told him.

'They'll only pay for us if we see their film,' Demelza said.

'That's blackmail,' their father agreed. 'No, we can't let them get away with that. We must make a stand.'

'Don't go to a lot of trouble, Dad. Just give us the money.'

The girls laughed. Dad laughed. It was going to be a good weekend, with their father prepared to side with them in opposition to anything the aunts proposed and the girls didn't like. They knew he enjoyed battling with mum's sisters, however friendly the argument. It drove Mum mad.

'How's your mother? Getting on with her writing?'

'OK I suppose,' Lamorna began. 'Actually, she's a bit weird. Sometimes she calls me Virginia ..'

'And me, Vanessa,' chipped in Demelza. 'The house isn't haunted with these people. It's all in her head.'

'You'd better sort her out, Dad, otherwise we'll have a crazy woman in the house.'

'Oh she's OK. You know what authors are like. They live in what they are writing. They go a bit odd. Probably she's named her characters Virginia and Vanessa.'

'I think it's weirder than that. She's thinking about Virginia and Vanessa – you know Dad, when they were children at Talland House,' Lamorna reminded her father.

'Nothing to worry about girls. You know she's forever reading Virginia Woolf's journals and letters. She's always been interested in the two sisters' lives. That's why I bought her a Vanessa Bell painting.'

'But Dad. Did you know she's brought it with her from London? Now that's weird. It's hanging in the bedroom. You'll see it in a minute.' Demelza persisted in her argument, ably backed up by Lamorna.

'She's brought it with her for inspiration,' Lewis explained, making this excuse as a point of loyalty to his wife. He persisted in dismissing the girls' comments about Rosemary and wondered why they were so keen to put their mother at a disadvantage. What did they want to punish Rosemary for? He surmised she had probably neglected them in some way and he had to admit, she did get a bit obsessive in her interests and subject matter.

He had known Rosemary pursue information for a book on particular artists to an embarrassing degree, ringing America in the middle of the night; interviewing artists, tracking down people who had any connection with them; spending days at libraries and exhausting herself writing up her research. In writing her novels she relied on her imagination. Fiction gave her endless freedom and self-reliance in making something out of the fabric of her experience, but it demanded different skills and a good deal of practice to write to a publishable standard. Lewis knew it was a scary situation and she was finding the transition difficult. He had to support her through the hard times.

'Read it to me, then I'll hear how it sounds and you'll get a feel for it,' he suggested.

But Rosemary was hesitant, fearing his disapproval and her disappointment. The only way he could help was to sanction her frequent trips to Cornwall.

Lewis turned sharp right at the Porthminster Hotel, crossed the road and, keeping to the left, entered the drive to the house. The girls, feeling guilty at a betrayal of their mother, stayed in the garden to play badminton, while Lewis went in search of Rosemary. He found her in their bedroom, standing on the balcony, looking down at the twins in the garden. She turned as he entered the room.

'You know, Lewis,' she said. 'I've examined every part of the garden and I can't think where the Stephen children could stand and see the steam train coming into St Ives station. Mind you, there were about eight carriages. The most they have now is four. It must have been when the garden was bigger and before the St Ives Bay Hotel replaced the smaller houses. Virginia Woolf distinctly mentioned the Lookout place. They complained about the Porthminster Hotel obscuring the view too. See if you can identify the spot. Listen. "This was a mound, grassy, unplanted, that jutted out over the garden wall. There one stood to look if the signal was down. If it were down, it was time to start for the station to meet the train ..."'

'Darling, can we talk about that later? I have to shower before we go to dinner and I need a cup of tea.'

Rosemary was immediately contrite. Why couldn't she say hello and leave her little problems, which weren't problems at all, until she had welcomed Lewis? She put down the book from which she had been quoting, kissed him briefly and said they'd have tea in their room, and a rest, before he had to run the gauntlet of the sisters.

In the lower flat an argument had broken out between Penelope, Miranda and Sylvia about who was cooking dinner and which film to see at the cinema. It was eventually decided that Sylvia should take the twins to see Harry Potter and because of her self-sacrifice she would be excused from cooking.

The twins, playing in the garden and hearing the arguments through the windows opening onto the lawn, intervened at that point, saying they were quite capable of sitting in a cinema seat on their own.

'But you don't know who might be sitting next to you. There are weird people who go to cinemas to sit next to little girls,' Sylvia warned.

Lewis and Rosemary, coming in, agreed. 'The twins can pay for you, Sylvia. I've heard from other forty-year olds that it's a good film, so I'm sure you'll enjoy it,'

'I'm thirty-five, Lewis, as you well know. And if you argue about it, I shall not take your precious daughters to the cinema, and you'll have to miss your dinner date and go instead.'

'Oh, yes please, Dad. We'd love you to come. Please.' Lamorna pleaded.

'Please Dad,' added Demelza.

'Oh now look what you've done Lewis!' complained Rosemary.

It ended with Lewis apologising, the twins moaning, the sisters laughing, and Rosemary warning the twins to behave themselves, and dragging Lewis off to Porthminster beach café before he could stir up any more trouble.

The day of the auction arrived with blue sky and sun. Rosemary and her three sisters piled into Penelope's car and drove to Marazion early to view the paintings before the sale started. The twins were left to fend for themselves, with money to buy drinks and lunch at the beach take-away.

'You'll be fine on the beach,' Rosemary said. 'We'll be back late afternoon. Take the mobile and give me a ring if you're worried about anything.'

'Worried! What about?' Lamorna snorted indignantly.

'We'll hardly be kidnapped from a crowded beach,' Demelza said. 'And what could you do five miles away? We might just as well ring Dad in London.'

Rosemary flinched under the criticism. Demelza was quite right. What indeed, could she do five miles away? but Demelza always gave that extra dig, or sharpness to her comments.

'Don't let them give you a hard time, Rosemary,' Miranda advised.

'They're old enough and ugly enough to look after themselves; as our mother used to say,' Sylvia added.

'Will you get in the car,' Penelope said impatiently. 'Twins, for goodness sake. Go.' She pointed imperiously towards the beach, and the twins started for Primrose Valley with never a goodbye or a backward glance. 'That'll teach them to go off without us,' their retreating figures loudly proclaimed.

Penelope was disappointed in not finding anything she wished to bid for among the pictures of early traditional painters, or even those of the more modern and abstract variety. There were the usual Scott Tuke's of nude boys bathing; a Julius Olsson seascape, an early Terence Cuneo, before his more famous railway paintings; a Stanhope Forbes, Terry Frost and Patrick Heron prints, and other Newlyn and St Ives artists. There were the usual number of paintings from unknowns, who had come on painting holidays, been disillusioned with their efforts, and left their unsigned pictures with unwilling landladies, who had also wanted them out of their sight and sent them to the auction house.

'There's nothing here for me,' Penelope said.

Rosemary was excited by two paintings. 'Look at these. I like the larger seascape with boats leaving Newlyn harbour. I can see that as a cover for my book. The smaller one of a Cornish cottage is very attractive too.' Both works were signed Mary Jewels.

'Who is Mary Jewels?' Penelope asked.

'Indeed. Who is she?' Rosemary repeated. 'I've never heard of her!'

Rosemary watched Roger Goodwood, the auctioneer, arrive. He gave her a brief wave, and began assessing his audience, greeting his regular clients, and noting the number of dealers. He was a brusque, cocksure young man, used to treating his audience to various insults and taking advantage of his knowledge of the depths of their pockets.

At one point he stopped proceedings, pointed with his gavel, and asked an old woman to stop bidding. She sat quietly for a short time, and then began again. He ignored her, but her voice was disruptive and competed with his. He leaned forward on his desk and addressed her in a loud voice.

'Listen, Esme,' he said, 'You buy £10 lots at the end of a sale. Please do keep quiet, and do not disrupt the serious bidding.'

'But I like that picture, Roger,' she replied.

'But you can't afford it woman,' he thundered, 'You are wasting my time and everyone else's.' Rosemary knew his next move. He would appeal to the crowd. 'This is what I have to put up with at every auction.

This little old lady will stir your sympathy and support, but she interrupts constantly, as these regulars will testify.' There were many noddings of heads throughout the room. The crowd, nevertheless, had been entertained.

He glared at Esme, but there was a familiarity between them that belied his fierce tongue, and indeed the woman was not in the least perturbed, but remained silent. Esme was Leah's aunt. Leah and Roger had an on/off relationship; Esme was a legacy of that friendship, tolerated by Roger as a means to Leah. But Leah couldn't commit, being a very independent person, fond of her personal and financial freedom.

'He's too powerful,' she said, 'He'll try and take over my life, and that will lead to arguments. It'll be a battle of wills.'

'Why don't you give yourselves a trial period; say three months of getting to know one another; excluding all others, and see how your life styles can fit together.' Rosemary advised.

Roger had agreed. Leah was thinking about it, and while there was still a chance, Roger had Leah's aunt Esme.

'It's the weirdest situation,' Leah said. 'Roger positively clings to Esme. He pretends to find her troublesome in the saleroom. I believe sometimes, she really is a trial. Then he takes her out to lunch so he can talk to her about me.'

Rosemary wondered whether Esme would literally be thrown out of his saleroom, if Leah turned him down.

Roger's assistant held up the Stanhope Forbes painting. There would now be some serious bidding from dealers and devotees of Forbes. Roger was slow to begin, letting the tension mount, seemingly engaged on some paper work on his desk, and discomforting the clients eager to bid. The room became electric. Suddenly, he looked up, about to launch quickly into the event.

'I know where that painting came from Roger. I've seen it in the house.' Esme's cultured voice drew attention to the centre of the room where she sat. The tension he'd created fell apart. Roger had lost his dominance over the proceedings. He held back his anger with an effort.

'This is where I either throw you out, or treat you to a cup of tea and a cake, Esme. Leave at once.' He pointed imperiously towards the door. The old woman got up reluctantly, escorted by one of the assistants. 'Don't let anyone sit in my chair Roger,' she commanded. The door closed on her. Roger gave a wry smile.

'I wonder how much that interruption cost him?' Rosemary whispered. 'Poor old Esme. I've seen it happen before. He holds off the bidding, looks as though he's going to start, and doesn't. The punters are like horses at a starting gate. Then along comes a little old lady and upsets his master plan. He loses his advantage. Unless he can recover, the floor has the upper hand.'

The Forbes went to a client on the telephone. The dealers left immediately, like a flock of raucous crows. There was now a more relaxed and jolly atmosphere for those people left to mop up the lesser known artists and works. 'Now we'll have some fun,' he said. 'Esme,' he called, 'You can come in now.' Esme arrived, smiling, in a flurry of silk scarves.

'Lot 239. Seascape. A rather naïve impasto work by a Newlyn artist, Mary Jewels.'

The bids soon outstripped Rosemary's purse and she found herself bidding for the smaller work, against one other bidder. She did not achieve that one either, and watched the Mary Jewels paintings being taken to the office for collection.

'Well, that's that,' she said, 'But now I've seen the work, I want to find out more about the artist.'

'Another picture is bound to come up again. It just means waiting.' Penelope said.

They were about to leave when the new owner of the small painting stopped them.

'Hello,' she said, 'I'm Mrs Fox. Forgive me for intruding but I believe you bid for my Mary Jewels. I'm sorry you didn't get it, but it happens to be a painting of my cottage, so you see I couldn't let anyone else have it.'

'Perfectly understandable,' Rosemary agreed. 'I hope I didn't make you bid over your limit.'

'It was lucky only you were bidding against me or I might have lost it. But you see I knew Mary Jewels, the artist, and her sister Cordelia, and I remember the afternoon when they both came for tea, and Mary began the first sketch.'

'How lovely,' Rosemary enthused. 'I'm quite interested in the artist, as well as her work. I've been studying Cornish artists for some time and she has completely escaped my notice.'

'Then you must come for tea. Any afternoon this week, and I'll tell you something about two very remarkable sisters.'

'Were they both painters?'

But the question remained unanswered. There was only time to exchange telephone numbers before Rosemary's three impatient sisters whisked her off to lunch.

Lunch was a long drawn out affair, with the sisters talking in more intimate terms than their sitting at the table in Talland House would allow, with the sharp ears of their nieces, constantly on alert. During the boring bits they clamped on their Walkmans. But listening in to the conversations of their aunts was one of the ways the girls learnt about the world. They developed the scheme of appearing to be engrossed in playing Scrabble, doing a jigsaw, or filling in a crossword. If they were addressed during these sessions they would look up startled, as though taken unawares.

Penelope's husband was about to be made redundant. He could maybe retrain, but they had to rethink their lifestyle. Everything was uncertain.

Sylvia was thinking of moving house, maybe to come and live in the West Country.

'I've got a friend living in Piazza flats. I must introduce you to her, Rosemary. I haven't seen her place yet, but apparently it's in a choice spot, right on Porthmeor beach. I'm meeting her during the week.'

Miranda was thinking of having cosmetic surgery to iron out the wrinkles round her eyes. 'And I don't even do a lot of laughing,' she said. They all laughed.

Lewis had told Rosemary over dinner at the Porthminster that the partners had acquired a big money account and were designing a prestigious web page for their client. 'If we achieve this one, it'll lead to others in their bracket. It could mean a great deal to the business as a whole.' Lewis was excited at the prospect. The business had survived its rocky first year and they were now looking to expand and build on a firm foundation. It was a crucial time in Lewis's career, with a team of two partners, and a staff of three whizkid youngsters fresh from college, with design and computer skills to match the best.

The twins arrived for their coffee at Porthminster beach café and were greeted by Brad and Dave. Demelza deposited their bags on the beach where they could see them from the balcony, and Lamorna secured their usual table.

'And how're our favourite twins this morning?' Brad asked.

'Where've you been?' Dave said.

Lamorna began explaining their late arrival. 'We've got three mad aunts staying with us. It's chaos trying to get out while they sort out their problems. One always loses her handbag, another can't decide what to wear and the place is littered with funny old clothes.'

'And the other,' added Demelza, 'takes ages over her make-up. And mum's flapping around wondering if we

are going to be abducted from the beach in broad daylight. What a joke.'

'That's mothers for you,' Brad said, 'Not much you
can do about them. My mum threatens to come out by
the next plane if I don't report every week, 7 o'clock,
Ozzy time every Sunday.'

'Don't look now,' Dave warned, 'but I think that guy
has arrived. The one taking the dodgy pictures.'

'Oh, I expect he's all right,' Lamorna said.

'He's alright for a thirty year old woman, not for
twelve year old girls.' Brad reprimanded them.

'We can take care of ourselves,' Demelza said, pretending to a certainty she knew that neither of them
felt. On the beach they greeted George lightly and sat
down.

'I've been looking after your stuff, waiting for you to
arrive, because I've heard that things get stolen from
the beach.' He talked pleasantly, telling the girls he was
staying at a B&B in town. 'Plenty of those Australians
there,' he said. 'Loud people. Full of themselves.'

George knew the girls were wary of him, but as he
continued talking they became more relaxed in his
company. They dared remove their wraps, ready for
another bout of sunbathing. They began to apply their
sun lotion, rubbing it on their shoulders and arms, liberally applying it to their legs. He watched and talked,
while they half listened, not making replies, and carried
on with their activity.

'St Ives was a big fishing town, relying on the
pilchard. When I came as a boy there were many old
chaps sitting on the wharf, telling tales of the sea. The

older ones walked up and down at Rose Lodge, so many paces up and the same number back. Do you know why they did that?'

Demelza and Lamorna shook their heads.

'It's because they were pacing the exact measurement of the decks of their boats. Those fishermen still working at sea would be lined up on the pier, mending nets.'

Demelza knelt up to rub the cream on Lamorna's back, but George snatched the tube from her, causing her to fall sideways. 'Sit down. I'll do that.' The girls were taken by surprise and didn't react to this unwelcome intrusion of a big hand rubbing Lamorna's back. He knelt behind her, liberally spreading the lotion, smoothing up her neck and shoulders, and down to the top of her bikini bottoms. This was so different from her sister doing it.

Demelza righted herself and watched, fascinated, realising it would be her turn next. The girls gave a covert glance at one another. Was it ridiculous to object? 'Careful,' was all Lamorna said, 'Don't rub so hard.'

Before it was Demelza's turn to suffer the embarrassing and humiliating experience of having this man's hand on her, she stood up. 'That's enough,' she said, taking the tube from him. 'Shall we go for a walk Lamorna?'

George protested. 'You've only just arrived, and I haven't done you Demelza.' He grinned, hanging on to her hand, dragging at her. She released her hold on the suncream. It dropped on the sand.

Then Brad and Dave appeared suddenly, like knights,

in their black wet suits, coming down the steps to the beach, carrying their surfboards.

'Something wrong, girls? Someone bothering you?' Brad demanded.

George released Demelza's hand, attempting to stand up. 'Nothing to concern you,' he said.

'That's for me to judge,' Brad countered, standing on George's coat so that he couldn't get up. Dave stood at the other side of George. He retrieved the sun cream and handed it to Demelza.

The girls began gathering up their things, saying nothing. Tears were on the brink of falling from Lamorna's eyes. She began walking away. Demelza hastened to catch up with her sister, embarrassed and troubled, leaving George pinned to the beach between Brad and Dave.

'I think he put his finger down the back of my pants,' Lamorna said as Demelza caught up.

'What do you mean, you think, he did?'

'Why did we let him do that, touch us? Why? I can't believe we were so stupid. It was such a surprise. I couldn't think what to do. Next time ...' Lamorna said angrily.

'Next time,' Demelza said. 'There won't be a next time.'

They stopped by the putting green, where they put on their robes. 'I think we should find somewhere else to sit.' Demelza said. 'Bloody nuisance, him making us move from our place. We'd better avoid him. He was OK just talking about the old fishermen.'

'Yes, but why is he hanging around us?'

They rang their mother's mobile. It was turned off so they left a message to say if she returned from the auction sooner than expected, they would be on Porthgwidden beach.

Over coffee, after lunch, Rosemary realised she hadn't turned on her mobile on leaving the auction. When she received the message saying the girls had moved from their usual spot, she guessed something more had happened. They didn't like walking about town in their wrap-arounds, and why should they tell her where they were going. It was such a slight thing, to move to another beach. The sisters laughed off her concern.

'They've probably met some other teenagers and gone off with them, or some pimply boys have splashed water over them.'

They assured Rosemary she was over reacting to a simple message. Rosemary accepted their explanations.

Mrs Fox, the owner of the Mary Jewels painting, lived in Newlyn. Rosemary had driven over there by herself, not wanting any extra chat from the sisters to interfere with her purpose of learning something of the life of Mary and her sister Cordelia. Rosemary drew up outside the cottage. Mrs Fox was in the garden picking flowers for the house.

'Hope today is convenient,' Rosemary said.

'Of course. Come in. I'll just put these in water.'

They walked through the hall. Mrs Fox stopped and pointed to a vibrant painting at the turn of the stair well. 'Mary and Delia's nephew, Peter, gave me that painting of the fishing fleet at Newlyn, because I used to look after them; not that I ever received any thanks from them.'

Mrs Fox left Rosemary admiring the painting, then called out from the kitchen.

'Do go into the living room. Be with you shortly.'

Rosemary sat in a chair by the window and was rather dismayed when two silky haired, large eyed dogs, sat at her feet and stared at her. Rosemary had never got to grips with breeds of dog, or makes of car - not liking either very much. She avoided the possibility of being unnerved by the dogs' stares by looking at the Mary Jewels painting, and trying not to sweat with fear. She was thankful when Mrs Fox returned, looking surprised that her guest wasn't fondling the long ears of her companions. They were probably surprised too, Rosemary thought.

'Don't you like dogs?' Mrs Fox asked.

'No. Afraid not,' Rosemary replied, knowing she was probably offending her, but unable to overcome her fear.

'Soft as butter. Wouldn't hurt a flea.'

Oh wouldn't they, Rosemary thought, as the dogs gnawed savagely at their tails. Like all the other dog owners Rosemary had known, she wouldn't understand a guest's refusal to melt into adoration of her canine friends. When she went into the kitchen to make tea Rosemary jumped up and followed, on the pretext of continuing the conversation. She wasn't prepared to suffer the ordeal of staring dogs again. In any case, she

47

only felt safe while their owner was in the room, and their doggy eyes were turned lovingly to her instead of the warning looks they gave Rosemary.

Mrs Fox had found photographs of Mary and Cordelia, standing in the doorway of the cottage. She launched straight away into details of the sisters' lives, while automatically filling the kettle, setting out the cups, opening a packet of biscuits, and pausing for the brewing of the teapot.

'Mary married a local boy, a carpenter, though how he would have fitted in to her later life, with all the artists, I don't know. Anyhow, the opportunity never arose; he was killed in the First World War, a few months after their marriage. His name is on the Newlyn War Memorial. Cordelia married an artist, can't remember his name. They lived in Newlyn for a while, with her mother at Vine Cottage, then moved to London.'

When they returned to the living room with the tray of tea things, the dogs were waiting. Again, they came over to stare and sit at her feet. Fortunately, Rosemary's attention was taken up with Mrs Fox's narration and the photographs. The dogs, being ignored, lay down and slept.

'The sisters lived to a great age. In their nineties they were. Could be very cutting in their remarks. Insulted people. I didn't take any notice. I was used to them. But they were quite waspish to me, even though I was cooking dinners and shopping for them. There was a family secret too, something that happened in South Africa. They were always hinting at it, but I never found out what it was.'

'If I find out I'll let you know.'

Rosemary discovered that Mary Jewels was self-taught, and took up painting when one of the early Newlyn artists persuaded her to do so, saying she had a natural talent and a good colour sense. Mary never doubted the truth of this and, from that moment, had great belief in her ability.

'I knew Mary and Cordelia from when I was quite young, being Cornish of course. They were privately educated. The sisters were quite something. Very provocative. Very vibrant. Flamboyant. You couldn't walk into a room and not notice them. They were very well dressed, very well connected, artist wise. They knew all sorts of people. I remember Mary used to wear designer clothes. Pure silk. Beautiful dresses.'

This was just what Rosemary wanted to hear, the personality of Mary when she was younger. Not the older character, fascinating as it might be. She wanted the Mary of those years when she was painting and exhibiting her work.

'Augustus John used to buy her paintings. He visited their cottage whenever he was in Newlyn,' Mrs Fox continued. She could not provide any evidence but remembered both sisters mentioning him. 'I believe he organised an exhibition for her in London, and he wrote an article about her. Can't remember in what magazine or newspaper.'

So, Rosemary thought, amazed. She had charmed Augustus John. She studied the photos of Mary and Cordelia that Mrs Fox had found, and saw the dark

49

raven-haired beauties that he would have admired. He had drawn and painted many gypsies, and the women were definitely of this type, rather heavy featured, prominent noses, bold looking. Very striking and attractive women. Augustus John had been an active supporter of the gypsies free way of life. Other artists connected with the West Country, including Laura Knight and Alfred Munnings, had also favoured paintings of gypsies, fairgrounds, and circus artists. Perhaps she'd look at some of their paintings too for a suitable cover.

Rosemary drove to St Ives feeling guilty at the time she had spent away from working on her novel, and being involved with the children. And then there was Lewis. It was hard to spread herself around. There was an email from Patsy, asking if she was sticking at her writing. Was she working every day? Had she found a painting for the cover of her book? The publishers now wanted to see several paintings by different artists so they could choose the most appropriate image.

Rosemary replied to Patsy's email. 'I am managing to write something every day, don't keep pushing. I am doing my best. Have found an artist named Mary Jewels, a naïve Cornish painter, who I think would be just right for the cover. I'm hoping to find a good image. I haven't considered other artists. I thought the publishers were relying on my judgement.'

The telephone rang almost as soon as Rosemary had

pressed the send button on the email. She picked it up with some trepidation.

'Who is Mary Jewels?' Patsy demanded. 'I've never heard of her.'

'She's a little-known Newlyn painter. I like her work. Apparently, Augustus John was devoted to her.'

'He's known for being devoted to women, very seldom for their painting. But do be good and bung in a few other artists' work. The publishers must be seen to be making their little contribution and given a choice of cover.'

'Well, I'm researching Mary Jewels at the moment.'

'I hope you're not spending too much time on research; it's not necessary. We only want an image, not a life story. Don't get too involved, Rosemary. I know you. Remember you're writing a novel.'

In spite of the dire warning not to get too involved, Rosemary pursued both the image and the person, to the detriment of writing. She would see the cottage where the two sisters lived and go to the private view at the Newlyn Art Gallery at the same time; after that, Rosemary felt confident she would tackle the novel again. She wasn't short of ideas, and when she started writing, things would flow. And so, comforted, she left the twins with their three aunts, who had decided to get a quick tan before going home at the weekend. The expedition set off for the seashore trailing bags of beach items.

George, watching out for the twins, and seeing the entourage of aunts coming down Primrose Valley, quickly disappeared to the busy harbour beach, where he took innocent photos of thieving gulls stealing ice creams and pasties from unwary holiday makers. The gulls, this year, were now attacking in screaming groups, leaving children crying and terrified.

Rosemary took the train from St Ives, leaving behind the beautiful harbour. The wooded area to Carbis Bay station filtered sunlight through leaves, shining on hedgerows and banks of purple heather and golden gorse. From there the tracks ran between the wide sweep of Porthkidney beach, with its white tide line, and the tufty sandhills and green golf course. Godrevy Island's lighthouse graced the bay further out, and Hayle Towans shimmered in light. The countryside beyond St Erth every year would provide a feast of yellow daffodils; and St Michael's Mount astounded with its brilliance, as the train came again to the sea towards Penzance.

Rosemary duly arrived at the Gallery. It was a mixed show of mostly abstract works of the members, with a construction resembling a boat and a wave in the gallery below, which reached from floor to ceiling. It would be dismantled and gone forever, apart from a few photographs to record the event.

Rachel, the twins' godparent, had told her to meet up with Tim Maynard, who would be there at eleven, holding the Newlyn catalogue, and looking out for her. Rosemary was adept at recruiting the help of friends and their friends. She approached Tim noting the blue bow tie and the dapper suit described by Rachel. Tim waved his catalogue, 'Ah, the lady with the red hat,' he said. They laughed, recognising Rachel's description of them both.

'Rachel tells me you have something interesting on Mary Jewels.'

'I used to be keen on interviewing remarkable people in Newlyn, where I live, and I remember I taped Mary and Cordelia talking together. I haven't seen it for ages, but I'll find it and give you a call if you're interested in hearing it. Afraid I haven't got any of Mary's paintings, though I saw lots of them at Vine Cottage, when I visited.'

'I'm happy to learn anything about Mary, and especially to hear her voice.' She thanked him, and they exchanged telephone numbers. 'Fascinating characters, fascinating,' he said, leaving the gallery. Rosemary was intrigued to know more.

3

The sisters were tired of sitting around on the beach. The sun was hidden behind a hazy cloud, and mist rolled in from the sea, leaving a damp residue on bare arms. Every now and then the lighthouse was partly obscured with a fine spray.

'We're walking to Zennor,' announced Penelope.

'And having lunch at the Tinner's Arms,' Sylvia added.

'The country route, of course,' Miranda said. 'Don't want to get stuck on the coast path, fall down a cliff, or break an ankle walking over the rocky track.'

To Rosemary's immense surprise, the twins decided to go along, too, and were already packing bottles of water and a few bananas for the journey. Rosemary declined to join the group, having that morning received a telephone call from Tim Maynard, saying he had found the tape of Mary and Cordelia talking about their lives, and would Rosemary like to come for coffee and listen to it? The decision to go was already made.

'Let Mum do her own thing,' Lamorna said, when the aunts began to put pressure on Rosemary. 'We can take you round Zennor; see the big water mill at the Folk Museum and sit in the old kitchen.'

'See the Mermaid in the church, and even show you the gravestones in the churchyard where Mum and Dad saw my Cornish name,' Demelza said. She pulled a face of disapproval.

Having reached Burthallan Lane, the group saw the first black and white posts that were to guide them over the fields and Cornish stone stiles, along a route dotted with pylons; an extra precaution for those likely to get lost on the way. They had taken all the available walking sticks at the house to ward off cattle, or geese and dogs, eager to defend their territory at the farm houses they would need to walk through.

Rosemary set off immediately to Newlyn, glad to have everyone out of the way. This time, instead of driving past the cottage where Mary and Cordelia had lived, she would knock on the door and ask if she could take a photo of the outside and walk in the garden; but first she must visit Tim Maynard.

The road to his cottage took her past the Newlyn Gallery, over the humped back bridge, past Vine Cottage, and up a steep hill, which wound deep into the countryside for over a mile. Tim's wife made her welcome, providing a substantial lunch

Coffee was taken to the living room in the older part of the cottage. Two deep windows would have looked out to the garden, except it was so overgrown, that the garden looked into the cottage. It suddenly started to rain, the sky darkened, and the wind tousled the plants, which had all the appearance of trying to attack the panes of glass and force their way in.

'I used to call in for tea at Vine Cottage,' Tim began. 'They were real Cornish, through and through. I'll let Mary and Cordelia tell you the story. Of course they were in their eighties when I made the tape and past their more lucid days.

Rosemary looked at Tim, delighted. 'That's wonderful. I'd love to hear their voices. Are they very Cornish?'

'No. In fact, very Bloomsbury, I would say. I haven't played it for years, so it'll be interesting to hear them talk again.'

The voices were clear and bell-like, and so similar Rosemary could not distinguish one from another. She began to form pictures of the two in her mind's eye based on the photos Mrs Fox had shown her. Both tall, with sharp features; noses prominent, dark thick hair, brushed back from the forehead and spreading in natural curls on their shoulders, or swept severely up in a bun. She decided they must have been a forbidding pair. As she listened she realised they were very good at dispatching poor Tim, who was a friend.

'Be quiet, I'm telling you in my own time,' one of them said as he attempted to ask a question.

'But you simply don't answer my questions,' protested Tim.

'And why should we?' came the curt reply.

'Grandmother was a little girl when the cholera came to Newlyn. She had three sisters and a brother. They would hide behind their nurse's skirts, and told not to look outside when the cart came to collect the dead. They wrapped up the victims in paper and they dragged one or two to Paul and pushed them in a deep hole. No one knows where they are buried. The grave was not marked, you know. There was only one family that survived. They lived behind the Red Lion pub. Mother was born in 1864. She was three weeks short of ninety-seven when she died. There was no greater person than my mother. She would take a book to bed and two candles and read all night.'

'We were born in Vine cottage,' Mary said. 'And our two brothers. One lived in Plymouth. The other went to South Africa, with father, and stayed there.'

'Have you still got family in South Africa?' Tim asked.

'We're not talking about South Africa. So stop prying.' Cordelia warned, and carried on talking in her own vein.

The sisters carried on about church affairs, constantly interrupting one another and frequently squashing Tim for asking questions, or complaining because he tried to steer them back to other issues from which they had deviated. It was very much a jumble of matters, which suddenly came into their heads.

'Mary has an eye for colour.' Cordelia informed Tim. 'A natural artist - not one of those art school students who have all their artistic instincts polished out of them by too much teaching; not enough freedom given to develop their own style, own way of seeing. Mary has artistic integrity. Real integrity.'

'That's plain to see,' Tim said.

'Cordelia is psychic,' Mary said, diverting attention away from herself.

'Yes. Did you know that? I'm psychic. I've been in touch with my family who've passed over. Close family. Very sad. Very sad.'

'Cordelia, we don't speak of that.'

'What don't you speak of? Have you contacted the other side?' Tim asked.

'Now just you mind your own business, Tim.' Cordelia said severely. 'If you've come to see Mary's paintings, I'll show them to you. Everything else is private. Family matters are for family, but never forgotten. No, never.'

'No never,' Mary reiterated. 'Father went out to South Africa to seek his fortune. There are still cousins out there, but I don't think they found their fortune. Poor father,' Mary sighed. 'No. Not family, Tim.'

'Very well,' said Tim. 'No family matters. What about some of the painters you knew? Were you very friendly with ...'

'Stanhope Forbes,' interrupted Cordelia. 'He sat out there in the garden and painted a picture of the cottage. It was accepted and hung in the Royal Academy and sold. He was delighted. He wrote to me and thanked me for being kind and making him tea when he was spending days at his painting. Oh, yes, the Forbes were quite close neighbours. Mary, find the letter. It's in the drawer.'

With the tape still running Rosemary could hear a drawer being opened, a rustle of papers, and then Mary's voice reading Stanhope Forbes' letter.

"Dear Mrs Dobson, I have great pleasure in asking you and your sister to accept the photograph of the picture which you both so kindly helped me to paint last summer. You will be pleased to hear it is beautifully placed in the Royal Academy. This morning I have heard the good news that it was sold on the opening day. I shall never forget the happy times I spent in your charming garden. Fondest wishes to you both. I hope to see you before long. Yours ever, S A Forbes"

'And there was Harold Harvey,' Cordelia continued. 'He used to leave his paints, and canvas in our cottage, rather than drag them up from Lamorna. We knew him quite well, being Cornish; and Gertrude Harvey, of course. She used to model for Harold, then she married him. Mother was fond of Alfred Munnings, though not everyone in the village liked him. Wild parties you see. He kept his horses down in Lamorna Valley. Alfred taught Mother to ride.'

'And then there was Augustus John...' Mary began.

'Don't be too free with your tongue, Mary,' Cordelia warned.

Rosemary already knew from other sources that Augustus John created a stir of disapproval among the Newlyn folk when he moved into Lamorna in 1914 with his beautiful wife, Dorelia, and family. His reputation as a womaniser preceded him. The Cornish Methodists were vociferous in their disapproval of visiting artists, with their free-and-easy lifestyle, their dress, their casual living, their disregard of Sunday observance. Artists came in for much censure from the locals. At least, Rosemary thought, they didn't get thrown into the harbour, easel and all, for daring to paint on a Sunday, as they did in St Ives.

'Augustus John,' Mary said, ignoring her sister's warning. 'Augustus liked - well he liked my work.' Rosemary thought she detected a certain archness in her words, a note of something remembered but left unsaid. A secret?

'Augustus John was a monster, my dear!' interrupted Cordelia.

But Mary carried on regardless. 'He had quite a few of my paintings in his own collection. He arranged an exhibition for me at the Warren Gallery, in London. He visited us quite often over a number of years. Yes, quite often. He was very fond of Mother. Always asked her permission to come and see my paintings. Always interested ...' Then the tape blanked out.

'I think that was the end of the tape,' Tim said, dismayed.

'Do you remember what she said? Was there anything more about Augustus John?'

'Not really, but Cordelia said something like, "You don't think he was interested in you, do you?" and she laughed in a wicked way. The mother and two daughters thought the world of John, according to stories bandied round among the artists. He was attracted to Mary and visited her whenever he was in Cornwall.'

Rosemary had heard of his fascination with Mary so many times, but it hadn't led her to any evidence. 'I'm going to investigate the biography of Augustus John,' she told Tim. 'There is bound to be something of his stay in Cornwall and his relationship with the sisters. After all, he did visit the family. And what happened?'

Tim's wife came in at that moment and raised her eyebrows. 'Did anyone escape the clutches of 'that man?' I know both sisters were admired because of their gypsy appearance, but their mother, Mrs Tregurtha, was a real stickler for the proprieties of behaviour and she probably kept him at bay. But who knows?'

Rosemary, with some trepidation, knocked on the door of Vine Cottage. The door was open. People were obviously in the house, but there was no response to her knock. She took the opportunity of peering inside, noting the long, worn slate passage, leading to a staircase, on either side of which were doors to inner rooms. Her second knock produced a woman, who came part way down the staircase. 'Did you knock?'

It was rather a foolish question, Rosemary thought, but plunged into her quest. 'This is the cottage where Mary Jewels, an artist, lived and I wondered if you would allow me to take a photograph of the house and garden?'

The woman, intrigued, came to the door. 'Well, I'm glad to know something about the people who lived here. Was she famous, this woman painter?'

'She was quite well known in her day, but since overlooked, but then that's the fate of most women artists. They get left out of the history of painting. But she was well connected with many of the more famous artists in Cornwall.'

'I must make a point of looking in the attic,' the woman laughed. 'I've only had the cottage for a couple of months so it's interesting to learn something of the history of the place. We haven't had a chance to furnish the cottage properly yet. Would you like to come inside and look around?'

'I'd be delighted, of course.'

'Trouble is, I can only spare about ten minutes. I'll have to leave you to show yourself around. I'm packing. We've got a taxi calling to take us to Penzance station. Back to London, worse luck.'

'Fine,' Rosemary assured her and stepped onto the flagstones, where Mary and Cordelia had walked, over all the years of their lives. The woman ran up the stairs to finish her packing, calling out as she did so, 'Girls, someone's coming to look at the house. OK?'

She got the feeling for the place as soon as she entered the parlour. It was where the sisters had entertained their friends to tea. It was small and she imagined a round table, with a tablecloth of shimmering white, iridescent damask, with generous matching napkins. The tea-set, with a delicate flower design, would be Royal Doulton. A silver teapot on a stand, with matching sugar bowl and tongs, would have graced the centre of the table. No common tea-cosy would conceal the tracery of the silver. They would, of course, serve home made scones with strawberry jam and Cornish cream, to emphasise the Cornish connection. On a sideboard would be a three-tiered cake stand, holding the more delicate fancies.

Behind the parlour was a room, smaller and darker. It was in this room where Rosemary imagined Mary had stored her paintings, and Cordelia had proudly shown them off to their visiting company. She had now seen several works and they were of Newlyn harbour with its fishing fleet, and the neighbouring village of

Mousehole, with its tiny protective harbour. The Cornish fishing fleet and seine boats were celebrated with bright vibrant colour, thickly applied, with no attempt at toning.

Lighthouses, piers and tumbling cottages on Cornish hillsides were in abundance. Rosemary could see a table covered with tubes of oil paints and brushes up to their necks in jars of turpentine. She somehow thought Mary would have an easel because Tim said she painted in every room in the house, wherever it was warm, or the sun shone through the window helping to enhance the vibrancy of her colours.

After viewing the paintings, tea would be taken in the parlour. Cordelia would decide on a price, while Mary sat shyly by and poured the tea. As Mrs Fox had explained, 'We would agree a price. I would go to the bank, after my third cup of tea, to get the money. By the time I got back Cordelia had upped the price. She was wicked like that. We had a lot of arguments about it. I refused to pay more and Cordelia refused to budge, and sometimes we ended up not speaking for a few months.'

Remembering these snippets of conversation made the house come alive for Rosemary. She walked into the hall and took the door on the left of the passage. This would be the dining-room, but through an archway was the kitchen, large and roomy, with an almost walk-in fireplace. This was where the present family socialised, not in a small parlour where the kettle had constantly to be fetched, refilled and boiled. Mary and Cordelia's Victorian mother would have left the kitchen to the servants, while she presided in the soft furnished sitting room and parlour, with their Victorian furniture, beaded fringe lamp shades, ormolu clocks, and china ornaments.

There was a moment of embarrassment as Rosemary entered the kitchen, where the woman's two daughters were sitting at the table. She hoped their mother's loud voice had carried and they knew a stranger was about to enter the room. She could have been a ghost walking through for all they knew, but their stares weren't hostile. She could have stepped back in time, and found Mary and Cordelia in these two young, dark haired, girls. 'Hello,' she said brightly, and made her way to a flight of stairs to the upper floor. She found herself in a long passageway

I wonder where Mary slept? she asked herself, and decided it was the end room. In it she imagined a large, high, brass bedstead with a feather mattress and a white coverlet. She visualised a large Victorian wardrobe and oversized chest of drawers, with a triple mirror and silver backed hair brushes. The room must have been overstocked with furniture but it probably helped absorb some of the cold. The windows to this room overlooked a small yard, and the front garden. In the garden, at one end, was a high brick wall nearly the height of the house, supporting higher ground with a footpath immediately at its edge, where the gardens of other cottages sloped upward.

To the side of the cottage and garden was the main road, once a country lane. Across the road, accessed by a bridge, was the pilchard packing factory, an industry in full production when the Tregurtha family were young, now a working museum but still exporting a limited catch of pilchards to Italy. Beside the factory ran a swiftly flowing river down to the little humped-back bridge. It travelled over a rocky path, between the backs of cottages, to the sea and to the fleet of Newlyn fishing boats lying along the quay and fish market.

The new owner of Vine Cottage said a polite, but hurried goodbye and Rosemary took photographs of the cottage from the garden. By this time the rain began pouring down in torrents and Rosemary drove home in appalling weather conditions. The car was sprayed with water from over-full gutters, and windscreen wipers could not keep the view clear. Dusk came early and the country route home to St Ives was ill-lit. Trees bent in the wind and the little car was almost bowled over as she drove out of the valley of Nancledra, up the hill, and onto the moorland, that unsheltered stretch of road beyond Cripplesease.

She arrived home to find the family safely enfolded in the warmth of the big kitchen downstairs; a casserole, which they had all prepared before leaving that morning, giving off a welcoming smell of goodness, and everyone eager to tell of their walk to Zennor.

'We decided to walk back,' Miranda began.

'It had started to rain quite heavily,' Sylvia added.

'We thought we'd cut up from the path by Tregerthen farm,' Penelope said.

The twins interrupted, 'We were just outside the cottage where D H Lawrence stayed when the rain came pouring down in buckets,' Lamorna said.

'And then, the woman who lives next door called out from her cottage to come in out of the rain,' Demelza said.

They had all taken shelter, had tea at the cottage, and rang for a taxi to take them home. 'The woman told us that Katherine Mansfield, a New Zealand writer, had lived in her cottage, right next door to Frieda and Lawrence.'

'Well, I've told you all that,' Rosemary said.

'We know, but this time we listened properly,' Lamorna confessed.

'Poor Lawrence. He was driven out of Cornwall with his wife Frieda, who was German you know. Of course it was the First World War. They were accused of spying,' Penelope said. 'Did you know, Frieda was related to Baron Von Richtofen? that notorious German pilot with his red plane?'

'Yes,' Rosemary said impatiently. 'I believe I've told you all these stories in the past, but you've always been too apathetic to listen.'

Penelope ignored her. 'All the English pilots had a mission to get the Red Baron, because he shot down so many English planes.'

'I know. I know. Why does no one listen to me?' Rosemary flounced off, gritting her teeth.

'Don't be such a child,' Penelope called after her.

Miranda took up the story. 'I liked the bit about Lawrence making Frieda wear red stockings. You can imagine how shocked the natives were when she walked into town.'

Their laughter followed Rosemary out of the room.

Next day was the end of the sisters' holiday week, but Sylvia decided to stay on for a few days in order to meet up with her friend at Piazza flats and introduce her to Rosemary. Lewis was escorted to the station and waved off on the train to London.

'Come again soon,' Rosemary called out after the train.

'Mum, how can he hear you?' Demelza said. 'You should have told him.'

The day after Penelope and Miranda left Talland House to return home, Rosemary woke up in a panic. She was stuck again. She couldn't write anything. There was nothing in her head except imagined voices from the past. Children continued to play cricket whenever the twins weren't around. Sometimes she heard laughter in the garden and thought she caught sight of a white petticoat just touching a small lace-up black boot.

She remembered what happened last night when she couldn't sleep and got up to look at the moon hanging over the sea. She stood out on her balcony. Next door she thought she heard Lamorna and Demelza talking. She was about to say, 'Go to sleep, girls,' when another adult voice said exactly those words. She was startled. She thought about the conversation she had overheard between two children.

'Are you asleep Vanessa? I can hear voices on the balcony.'

'It's only Mother and Father talking. Go to sleep, Virginia.'

'I can hear the waves too.'

'They're telling you to go to sleep, Ginia.'

'I know. They say 'shush' very softly and quietly, like a lullaby. They whisper on the beach.'

'If you keep on talking, Virginia, we can't hear the lullaby.'

'The light is keeping me awake, Nessa.'

'Well close your eyes.'

'I don't want to. I love watching the light on the nursery wall. I always miss it when we're in London. We're part of the lighthouse and the light in Talland House. I shall always remember the lighthouse.'

'We're part of it now, tonight. Don't sound so sad, Ginia. We're here in our favourite house at St Ives on sea.'

'Oh Nessa, you make it sound so common. St Ives isn't like any other place. I hope mother and father will always have this house.'

'Of course they will. They love it here as much as we do.'

'I can't hear voices anymore. I think they've gone to dinner. Shall we let the basket down, Vanessa?'

'Was Sophie in a good mood?'

'When I said goodnight she gave me a wink.'

'That means she's all right. What was she cooking, Virginia?'

'I think it was fish.'

'Well, she wouldn't put fish in the basket, silly. What did you see for pudding?'

'Rhubarb tart. Ugh! We don't want any sour old rhubarb.'

'If she doesn't feel like it we won't get anything. I'm

going to let the basket down.'

'Help me open the window, Ginia. I'll tie the knot. We don't want it coming undone and tipping custard all over the cat.'

'I felt a tug. Cook's taken the basket in. Will she, won't she, send us any supper. Yes, she will.'

'Give me the rope. Gently. Grab the basket when it gets to the windowsill.'

'What's in it?'

'Strawberries. Strawberries Nessa! And a little dish of Cornish cream with brown sugar. I'll write a special thank you note and send it down in the basket.'

'Eat the strawberries first, Ginia.'

'I wonder if Father will take us to the lighthouse tomorrow. If all of us want to go there won't be room in the boat and of course the boys will get first choice.'

'We'll have to wait and see. But he'll have to take Rupert ...'

'Rupert Brooke is only six!'

'He'll be treated like a man – but he is a guest. Anyway, what makes you think Father is going to the lighthouse tomorrow?'

'I was reading the notes and papers on his desk.'

'You shouldn't read other people's letters, Virginia.'

'It wasn't a letter; it said St Ives Arts Club. I can remember what it said, 'It was resolved that when members had finished reading the magazines they should be disposed of by being sent to the keepers of Godrevy lighthouse. All the magazines were piled on the chair.'

'Vanessa, Virginia. Go to sleep girls.'

'Yes, Mother – goodnight.'

Rosemary was troubled. Her hands were hot and sweaty with anxiety and her head began to throb. The twins were probably right. She was mad. They told her frequently and, worse still, implied it with the looks that passed between them. Or perhaps after a week of activity when her sisters were around, the quiet house was returning to normal. That's why she could hear the voices again; or was it simply that she was so full of the journals and letters of Virginia that they appeared like voices, but they were actually inside her head? She could recall whole passages of writing, and then again, she was able to create happenings from just a brief description, like letting down the basket from the nursery to the kitchen window for tit-bits from the dinner table for Virginia and Vanessa.

Rosemary, panicked by her thoughts, woke the girls early. 'We're going out to the country to visit Rachel. You can ride the horses and have a lovely time.'

They lay, looking at their mother. Now what was she running away from? It was more than wanting to see Rachel. Something had upset her. They hastened to get dressed, without fuss, or question, knowing they could help restore her calmness if they weren't argumentative.

Rachel, as usual, was delighted to see her two god-daughters and their mother. 'We'll have to go and get the horses from the field. They won't be any trouble. You girls can go to the stables and sort out the tack.'

As they emerged from the woods the two horses came trotting across the field to greet them. They nuzzled into Rachel's shoulder and began to push the women along from behind. Rosemary shivered. She was nervous of their height and strength, never having been accustomed to horses.

'They terrify me. However, gentle and lovely they are, I could never overcome my fear.'

'Don't worry. They're perfectly OK,' Rachel assured her. 'They're taking us to the kitchen door for a feed. Desmond feeds them carrots and apples. They just want to make sure we don't dawdle on the way, so keep walking and they'll behave like gentlemen.'

'Some gentlemen,' Rosemary said. 'One of those gentlemen is the reason for you having your hand X Rayed this afternoon.'

'Well, wouldn't you be startled if a rabbit popped out of a hole at your feet?'

'What is it that makes animal owners find excuses and forgive them for everything they do?' Rosemary asked.

For asking such a question Rosemary was nudged quite forcefully in the back.

'Better keep walking,' Rachel advised.

They were escorted to the rear of the house and the Elizabethan exterior. Rachel had a job restraining the pair while Rosemary ran forward to open the stable door to the kitchen, letting Rachel in and closing the lower half, while the horses thrust their heads over the top.

'Now then, Rosemary, put your hands into those sacks under the bench and pull out a handful of apples. I'll get the carrots. They'll go away after they've had a feed, and if we ignore them. Then the girls can take charge.'

Rosemary made her offerings very tentatively, copying Rachel's way of feeding them. When the horses were satisfied and had been taken off by the girls, Rachel prepared salad and filter coffee for lunch. They took themselves to the drawing room and sat with plates on their laps in armchairs either side of a huge log fire ready to be lit in the evening.

'Rachel, this house is so beautiful. I could never imagine living in a house like this.'

'I know,' Rachel said, with a sigh of pure joy and contentment. There was no attempt at apology for her good fortune, or pretence that it wasn't all that special. 'I wake every morning and look out of any window, to the fields and woods and know they are mine and Desmond's. It's such a wonderful feeling. I love it. I truly love this place.'

The house was full of antique furniture, inherited from previous generations. Portraits of ancestors hung in every lofty room and hallway. The wide wooden stairs from the main hall would take six people walking abreast.

They had chatted for an hour when Rachel, with a worried expression said, 'Desmond should be home by now. He was supposed to have lunch with us and then take me to the hospital for my X Ray. You can't afford to cancel appointments these days, or you won't get another for ages.'

Rachel got up to look out of the windows to see if he was coming up the drive, but the telephone rang. She listened and then turned to Rosemary, 'The car's broken down. The AA's with him now but he doesn't know how long it'll take to fix. I hate going to hospital on my own.'

'No problem,' Rosemary said, 'I've got nothing on this afternoon. I'll drive you.' Rachel relayed the solution to Desmond, while Rosemary's thoughts strayed to perhaps getting back late enough to see the log fire alight and to be offered tea, sitting in that cosy room without the intrusion of electric light. As if knowing her thoughts Rachel said, 'We'll light the fire when we get home. We usually sit for ages in candle light, just talking. Just being here.'

For their own safety, the twins were hastily deprived of their mounts, amid much moaning and complaining, and left to eat their late lunch in the kitchen and to occupy themselves cleaning some silver, rather than sit in a hospital waiting room.

It was while walking down one of those long hospital corridors with windows overlooking courtyards and gardens, and the other interior wall plastered with advisory notices in between a variety of paintings and prints, that a particular picture flashed upon Rosemary's eye. It seemed to call out to her. She stopped in her tracks. She was now familiar with Mary Jewels' bright splashes of colour, and this one practically leapt off the wall.

'It's a Mary Jewels,' she squealed, peering hard at the signature in the left hand corner. Rachel joined her, studying the picture closely. 'Yes, it is,' she confirmed. 'Isn't that brilliant. And there it is, signed.'

'While you're having your X Ray I'll see what I can find out about the painting. How it got here and such. OK?' She went in search of the clerk of works, or whoever was responsible for fixtures and fittings. In an office a secretary looked into her filing cabinet, pulled out a file marked paintings and, on shuffling through, told her the painting had been donated directly from the artist, Mary Jewels, after a short period of hospitalisation. 'It is now our property,' she said, as though Rosemary might be trying to claim it. She advised her to write to the hospital trust requesting permission to photograph the painting.

The evening was spent as Rosemary had hoped, with supper in the huge kitchen, and coffee, sitting by the log fire in candlelight. Rachel's X-ray revealed a small fracture, Desmond's car was fixed, the twins were racketing around upstairs in the attics, and Rosemary felt refreshed and ready to attempt her novel again.

When a couple of years ago Patsy said Rosemary should try her hand at novel writing, she jumped at the opportunity. She was looking forward to having a rest from phone calls, letter writing, interviewing people, taking photographs of paintings, searching through newspaper articles, photocopying, visiting art galleries, reading reviews, organising her material, writing and rewriting, and everything that entailed compiling information about artists. However, from the moment she had seen the paintings by Mary Jewels, and met people who knew her, the painter began to live in her head. The more Rosemary delved, the more interesting the artist became and she wanted to chase after the details of her life and, more than anything, find some of her paintings.

Next day, Rosemary was struggling with this third intractable novel when the phone rang. It was Patsy, sounding friendly and approachable.

'Sorry to disturb your writing,' she said. 'I know you're doing really well. It does seem to have worked for you, going to Cornwall. Perhaps it might work for some of my other poorly writers, suffering writers' block. Though with you, dear girl, I don't believe there is such a thing. Splendid. Splendid.'

'Something else is on your mind Patsy. Something you have to persuade me about. What is it?' Rosemary said sharply.

'Well, and how are you?' Patsy replied.

'Just tell me the bad news,' Rosemary said, ignoring the sarcasm.

'Calm down. I have set up an interview for you with a magazine. It's on writing and writers, mostly for the amateur market ...'

'I can write it.'

'No you can't. This is a question and answer on your approach to writing novels; non-fiction on specialist subjects, articles, and the requirements and differences of each discipline.'

'I can answer all those questions over the phone.'

'No, Rosemary. The interview is called Face to Face. They must be honest with their readership, and they also want to take a photo – a new one. The interview is in London, and to provide you with an extra reason for leaving Cornwall, I know a man who has some Mary

Jewels paintings.'

'What! Are you absolutely sure?'

'Absolutely. I've been doing some homework too. He's prepared to meet you in London.'

'Well, why didn't you say so in the first place?'

'Priorities, Rosemary, priorities. Found him through the West Cornwall Art Archive at Trevelyan House in Chapel Street. I beat you to it, didn't I?' Patsy laughed.

'I would have got round to the Penzance archive, eventually,' Rosemary assured her, 'but I've been trying to write a novel.'

'Of course. Of course. Now, I hope you won't get too carried away with Mary Jewels.'

For reply, Rosemary demanded the names of the people she had to meet and thereafter all thoughts on the new novel ceased. 'I shall be able to concentrate on writing on the train,' she consoled herself, putting away her writing materials and preparing for her trip the next day. Sylvia was looking after the girls, but they complained about being orphaned off to an aunt.

'We're always the last people to be thought about,' Lamorna said.

'I wonder why you bothered to have children, for all the notice you take of us.'

Demelza's comments were always the ones to hit home hard. Rosemary was made to feel distinctly ill-at-ease and guilty. Why did they do this to her? They seemed to take some perverse joy in making her uncomfortable. Their father didn't receive this kind of treatment. He was welcomed with open arms when he came to Cornwall for the weekend. Why didn't they make him suffer for being away from them during the week? It really was puzzling. And yet, when she and the twins were together, they treated her as part of the furniture and had to be cajoled into taking part in any activity.

Rosemary telephoned Arthur Bridges, the man who had a collection of Mary Jewels' work, and arranged to meet him in London at his Club, which was the between stage for each of them, he coming from Sussex, and she from Cornwall. The train journey was delightful, as ever. She enjoyed just being, having no responsibilities, except to stare out of the window, enjoy the countryside, think, sleep, eat, read, or jot down questions for her meeting with Arthur Bridges. All of which she did.

The one thing that evaded her was the ability to write, or think about the current writing of her novel. As the train pulled her away from Cornwall and over the Tamar bridge, her mind went blank. She couldn't remember at which point she had left the last chapter, or what thoughts she'd had for continuing into the next. She felt quite panicky about the situation. It was another set-back she would have to deal with. She realised she'd have to return to Cornwall in order to pick up the thread again. Meanwhile, she couldn't allow the worry of it to interfere with her forthcoming Face-to-Face interview, or her meeting with Arthur Bridges at his club.

She arrived at the Travellers' Club in Pall Mall. As she entered the building, two men in reception looked up and met her with a hostile gaze. One came out from the desk and stood in front of the inner door to the Club. It made her imagine that bounding up the steps behind her were half a dozen Suffragette women in lace-up ankle boots and long skirts, leg-of-mutton sleeves on short waist-nipped jackets, with a variety of hats, surging through the doorway shouting slogans, and ready to storm the building.

'I have an appointment with Mr Arthur Bridges at 2.30,' she said, unsmiling, and in her most un-put-downable voice.

'May I have your full name, madam,' the receptionist said, equally unsmiling.

'Rosemary, Euphemia, Maud, Constance, Virginia, Katherine, Knight.' Rosemary said, trying not to smile at the stunned look on his face, 'But I expect the first and last name will be adequate for this purpose.' She didn't remind him of the first name, which she hoped he'd lost in the list of other names she'd made up to confuse him, and put him at a disadvantage. It had the desired effect. He consulted his list, nodded to the other man, and he, whilst opening the door informed her, 'At the moment, Mr Bridges is out but is expecting you. As soon as he returns I will inform him of your arrival. Would you care to go through to the lounge and help yourself to coffee?'

He directed the way, polite but ungracious, and she pushed through the door indicated. Before her, at the far end of a very large room, a fire was burning in the grate, armchairs were liberally planted in groups round coffee tables, indoor plants proliferated, two writing desks were available with club headed paper, and on the centre table, were carefully placed, *The Times, The Tatler, The Field,* and other magazines and newspapers suitable for their members' tastes.

She made straight for the fire and sat on the nearest sofa. While acquainting herself with the room, she saw the table with a filter coffee machine and got up to pour heerself a cup. She wandered around the room thinking, so this is what a gentleman's club is like. She had never expected ever to find out. A woman entered the room, and seeing her, asked if she'd had coffee. She was obviously there as a house mother, or matron, Rosemary thought, to remind them of their prep-school days, to make the members feel secure. She asked the woman to direct her to the ladies room. She did so, with a kind of apologetic dismissal.

The staircase was grand enough for a large country house, with portraits of distinguished members looking proudly and disdainfully down at her. At the turn of the stair she entered a door and found herself in a windowless cubbyhole. It must once have been a broom cupboard, but this lowest of low storage area was deemed good enough to turn into a ladies toilet. Obviously, one wouldn't want to encourage this other sex to overstay their welcome. She squeezed through the door.

Afterwards she continued up the stairs. She came upon a large oak door, furtively opened it and peeped inside. Drifting up from armchairs facing the window was a pall of smoke. A rumble of voices issued from these unseen bodies. This was obviously the smoking room. Sprawling either side of the fire were two old gentlemen, fast asleep with their mouths open. She closed the door on them. She was trespassing, and made her way back downstairs.

In the lounge Rosemary made herself comfortable waiting for the unknown person to turn up. Each time the door opened she expected him. Ten minutes after the appointed time, she gave up bothering to look up with a welcome smile, and sat with her head in a magazine. When Arthur Bridges arrived she was deep in an armchair and engaged in reading. She lifted her head as a shadow imposed itself on the page, and smiled at a tall, imposing man. He was a most suitable figure for this exclusive club.

'Sorry I'm late. Got held up.' They were immediately quite at home with one another, and he ordered more coffee, brought to their table by the resident hostess.

'Well, so you're writing something on Mary Jewels. I remember that parlour at Vine Cottage so well, with Mary and her sister Cordelia. I worked for the Craftsman's Council and was often at Newlyn where my mother used to live. When she died it was home from home for me when I was on business in the West Country. I stayed with the Tregurtha family many times.

I've brought along some photos of the work I have at home. I've got nine paintings, from the fifties through to the seventies, bought over a period of years, direct from the cottage in Newlyn. They always served tea, and then the business of pricing the paintings began. It was a traditional process. It couldn't be hurried.'

Rosemary looked through the photos, marvelling at the subject matter and the colours used so liberally and delightfully. 'That one,' he said, 'I loaned to the Tate but most of these haven't been exhibited so have never been seen in public.' Rosemary did not have to bother with questions; he was ready to pour out his memories of the times he spent in the company of Mary and Cordelia.

'I remember one tale,' he said, with schoolboy delight. 'They had invited Ben Nicholson to tea. At that time, they told me, he was quite a dandy. Anyway, he arrived on his motorbike in one of his difficult moods. He was all the time on about aesthetics, the placing of things on tables in the right order, arranging pieces to please his eye. That afternoon nothing seemed to please him. The table was laid, the best china set out, and he'd no sooner sat down than he was on his feet again. He pulled the tablecloth from under the tea things and they scattered and broke all over the floor.'

'Nicholson left abruptly, without a word, and drove off on his motor cycle. The sisters were appalled at his conduct. Within a few days, a parcel arrived from Heals, with an apology for his behaviour, saying he hadn't liked the tea set they had used and would they please accept this one in recompense.'

'Well, I expect they were really shocked by his behaviour. I'd always understood Ben Nicholson to be a master of sophistication.' Rosemary said, unable to think of anything more appropriate to say. 'That is truly fascinating. I expect the new tea set was ultra modern.

What a wonderful story.'

The afternoon was coming to a close, and apart from a few other details, there seemed little more he could tell her about Mary Jewels. Rosemary expressed an interest in the club and the building. 'Have you a library here?' she asked. With that question his benign expression changed to one of embarrassed reticence.

'Ah, please excuse me a moment. I won't be long.' What had she said to cause his discomfort? He returned with a look of relief on his face, bent towards her and in a secretive whisper, told her, 'I'm afraid ladies are not allowed in the library, but there's nobody there at the moment and I can sneak you in.' She didn't decline with dignity, as she was sure Virginia Woolf would have done, but instead, followed him up the broad staircase. They were both silent and furtive.

They passed the smoking room, which she had defiled earlier by peeping through the door. He held up his hand to indicate the preciousness of that inner sanctum. On arriving at the top floor, he turned to her and with a final 'Shush!' warned, 'If there's anyone in there, don't say a word. Keep completely silent. And don't touch any of the books.' She wished again for a posse of Suffragettes storming behind her, ready to take the books off the shelves and read them.

The room was empty of studious members. What a shame, she thought. They crept about; she stealing along behind him. Sometimes he turned and put his finger to his lips as though to stay any exclamation she might make. But what a beautiful room! Windows were floor to ceiling with a balcony opening onto an inner garden. Books were also floor to ceiling. There was a grand fireplace. A huge round table at one end showed where members held their most secret meetings and exchanged confidences, unknown to mere women.

Arthur Bridges had been most helpful and promised to take photos of his collection, which might be good enough for reproduction for the cover of her book. He helped her with her coat and came down the steps to hail a taxi for her. It had been an enlightening visit, an experience which wouldn't have been open to her had he not been a friend of Mary and a member of the club. The quest for Mary was becoming really exciting. She now knew what she looked, and sounded like. She must seek out more paintings. She emailed Leah.

'I've found my artist, Mary Jewels. Am in London and wished you were with me when I was sneaked around the hallowed ground of a gentlemen's club. However, I know you would have burst into laughter at their quaint rules of only allowing women entry by invitation. You would probably have used the gent's loo, saying you couldn't get through the door of a broom cupboard, so perhaps it's better that I was on my own and able to conserve my dignity. You would have had us thrown out. Anyway, have just seen several photos of Mary Jewel's paintings. Found a lovely one suitable for the cover at Roger's, but was outbid for it. Do keep a look-out for me. How are things between you and Roger? Expect a chapter of the novel shortly. Be critical, but kind. I'm fragile. Will pop in and see you when I get back to St Ives. Love, as always, Rosemary.'

4

Because of her interview and meeting with Arthur Bridges, Rosemary had been able to spend two nights at home in London, with Lewis, without the twins. It offered a freedom they hadn't enjoyed very often since the days before their birth. They luxuriated in walking naked around the house after their showers, making love wherever it happened, and giggling about it. Even the garden shed wasn't sacrosanct.

Their intention was to find a bit of trellis as extra support for the climbing roses. They had hoed and watered the garden, sorted through the flower pots for new seedlings when Rosemary said, 'I find it humid in here Lewis, and the earthy smell of those geraniums is quite heady. Don't you feel the same way?' She smiled invitingly, lifting the tee shirt over her head. She saw him turn towards her, eyes wide and looking pleased. 'Fantastic,' was all he said, before they were struggling on the beach mats hastily thrown down on the shed floor.

'Now I know how the gardener felt making love with Lady Chatterley, if this is anything to go by,' Lewis said, extricating them both from the pile of rakes and brooms which had fallen on them. 'Do you think the smell of geraniums is an aphrodisiac?, or were you just feeling ...'

'Don't be silly Lewis – they're pelargoniums,' Rosemary said. 'Help me up.'

'Come on, let's go in the house. We'll try the wardrobe.'

'What if we get locked in?.'

'You can always scream for the neighbourhood watch brigade.'

'I'm afraid all my passion's spent.'

'Well, that's a phrase designed to make any passion wilt.'

'I rather think, Lewis, that our behaviour is ridiculous. It's totally out of character. What were we thinking of?'

'I know what you were thinking of Rosemary, and I was only too happy to oblige.'

'Oh don't!'

'Relax, Rosemary. Let's enjoy ourselves, like we used to. We used to take risks in the most unlikely places. It was fun. We were fun.'

'It may have been all right years ago – but not now!'

'But we enjoyed it. Didn't we? Didn't we?' Lewis laughed, 'And we still have a few hours to indulge ourselves.'

'I have to go out. Get my hair done before the interview, ' Rosemary protested.

'But I've taken the day off!'

'Tough.' Rosemary replied, but then relented a little. 'Tell you what though, think of something different for this evening. I'll even try the attic if you'll get rid of the spiders.'

Rosemary ran laughing from the shed, chased by

Lewis, aware that heads were popping up over garden fences on both sides, wondering what their usually well-behaved neighbours were up to. Rosemary ran up the stairs to shower, with Lewis clutching at her ankles, but she sped away, screaming, and locked the door. Really, they behaved so stupidly when the girls weren't around.

'But I need a shower, too. You're a cruel and heartless woman. Let me in.'

'Use the twins bathroom,' she called out.

He hammered on the door but she took no notice, and began singing to drown out his calls. He'd quieten down eventually, and she took her time. In their younger days they often showered together, but not anymore. Time was split into before and after the twins. Then came a gentle tapping on the door.

'Darling, I'm going to make some tea. You've got hours before your interview, and you'll only be tired if you go shopping and get your hair done. Stay with me and we'll have a nice quiet time together. We don't often get the chance with those two rampaging about the house. No sex, I promise.'

'I know you Lewis,' Rosemary said, coming out of the bathroom. 'Whenever you say I promise, it means it'll be broken at the first opportunity.'

Lewis was sitting on the stairs looking forlorn. She knew she had forced this change by choosing to keep her hair appointment, rather than being at home with him. 'I hope you're making plans for later,' she said, to encourage the return of his good mood, and was rewarded with a wicked grin. 'Are you staying?' he asked. She looked at his face, expectant and hopeful. 'I'm staying,' she said. 'You've got cobwebs in your hair. Better shower first. I'll make the tea.'

While Rosemary was in London, Harbour Day was taking place in St Ives. Brad and Dave had recruited the twins to be two mermaids, representing the Porthminster Beach Café and Caffé Pasta in the Raft Race. The young people of the town and neighbouring area had an annual race where the teams built rafts of various materials that would stay afloat. The crew of four rowed, or propelled their raft to the end of Smeatons Pier, gathered up a waiting mermaid, rowed to West Pier and carried her to the Lifeboat Inn. There they celebrated.

At the start of the race from the harbour slipway the teams pelted each other with bags of flour to impede progress. The crews hoisted their flags and paddled desperately towards the end of Smeaton's pier. Waiting in excited trepidation for Brad and Dave were the twins. Quite by accident they met up with George. He was hastening towards them along the pier. The girls were dressed in flimsy, sea-green, see-through garments draped over their bathing costumes. They wore long blonde wigs decorated with various sea creatures. Sylvia, the designer of their costumes, stood by her nieces.

George arrived and greeted the girls, saying, 'One for the album, twins,' and took out his camera. Sylvia wanted to be introduced and commanded his attention, and somehow the picture didn't get taken. Demelza and Lamorna lost themselves among the girls in their mermaid finery. George, and their chatting Aunt were ignored. The mermaids hung over the railings and shouted to urge on the strenuous efforts made by Brad and Dave and the other jolly boatmen. Brad's crew of pirates were first up the steps, followed by Dave's policemen.

The crewmen kept the raft as near the steps as they could while Brad grabbed Demelza, threw her over his shoulder and began perilously to descend the granite steps. The other mermaids suffered the same treatment. Lamorna, declining the fireman's lift from Dave, walked down the steps with him. By that time most of the crews of clowns, babies, nurses and nuns, had picked up their mermaids and the rafts were heading for West Pier.

The clown's raft lost their mermaid overboard. The crew dived in after her and were struggling to reboard, being weakened by their efforts and their laughter. This allowed Brad's pirates to arrive first, closely followed by the babies. The crews of four carried and ran with their mermaids to the Lifeboat Inn. The losers awarded drinks to the winning crews.

Waiting for them at the Inn were Sylvia and George. Sylvia immediately took charge, helping the twins to dry off and put on some warm clothes in the room provided for the mermaids. Already there was much argument and controversy about the light weight of the mermaid in the pirates crew, but Brad was able to defend his win with Demelza by pointing out that light-weight Lamorna had come in last with her team.

The twins were not allowed to stay and enjoy the entertainment and celebrations, but were taken to Talland House and promised a cream tea. George, to the consternation of the twins, had also been invited.

'Why did you invite him?' Demelza demanded of her aunt.

'I thought he was a friend of yours.'

'How can he be a friend of ours? He must be the same age as you!' Demelza said, exasperated, 'We've only met him on the beach. We're trying to get rid of him. Brad and Dave thought he was weird.'

'I should watch out for those two Australians. Wouldn't trust them an inch. They're known for bumming around Europe, getting up to all sorts of tricks,' Sylvia replied, rather discomforted by the twins outburst against George.

'They don't bum around,' she was told severely. 'They work, then they travel.'

'Whatever they do, you should be cautious. George seems nice enough to me. We had a long chat. I do think you ought to give him a chance to take some photos of you for his project on twins.' Sylvia shooed them out of the kitchen. 'Go and entertain the poor chap while I make the tea.'

The girls went into the living room where George had planted himself in the middle of the huge sofa, looking very pleased with himself. He patted the seat each side of him for them to come and sit down. They ignored the invitation and stood looking out of the window into the garden.

'Haven't seen much of you in the last couple of days. I've missed you. I thought you might be trying to avoid me for some reason. Can't think what,' George said, looking to them for an explanation, a slightly hurt but amused expression on his face.

'We've been moving around,' Lamorna said. 'Want to get our West side sun-tanned, as well as our East side.'

George laughed. 'I find these girls so amusing,' he said, as Sylvia entered the room carrying the tea things.

'Do you?' said Sylvia, surprised. Thinking only of their decidedly unamusing sulks. 'You must tell me some of your jokes girls; I shall be only too pleased to laugh. Now, give our guest some tea and scones.'

'He's your guest,' Demelza said boldly, being already in a bad mood by missing the fun at the Lifeboat Inn.

George and Sylvia exchanged a knowing, surprised look. It was George who poured the tea, asked who took sugar, handed round the plates and scones, and made himself charmingly attentive to Sylvia. The twins sat glowering in a far corner, reluctantly accepting tea and scones offered by George, who had to walk across the room to serve them. Sylvia began to look decidedly displeased. The twins excused themselves as soon as possible and went up to their room, leaving Sylvia to show George the downstairs flat and escort him round the garden.

'I've never known such rudeness,' she complained on the telephone to their mother later that evening. 'He was a perfectly nice young man. I liked him. He's doing research on twins with a friend of his. Wants to interview the girls. If it's a thesis of some sort it might even be published in a book.'

Their mother was more circumspect. 'The girls have never mentioned him to me. I'll have to see him myself. But if they're not keen to be interviewed, then I'm not going to persuade them.'

'I expect they've never mentioned him because you've been too busy with your writing.' Sylvia made a sharp dig at her sister. She, after all, had been looking after the twins, while their mother had gone off to London to be interviewed, and if she didn't trust her judgement, well then, she wouldn't be available another time. She pushed her point home by telling Rosemary, 'If I didn't think him perfectly nice, I wouldn't be meeting him again.' She put the phone down on this last remark.

Sylvia's next meeting with George took place on the beach at Porthminster. She had come down Primrose Valley intending to join the twins for coffee. She found George sitting by her nieces' towels and beach mats. 'Where are the girls?' she said. He waved his hand dismissively up at the café terrace, where they were having their cappuccino and laughing with the Australian waiters, who today were off duty and dressed in wet suits.

'I'd keep an eye on those two,' George said belligerently.

'I am. Their mother's gone up to London.'

'No. I meant those two chaps. Always there. Up to no good. The sort that take advantage of young girls who can easily be flattered. They're only out for what they can get, cruising around, showing off on their surf boards.'

'I've already warned the girls about Australian lads coming to this country; for what? I'm sure they've got better surf in their own country, and better jobs.'

'Auntie,' Lamorna called from the terrace, 'we're going to watch the surfing.' The two girls leapt to their feet and were away, following the two lads before Sylvia could reply. She and George were left to continue voicing their disapproval. She suspected a threat to the twins, confirmed by George's opinion.

The girls were lost to view behind the café. Sylvia could only sit there. They hadn't asked her permission, or advice, or opinion. But then, what danger could there be from boys in wet suits? She almost smiled at the idea. They were like straight jackets. You were simply helpless dressed in one of those. So she relaxed, and turned to George.

'Would you like a coffee?' she asked.

His face was like thunder. He looked even more put out than she was by the twins' departure. He didn't reply, just sat there glaring. She got up anyway and bought two coffees from the take-away. By the time she returned, he had composed himself.

Further along the beach the Australian lads were heading a group of youngsters in their wet suits in a jog along the water's edge. Today they were teaching at the Surf School.

When the twins returned two hours later, Sylvia and George were in friendly mode. George had suggested that Sylvia might like to accompany him to the

Marazion marshes for a spot of bird-watching. There were dry paths among the water pools, but to wear good boots, just in case. 'Perhaps the twins might like to come,' he said, as they arrived.

'Bird watching!' they chorused, in disbelief. 'We're going surfing. Brad and Dave are teaching us. Did you see them? They're really good. Can we have lunch on the beach? It's too far to go trudging up the hill to the house. We can get a take-away.'

Sylvia acceded to their demands for lunch, thinking that later she might be able to persuade them to go bird-watching tomorrow with her and George. If they didn't come, could they be left safely on their own?

At lunch the twins sat apart from Sylvia and George. He chided them for being stand-offish. 'Don't want to know me now,' he said, much to the annoyance of Lamorna and Demelza, who wanted to put him in his place and make it clear that he was no friend of theirs.

'You can have a private chat with Sylvia. You don't want us overhearing all your little secrets,' Lamorna said cheekily.

'People of your age don't want young ones, like us, interfering in your affairs,' Demelza added, meaning-fully. They giggled.

Sylvia gave an embarrassed snort, and George moved a little further away from her, demonstrating there was no commitment on his part with Sylvia. Nevertheless the girls felt they had dealt with George. And if Sylvia was attracted to him, they'd be delighted. It would stop him hanging around on the beach every day, waiting for them to appear, and having the cheek to look upset when they had coffee on the terrace and chatted to Brad and Dave. They didn't ask George to sit like a dog looking after their things on the beach. Their stuff would be perfectly OK without him, and so would they. Brad said they should tell him to shove off.

'That bloke's got a fixation on you two,' Brad told them that morning as they walked along the beach to the surfing centre. 'I can't make out what he's got in mind, but it ain't healthy.'

'Well, he's just hanging around. Can't really say he's doing any harm,' Lamorna said, doubtfully. 'We don't want to appear rude.'

'You be as rude as you like,' Brad told them. 'He's no right to bother you. And don't let him take any more kinky videos of you. If you want me to, I'll tell him to get lost straight to his face,' he offered.

'Oh no, Brad,' Demelza said, 'It would be too embarrassing. In any case, we think our Aunt's keen on him. Don't want to deprive her of an opportunity of a romance. Must be about her age, and she's not married.' They laughed heartily at the idea of Sylvia being attracted to George.

Next day Sylvia managed to persuade the girls to come bird-watching, reminding them that they were her responsibility while their mother was still away; she didn't want to have to worry about them, or those two Australian boys they were hanging around with. 'We're not hanging around with them. They're teaching us to surf.' The girls were rightly indignant.

The Nature Reserve for wild fowl was part of the RSPB's site on Marazion marshes, overlooked by St Michael's Mount. They took the bus from St Ives and, after a short walk, mounted a stile and walked a grass path in between reed beds and deep water troughs. The twins disliked the area immediately, being afraid of the soggy marshes and walking through tall plants of cow parsley, reeds, honeysuckle, meadow sweet, bramble, nettles, and gnarled lichen covered small trees. They couldn't admit to the sweetness of the various plants giving off their perfume and only complained of the number of voles lying half-eaten on the trail.

George led them in single file, crossing a wooden bridge over a reed filled dyke into the hide, where George cautioned, 'Be quiet, or you'll warn the birds we're coming.' Lamorna and Demelza exchanged looks. They hadn't said a word all the way, making it felt that this wasn't their idea of entertainment. Whereas Sylvia had chattered all the way, asking George about the names of plants, and what type of birds inhabited the nature reserve. As far as they were concerned, he didn't show any expert knowledge, was irritated by the questions, and was as ignorant as their aunt.

The hide was a surprisingly substantial wooden building. There was a bench to sit on and George opened several oblong shutters overlooking a pool, surrounded by tall reed beds. He forced a space to sit between the twins, pushing them roughly apart. He peered through his binoculars and pulled the girls towards him one at a time, pointing at the water, 'See, there, there,' putting the glasses to their eyes, stretching the short cord, which was still round his neck, so their faces were touching his each time, and he had his arm positioned round their shoulders.

Not one solitary bird settled on the water or appeared in the sky. What George saw in the ripples on the surface of the brown pool, they could not see. Neither could Sylvia who, being tired of the attention focussed on the twins, took the glasses from George's neck and tried to see what he was pointing at. The girls saw this as a release, and quickly got off the bench and left the wooden cabin. Outside they rubbed their bruised shoulders where George's hands held them and wiped his sweat from their cheeks.

'I don't know what he's doing in there to Sylvia, but next time he grabs me I'm going to tell him to sod off,' Demelza said vehemently. 'Me too,' agreed Lamorna, remembering with shame their ordeal on the beach when they hadn't told George to sod off, but had left it to Brad and Dave to release them from their ordeal. They were still sorely aware of not having known how to assert themselves.

Emerging from the cabin George was telling Sylvia, 'There are twelve pairs of nesting herons, warblers, moorhens, lots of dragon flies, and toads and frogs.' Sylvia was listening intently. Demelza whispered to Lamorna, 'I read that too, in the notice in the hut.' They nodded sagely. He certainly didn't know anything about birds. They didn't even see one, let alone identify any. They thought it more likely that rats inhabited the area and had killed off all the other wildlife.

George took another path back over a stout wooden bridge, crossing the railway line, and passing through a small copse of dark firs. The earth was so thickly covered in pine needles that nothing grew on the ground.

A walk to Marazion on the road with fast speeding traffic only further alienated the twins. Never again, they decided, would they accompany Sylvia on a trip with George. He was odious. Why couldn't she see it? Why didn't he put his arm round her. She would welcome it. But who knows what went on in the hide when they weren't there? It was the only thing that amused them the whole afternoon.

The magazine's offices were in Charlotte Street. Rosemary announced her arrival over the intercom. 'You're ten minutes early,' the receptionist said as she entered. 'Would you like to take a seat and Miss Sanders will be with you shortly.'

Precisely on time, Miss Sanders arrived, a vision of immaculate matt foundation, with glossy lips and hair that wouldn't move in a gale. She introduced herself, while looking critically over Rosemary's face and hair. 'Our photographer always comes with make-up, stroke hair stylist, so no need to worry, Mrs Knight. We'll go right through to the studio.'

Rosemary dutifully followed, feeling piqued at her mistake of arriving early and obviously needing major repair work. She shouldn't have let Lewis persuade her to miss her hair appointment. The photographer,

Graham, also eyed her with unflattering appraisal. She was beginning to feel rejected all round.

'Do sit down, Rosemary,' he said. 'You don't mind if we touch you up a little bit here and there?' He danced attendance round her, hands poised to tweak at her hair. 'Everyone needs a little colour, a flattering shine on the old tresses. Don't you think?'

She was about to give a sharp retort when he raised his voice and called, 'Deirdre!'

Deirdre emerged from behind a curtain, looking like Bubble from a sketch from 'Absolutely Fabulous.' She was wearing a large blue and white checked cotton dress with huge matching hair bow on her short blonde hair. Below the dress, her lime green shiny shorts reached to above the knee. The rest of the legs and feet were covered in a pair of blue boots with thick soles and block heels. She was carrying a huge pink case.

'Now don't worry about a thing. We'll soon get you sorted,' she said reassuringly. Dierdre took charge, pulling out a chair in front of a mirror, and hoisting her huge pink case on the shelf. Miss Sanders and Graham left. 'Surprise us, dear,' Graham said as they disappeared.

Dierdre set to work immediately, gathering Rosemary's thick hair behind an Alice band, and a pink bib round her neck. She looked thoughtfully at her face; 'Cleanser, toner, moisturiser, foundation, blusher, to start with,' she said, and began lathering Rosemary's face with a smooth cream, wiping it off immediately, and applying a cool lotion. Her attention to the job required no participation; her remarks were purely to make judgements about her choice of colours, 'Skin tone tending to darkish peachy, I think.' Then there was a period of silence while applying her lotions. 'Not even dark brown for the eyes, it's got to be black.'

Rosemary watched the transformation and was really rather impressed with the vibrant face that looked at her from the mirror. Her hair was then brushed, combed, squirted with a liquid, while Deirdre held a shell-like shield over Rosemary's face. Half an hour passed and Miss Sanders and Graham came in and beamed at Rosemary. Deirdre packed up her huge pink case, waved her fingers at everybody, and went.

Graham took over, sitting the two women face to face on two armchairs in front of a curtain. 'We can do the background later,' he said. 'Now you two relax and don't take any notice of me.' He positioned himself behind his camera. A sound man asked them to chat, and put on his ear phones. The two women sat and stared at one another.

'This is not the interview, Rosemary,' Miss Sanders informed her in a friendly tone. 'We'll do that later. I must say your hair suits you in that style. Do you think mine looks all right? I've had the same treatment as you. I hardly recognise myself. I could never achieve this look. She really is a genius that girl.'

Rosemary began to warm to the woman with this new approach. She didn't feel quite like the freak she was when first looked over, and found wanting, and with the realisation Miss Sanders, had also been 'done over' things weren't so bad. They began to discuss various aspects of their lives and found some common ground.

'As soon as Graham's finished, we'll have a drink, sit comfortably in my office and just have a chat. It's so good of you to go through all this process, but I hope it does you some good too. I'm sure our readers will appreciate your advice and your approach to the various aspects of your work.'

What Rosemary couldn't give advice on was writer's block, and wouldn't be drawn to discuss whether there was such a thing, and if so, how to overcome it. 'Each person must deal with the problem in their own way.'

'But do you experience this particular dilemma?' Miss Sanders insisted.

'Sue,' she replied. They were now on first name terms, 'I have dealt with all your questions and answered them honestly, admitting to difficulties in my writing career, but for the moment, this is a delicate and sensitive area. I cannot discuss the hitch, which is only temporary, or it looms too large and scares me.'

Sue was at once sympathetic, pleased that Rosemary had confided in her.' I'll tell editorial to erase that piece of conversation from the tape, unless,' she said, 'they feel that it is needed to provide some interest, or conflict. I have no final say, or control over their ideas.'

By the time Rosemary left that afternoon, she felt quite good about the whole experience. She arrived home to find Lewis cooking the evening meal, table laid with flowers from the garden and wine glowing red in the best Waterford crystal glasses. 'You look absolutely stunning,' Lewis said appreciatively. 'Hair's great.

Your eyes look marvellous. I'd like to kiss you but I don't want to spoil your lipstick.' He did kiss her in spite of that.

'You intended spoiling it anyway, I'm sure, with all this preparation and foreplay.'

'Cooking – foreplay?'

'Yes. Modern man's seduction method.'

'Well, let's hope it works.'

Lewis accompanied Rosemary to Paddington station and saw her off on the train with magazines, a cross-word book, a new audio cassette for her player and an assurance that he would be in Cornwall again for another weekend. Rosemary had also brought her painting of Penwith landscape, by Isobel Heath. She had bought it from the artist's studio in St Ives. It reminded her of the time before the twins, when she and Lewis had tramped the country route to Zennor, and climbed over Cornish stiles and stone hedges. The painting was of such a hedge with an abundance of wild flowers. Taller than everything, were the foxgloves growing among the grasses.

'I thought you loved that painting,' Lewis protested.

'I do, Lewis, but if I get the chance of a Mary Jewels, I'll put this one in the next auction to help pay for it.'

On crossing the Tamar into Cornwall, Rosemary turned her thoughts to her novel. It was imperative that she get to grips with character, plot, and take up the story from where she left it two days ago. She found it difficult. The novel needed continuity. The main subject of the tale was changing from a fair haired, small woman of equable temperament to one with dark, raven hair, and a fiery personality. In her mind's eye the character was becoming Mary Jewels. The thought shook her. Should she allow the change of character to happen, or take a firm hold and exert her will on the happenings and behaviour of her heroine? She put away her notes and decided to wait until she was once again sitting in the garden at Talland House, where her thoughts would become clearer, she was sure.

Waiting at St Ives station were Lamorna and Demelza. They burst into a catalogue of complaints about Sylvia, and her insistence that the girls accompany her and George to the water bird marshes at Marazion. 'We didn't want to go, Mum. We wanted to go surfing with Brad and Dave. They gave us the first lesson free. And George is such a creep. He hangs around. And Sylvia thinks he's lovely and we ought to let him take photos of us. And we're fed up with him. She's even told him which school we go to in London, so he can pick us up after lessons and take us to his friend at Camden Town for interviews. Don't make us go, Mum. Tell Sylvia to mind her own business.'

'My goodness,' Rosemary interrupted, 'You don't have to do anything you don't want to, within reason. It seems I must meet this George person, and Brad and Dave, who at least you seem keen on. But perhaps we'll wait until the weekend when your father's here, and we can both meet George. Invite him up for a drink.'

'Oh no!' they both said. 'Don't invite him to the

house. He's already haunting the place now that Sylvia thinks he's so wonderful. Honestly, Mum, we thought it was a joke at first, but she's practically throwing herself at him, and he doesn't seem to be that interested in her.'

Sylvia watched the twins escorting their mother up the path and hastened to make the tea. She didn't know where to start with her list of complaints about the girls' behaviour and their continued rudeness to George, who was kind and considerate to a fault. He always asked after them and was interested in everything they did. Sylvia couldn't understand their obstinacy and refusal to cooperate in his project on twins.

'I shall have to think twice about going away again. You three don't seem to have had much fun together.' Sylvia, Lamorna and Demelza nodded their heads in agreement.

To soothe away the unhappy experiences of the last two days, Rosemary took the three of them out to dinner at Caffe Pasta overlooking the harbour. The air was warm and still, the boats in the harbour barely stirring. People had left the beach to have their evening meal, or like them, enjoy it in one of the many excellent restaurants in St Ives. The absence of people walking along the harbour meant that the gulls were not marauding and attacking pasty and ice-cream eating tourists. They sat at a table outside at the insistence of the twins, who ate pizza. The women opted for pasta dishes and a glass of red wine.

'I'm probably going home shortly,' Sylvia said, 'but before I do I want to introduce you to my friend at

Piazza flat. She rang me today to say she's back from seeing her mother up north and would be pleased if we came for coffee in the morning.'

'Suits me,' Rosemary agreed. 'I don't know about the girls.'

'Now you're back, Mum, we want to learn to surf. It's quite safe on Porthminster beach, and there are trained instructors and lifeguards, so we'll be OK for a couple of hours while you're gone. Please,' they said together.

'I didn't let them go off on their own,' Sylvia said. But to their contentment, Rosemary agreed. They cast a triumphant look at their aunt.

Rosemary awoke early and stood on the balcony. Godrevy lighthouse was gleaming white in the pure sharp light of morning. It was going to be another sunny day. The air was already losing its chilliness, and the sun drying the moisture on the grass and hedgerows in the garden below. Today Rosemary would seriously tackle her novel, but first, to please Sylvia, she had to meet the friend at the flat in Piazza.

They accompanied the twins down Primrose Valley to the Surfing School at the end of the beach. Sylvia looked out for George, but there was no sign of him. He rarely made arrangements for them to meet, but seemed to turn up suddenly. Sylvia found this a little disconcerting, since she liked a definite structure to her day, and making plans was part of it. To the twins' disappointment, Brad and Dave were not instructing that day, so Rosemary couldn't meet them. Other local lads and girls were teaching the youngsters. The twins looked like eels in their hired wetsuits, their mother thought. If they took to surfing, which she doubted, she would buy them more fashionable garments.

The Piazza flat was on the second floor. As they entered the room it was flooded with light from Porthmeor beach. The mixture of fine whitish sand, the sea and light reflections from the sun on water, made it a breathtaking experience. 'It's lovely,' the sisters breathed together, ignoring the friend, but going to the window to take in the whole view of the beach. They turned and apologised.

'Don't worry,' Ruth said, 'Everybody does it. I have a friend who is a painter. She has one of these flats as a studio and if a gallery, or buyer, wants to view her work she pulls down the blinds before allowing them to enter the studio, so they can see the paintings before being bowled over by the light.'

Ruth made coffee and they sat on the window seat. Before them were the beach and the crashing waves of the Atlantic. To their right was the mound of rock, known as the Island, topped by greenery and a small chapel. The sandy beach had long clogged up the passage where, in former times, the sea ran through and created the island. To their left was the rock known as Man's Head. Further along was Clodgy, where five bays could be viewed from its topmost point. The coast path then led to Zennor, Gurnard's Head, St Just, Sennen, and Land's End.

'I shall be sorry to leave again, so soon,' Ruth said, 'but I have to go to New Zealand to the christening of my first grandchild. Not that it's a problem, of course. I can't wait to see her, but I didn't want to leave the flat empty. I hoped my mother would stay here, but there were problems, so ...'

'So, could you let it to me?' Rosemary asked, almost before she had thought about it properly. 'I'm leaving Talland House shortly. The girls have to return to school and I need to be away from London to work on my novel. I feel I can write in Cornwall.'

'Well,' Ruth replied, taken aback. 'A sister of my friend Sylvia seems to be the answer to my prayer. You don't smoke,' she added fearfully, 'And if the answer's no, then let's come to an arrangement right away.'

Sylvia was as astonished as her friend. 'Well, aren't old college friends accommodating,' she laughed, 'And aren't sisters a surprise when they suddenly make up their minds to something. I shall expect to come for a weekend, as a bonus for the introduction.'

The twins were full of the morning's adventure in learning to surf and were keen to repeat the experience. They showed their lessons in the garden at Talland House as Rosemary sat at her writing table. 'You put one foot in front of the other on the board and hold out your arms.' They demonstrated with outstretched arms to balance and combat the imaginary waves they would be riding. They swayed, and pretended they were thrown off the board, and argued who had been the best. Their mother watched their playful antics. They were in a good mood, but if she left them to work, there would be all the complaints about neglect and lack of interest, so her writing materials remained untouched. She walked round the garden with them as they explained all the complexities of surfing.

Sylvia had gone to find George. He was on the beach, sitting close to the water's edge, filming a family of small children, running in and out and jumping over the waves as they chased them up the shore. The little ones were all naked, boys and girls.

The children bent to pick up shells and crouched down to dig in the sand, quite oblivious of their bare bottoms exposed to the air. They shrieked and splashed. Sylvia identified a group of four adults, sitting behind their windbreak, smoking and talking. Apart from an occasional glance at the youngsters, they were far more engaged in their conversation than with the children's activities.

'George,' Sylvia said, coming up behind him. 'I've been looking for you.'

He turned a terrified, nervous face to her, jumped out of his skin, and leapt up as the sea threatened to soak his trousers. He gave a grey, wavering grin, and stumbled away up the beach, stuffing his camera in his bag. Sylvia was amazed at his antics. Why was he so frightened? She followed him slowly as he continued running away from her. She caught up with him at the Pedn Olva hotel, where he sat down, hugging his knees to his chest and breathing hoarsely.

'What do you want with me? Why are you following me?' He looked hostile and threatening. 'Is there anyone else with you? Leave me alone,' he wailed.

'Calm yourself,' Sylvia said quietly, and reached out a reassuring hand to touch his shoulder. He shrank away from her and shivered. She withdrew her hand. She made no reference to his strange behaviour, though it alarmed her, and made her anxious. 'I'm going home tomorrow. I thought I'd let you know, that's all. I've had enough of the twins.'

George was having trouble composing himself. He looked wildly around as though expecting someone to pounce on him, then he began building a wall around his feet, patting the sand into piles. He made no reply. She said, 'Just wanted to say goodbye,' and stood over him, willing him to look up. When he lifted his head to look at her, his face was vacant, and none-too friendly. She continued speaking to ease herself through the embarrassment of following him across the beach. She should have backed off.

'Rosemary wants to invite you for a drink on Friday evening. Lewis is coming for the weekend, and you can meet them both. You can tell them about the project of the twins. They'd be pleased to know.'

'Oh,' he snarled, 'Everybody seems to know about the bloody project. I have to explain myself, do I? I have to give my name and address. I have to answer questions. I have to authenticate myself. I have to present myself for approval.'

Sylvia was dismayed at his attitude. 'Well George,' she replied, 'the twins are only twelve, you must expect to have permission from the parents to interview them.'

'I thought you were giving me bloody permission,' he said, bitterly.

'I said I thought it would be all right. I can't have the final say.'

He continued to sulk and mumble about people spoiling everything, complaining they didn't understand, and what was wrong with it anyway. He got angry. 'People are always getting in the way, interfering. If they weren't so bloody nosey, well ...' He left the sentence incomplete, and Sylvia was at a loss to know what he was actually talking about.

'What is it with you?' she said, suddenly angry herself. 'You seem to be more interested in the twins than in me.'

George stiffened, and at once came to his senses; he got to his feet and guided Sylvia up the steps and into the Pedn Olva Hotel for coffee. 'Sorry,' he said, 'You see I'm not getting the results I need to present to my tutor, so it's important to complete the assignment. I haven't slept. Been awake all night.'

'Oh poor George,' she said, in sympathy. 'I'll help all I can, but you can see their parents on Friday, and I'm sure all will be well.' She leaned over and gave him a brief kiss on the cheek, in spite of the brush-off she had received. 'We can get together about it when we're in London.'

He attempted a smile, satisfied that Sylvia was on his side and prepared to pave the way for access to the twins. 'My friend in Camden Town will be pleased to know.'

Sylvia and George parted on cool but good terms and exchanged phone numbers. George agreed, reluctantly, that they would meet and have coffee and discuss the progress of his project when they were at home. Sylvia went to pack.

George went searching for the twins on Porthminster beach. They were having a surfing lesson and were intent in their activity. They were completely unaware of him watching from a distance. He wanted one last look before going back to London.

Lewis arrived in the afternoon on Friday. It was their final weekend. They would all be travelling back on the train on Sunday. Rosemary had several issues to discuss with Lewis and was glad the twins were out of the way.

'We have to see this chap George tonight, who Sylvia and the twins have got to know. According to Sylvia he's a proper gentleman; whatever that means. His study on twins involves interviewing the girls.'

'Is there a problem with that?' Lewis wanted to know.

'According to the twins, there is. They consider him a creep and from what they say, he's always hanging around. But young girls can put wrong interpretations on things. He's Sylvia's age and is obviously interested in her. It just so happens they're often with her, especially when I was away in London. Then there's the Australian lads.'

'Don't worry about it love. We'll talk to the girls, and we're seeing this chap George tonight. We'll be able to assess the situation.'

Lewis was quite happy to leave it there, rather than talking endlessly about people they hadn't met.

Rosemary never had a chance to mention her other concern about renting the Piazza flat, because Lewis was kissing her and smothering any talk coming from her lips. 'I've missed you. It's been a whole week.' He continued exploring her mouth. She gave in, and allowed herself to be led to the bed to make love. They both fell asleep and were awakened by shrieks of laughter from the girls as they returned from surfing. They guiltily and hastily dressed.

5

On the train going home Rosemary and Lewis discussed why George had not turned up to meet them on the Friday. They couldn't contact him, not knowing where he was staying, and were puzzled he hadn't tried to get in touch with them. The twins were equally puzzled, but pleased. 'We didn't want him to come anyway,' they declared. He hadn't been on the beach, as far as they were aware, but in any case they were surfing and made sure not to leave any of their clothes around, which he could identify and 'mind' for them.

It was always strange coming back from Cornwall. The twins were disorientated, thinking only of when they could return and take up surfing again. London seemed dark and noisy. The weather had changed, even in the west country, but they only remembered brightness, the sea and soft warm days on the beach. Lewis was happy having everyone in the house again, enjoying the twins' music and their laughter, and Rosemary taking control of the kitchen and organising their lives.

Rosemary was the most disturbed. She attempted writing her novel but nothing seemed to flow. She struggled with her changing characters and decided to let them take over, altering previous chapters to fall in line with the present mood. She had still not broached the subject of the Piazza flat, which would be hers from the first of next month. The opportunity arose when, on a humid, sultry, Sunday morning, they walked from West Hampstead, through the heath to Kenwood. Lunch in the sweltering heat of the garden caused the twins to recall the cool breezes from the sea at St Ives.

'When can we go back?' they asked.

'Well, as a matter of fact,' Rosemary began, taking a covert look at Lewis. 'I've more or less got an option on a flat at Piazza for a month. One of Sylvia's friends said I could have it ...'

'This is the first I've heard of it,' Lewis interrupted, beginning to feel more and more left out of his wife's plans. Rosemary wasn't the only one fed up with this novel. All the family were suffering.

'But she hasn't decided, Dad. That's why you didn't mention it, isn't it, Mum?'

The twins, bless their hearts, had guessed Rosemary's predicament and come to her aid. It was all to their good that their father shouldn't be put out by this arrangement, and though their mother would be away from home, they weren't going to protest at their neglect; not this time anyway. They would certainly do so if Rosemary didn't let them come for the weekend. Wisely, they left the parents to come to a decision but gave impetus to their mother's argument as they departed. 'You will let us come Mum, won't you?' Lewis gave in reluctantly, not wanting to deprive his youngsters of their surfing. Fortunately, Rosemary, wouldn't have to lose the deposit already paid on the flat.

Sylvia was on the doorstep when they arrived home exhausted from their long trek across Hampstead

Heath. The girls went off to shower and rescue their sweet perfumed skin from the sticky sweat of heat and dusty soil of the walk. Lewis went to battle with work problems in his study, and the women settled in chairs in the garden with a cool drink.

'Well, what did you think of George?' Sylvia asked.

'Not much, since he didn't turn up on that evening you arranged for us to meet him at Talland House.'

'Oh, what a nuisance. Didn't he ring to cancel?'

'No. So much for the perfect gentleman,' Rosemary teased.

'Perhaps I gave him the wrong number. Mind you, now I think of it, he was in a funny mood, or he was ill. He was certainly hot and bothered about something and acting very strangely, so he may have forgotten. He was like a different person.'

Sylvia was making all sorts of excuses, not wanting him to appear in an unfavourable light in her sister's eyes. Or for her to feel she had misjudged him. However, she was angry, despite her reasoning explanations for him letting them down. She would ring him at the first opportunity. That would be her excuse. He hadn't been in touch with her since she had returned to London.

However, she was uncertain of his reaction and left ringing for a few days, hoping George would make contact. He didn't. When she finally plucked up the courage to ring, he was cool and inattentive. When he answered the phone, she could hear noises in the background. It sounded as if he was watching television.

'Hello,' he said vaguely, as though his interest was on

114

something else.

'It's me, Sylvia,' she said. There was a scream from the programme he was watching.

'Are you busy? I could ring back.' She thought she heard him say, 'It's her.' Then he said, 'Hi Sylvia.' The disturbing noise from within the room ceased.

'We're watching a video. The friend I'm making the programme with on twins.' She heard the friend laugh.

'Actually, that's what I was ringing for. My sister said you didn't turn up at Talland House and meet them. I was wondering ...'

'Yeah. Well I cut short my holiday, and I didn't feel like an interrogation.'

'I just thought you'd like to get to know the twins' parents, that's all.'

'So when are you going to bring the twins round?'

'Well, perhaps we could meet and talk about it.'

There was another laugh from the friend.

'There's nothing to talk about. We just want to ask them a few questions. It's very simple. Then perhaps you and I could have a drink afterwards. Give me another ring when you've got it sorted. OK?'

Before she could make a reply, he had rung off. He had made her feel ridiculous, ringing him and questioning why he hadn't done something she had organised for him. Surely he could see it was the right approach; but obviously he thought it was unnecessarily complicated, or formal. She seemed to have made a blunder in trying to progress their relationship. She would have to give this some thought, or make amends; or forget about him altogether. It made her angry to think he was calling the tune. Now what should she do? The next move was obviously up to her. He had made that clear.

Rosemary arrived at Piazza in pouring rain. She collected the key from the woman in the flat below, declining the cup of tea, but hoping they would meet up again quite soon. The air was warm as she entered the flat. The tide was full and the waves swept up the beach and almost threatened to swamp the balconies of the flats beneath. It was exciting, watching that huge sea flinging itself on the beach and making mountains of sand at intervals along the shore. The sea made many changes to the beach, sometimes throwing up clusters of stones, grading them in size, and rounding the sand into perfect embankments.

It was a joy putting away her clothes, becoming familiar with the kitchen, laying out towels in the bathroom and finally setting up her writing table in front of the window, from where she could look out and watch the sea; to gain inspiration, she hoped. She rang home. 'Don't forget we're coming for the weekend,' the girls reminded her. 'Dad said he'd put us on the train.'

Lewis said, rather gloomily, that he hoped she'd find her muse, because if she didn't then she might just as well be home in London, comforting him. Rosemary determined not to feel guilty; after all Lewis had to go on trips for his work, and this was her work, it wasn't fun. No. It wasn't fun, she thought. What would be more enjoyable was to seek out more paintings and information on Mary Jewels. She somehow persuaded herself that this would help in the characterisation of her novel.

After the roar of the sea all night, it was now quieter. Rain was falling gently and promised to clear away by mid-morning. Rosemary set out for the local library, and a biography of Augustus John.

'Sorry Rosemary, it's not available locally,' Greta informed her, 'but I could order it. Should be here in a few days.'

Rosemary declined, and took the sixteen bus on the country route to Penzance to the Morrab private library, a detached house in Morrab Gardens. A beautiful house filled with books in every room. She'd always loved the house and the park, with its bandstand, fountain and exotic plants. From the first floor of the library she could look out to the sea at Mounts Bay, and below were the trees, lawns and flower beds.

After a cheery greeting from Annabel and Jan she sat in the main room downstairs with the books, the grandfather clock gently ticking in her ear, the quiet ambience of the room seeping through her. There were two volumes of John's biography by Michael Holroyd. She eagerly browsed through the books, feeling the excitement of coming across interesting snippets of information, before searching the index. There was no mention of Mary Jewels.

'Hello, Rosemary.' A voice caused her to look up. Before her stood her old friend Eric Quayle; writer, expert in every aspect of book valuations and collections. The library housed some important books and

Eric's invaluable advice was always available to them. 'Eric,' she said on a thought. 'Do you know anything about a Newlyn painter, Mary Jewels?'

'Of course. I've got two of her pictures.'

'Oh fantastic. When can I come and see you?'

'Any time. I think I may even have a portrait of her. And you can browse among some of my letters, too. Come over to Zennor and see what you think.'

Although disappointed in her search for written evidence of Mary in her visit to the Morrab Library, she was pleased she'd met Eric, with the positive knowledge that he had two of her paintings. She took the return journey to St Ives by train from Penzance. The line passed directly along the sea front. There was St Michael's Mount, standing out in the sea with its flag flying to show that Lord and Lady St Levan were at home.

D H Lawrence had described the mount as a 'dark little jewel.' Alfred Wallis painted it as a threat to boats sailing too close to its rocky shore. Bryan Pearce revealed all was safe and calm within the walls of the tiny harbour. They painted the subject with a very different approach. She had discussed their life experiences in her book on these two artists and how these influences had informed their work.

St Michael's Mount was forever popular with artists. In summer the trippers would walk across the causeway at low tide to visit the castle and gardens. Quite often, those same people would make a return journey by boat, or run along the path getting their feet wet as the tide flowed swiftly along behind them to cover the walkway.

At the flat Rosemary attacked her writing in a fury. She must write and hope something would come of her effort. If Patsy rang, she wouldn't be able to pretend she had been working, if she actually hadn't. Patsy had asked for a couple more chapters, but Rosemary was loathe to send them, having changed so much of the character of the heroine. The whole thing was taking on a different shape and she was forced to follow its lead. The rewriting was difficult and required concentration.

Patsy rang. 'How's my favourite author?' she began, with her cajoling voice.

'Pretty good, Patsy. Pretty good,' she lied.

'Good. That means I'll soon have something more to read. I look forward to that, just as soon as you can. Meanwhile, carry on with the good work. I won't press you too much, but when the publisher asks if you're going to meet your deadline, I can say, yes. Can I Rosemary?'

'Of course,' Rosemary said, with conviction. Panic invaded her chest, and her breathing became shallow and restricted. She had written all afternoon and evening in order to allow her time tomorrow to visit Eric. Today's big effort would salve her conscience, and now, she was hungry. She deserved her evening meal. The Seafood restaurant in Fore Street satisfied her appetite. Really, St Ives had some of the best restaurants of any small seaside town in the west country.

The next morning, sitting at her computer at the window overlooking the beach she began to transcribe the shorthand notes written in yesterday's big effort. It was a wild day with gusty winds blowing the tops off the six-foot surf into flowing mists. The on-shore winds whipped the few beach walkers along at a fast pace. Salt spray moistened their lips and took their breath away. There was salt and sand on the windows, needing a good rain shower to wash them clean.

The day was desolate, grey and lonely, with a heavy surging sea, which pushed the beach sand into mounds outside the flats. The bulldozer would be brought in to drive the sand back towards the sea, smoothing it out after severe storms. In times past the sand had invaded the town, crushed windows, piled up inside cottages and in studios, and buried fishing gear in net lofts, built on the beach at the very fringe of high tides.

Now was the time to get out into the countryside. Eric lived at Zennor with his Japanese wife, Sachiko, in a house in a valley, where natural spring water ran down to the sea. He had dammed the water to provide a trout stream on his land.

Eric Quayle's knowledge of books was legendary. A bibliophile, he had a weekly programme on Radio Cornwall where people called in describing old or precious books. He always knew the book, its value, its importance and its place in history. He was truly remarkable.

Rosemary had always felt an affinity with Zennor. It was one of those places where a great number of artists and writers had lived at some time, although it was hardly even a village, and yet Sir Alfred Munnings had lodged there, stabled his horses nearby and painted hunting scenes. D H Lawrence and Frieda had a cottage some few fields away from the centre of the village, and in that tiny inconvenient cottage, Rosemary recalled, he had written a major novel, *Women in Love*. Lawrence had referred to Cornwall as "a magic country with invisible walls and one is kept in by enchantment."

It was one of those unsolved mysteries why so many creative people had chosen to live in Cornwall. Rosemary was certainly drawn to the area. She came, plugged into the ambient magical current, and wrote. That is, she wrote about artists; the novel was something she was still learning about, through a rather painful process.

The big house on the hill above the row of farm cottages was Eagles Nest, where Virginia Woolf had stayed with her friends, the Arnold Forsters. They sat among the huge boulders in the windswept garden watching the sun drop behind the cliffs towards Land's End. The artist Patrick Heron had his first experience of staying at Eagle's Nest at the age of five. It was the fulfilment of a dream when, in the mid nineteen fifties, Patrick bought the house with his wife Delia, and their two girls. She enhanced the design of the garden. He painted from a studio in the house and from a Porthmeor studio in St Ives, where his very large canvases were created.

Rosemary remembered Patrick's funeral at Zennor church. The church was full to overflowing, everyone standing, rather than dare to occupy the magical seat.

But Rosemary boldly sat in the mermaid's chair. She felt she had that strange kinship with the mermaid. It was sitting in this chair where she experienced the first pangs of childbirth. She had wished for the twins to be born in Cornwall and, as far as she was concerned, the mermaid had granted her wish.

After the church service for Patrick, the house and garden at Eagle's Nest was the scene of a celebration of his life. The spring day was extraordinarily beautiful and Rosemary couldn't help wishing that the artist had been there to enjoy it, instead of newly buried with his wife, who had died twenty years previously.

It was a moment of poignant sadness to see Patrick's pink shirt in his bedroom and his bright pink scarf, the one he had worn to escort her round his garden, years ago, when she had interviewed him. Other items of clothing, so evocative of the personality of the man, were in neat folded piles in the room. She had a vision of seeing Patrick and Tony O'Malley, friend and fellow painter, walking at the water's edge at Porthmeor beach, deep in conversation, and had regretted not having her camera handy.

Fortunately, the summer bus timetable was operating. Rosemary took the open top bus to Zennor to see Eric. It travelled one of the loveliest roads in the county. From the top of the town, away from the sea and the harbour, the countryside spread out to old farm buildings, fields, heather, gorse, and the distant sea. On one side of the road were the wild hills, with a footpath known as the Tinner's Way, which led to the abandoned tin mines of long ago.

These hills held a dangerous legacy of mine shafts, many uncapped, which could easily swallow a horse and rider. On the other side of the road small green fields, bordered by ancient stone hedges, led directly to the cliff tops and the sea. From her vantage point on the top of a bus this luxurious treasure of countryside and sea opened up before her. The winding road coursed up and down hill, making vistas appear to please the most critical eye.

From the bus she walked to the centre of Zennor, past the Tinner's Arms and down a lane towards the sea, for about a quarter of a mile. She stopped at Eric's gate. Before she could press the button on the intercom, Eric's voice said, 'I saw you coming. Push the gate. It's open. Don't worry about the donkeys. Just come on down. They won't hurt you.' Worrying about the donkeys, she nevertheless obeyed the command and opened the gate. The two donkeys were on the far side of the grass area, which dipped down towards the house. They looked up on hearing the click of the gate but thankfully didn't find her sufficiently interesting to come over and investigate.

Eric was alone in the house, his wife having taken the children to Penzance for shopping. 'Come through. I'll make a cup of tea and we'll have it on the terrace. I've been waiting for some visitors to arrive.' Rosemary wondered who the visitors were. She walked through the dining room into the living room and on to the terrace. Everywhere there were books and paintings.

They were looking over the balcony down to the trout stream when they saw a flash. A bird streaked from the sky and skimmed over the water. 'The swallows. The swallows have arrived!' Eric exclaimed. 'My visitors. They come every spring and this is their first watering hole from their long journey across the sea. It's their first sip of water. Isn't that wonderful?' They watched while the bird flew backwards and forwards over the stream, dipping and sipping on the wing, and then it was gone.

'Won't be long before the others arrive,' Eric told her. 'They come swooping in from the Atlantic.' They stood watching the sea, hoping the whole flock of birds would follow the leader into the valley, but they were disappointed.

In the dining-room Eric pointed out his two Mary Jewels paintings of cottages and trees; two fairly small pictures, but with the full rich colours of her palette, giving them a fulsome look. Pleased though she was to see the paintings, they were not suitable for the cover of her novel.

'Now; about the portrait. It'll be interesting to see if it really is a picture of Mary Jewels. I've seen enough photos to identify her fairly positively.' They moved into the next room and saw a disappointingly blondish female with no relation to the dark features of the Romany beauty that was Mary. 'Ah,' she said, 'it isn't my Mary.'

Books of an exquisite nature surrounded her in Eric's library. Rare books, first editions, unique volumes, and illustrated manuscripts. It was a pleasure to see her own books on artists of the area. She sat in a chair facing down the valley and out towards the Atlantic ocean. The sea was fairly choppy on this day and the wind boisterous. Eric had known a time when he felt the sea would rise up and swallow the valley. The wind had been so strong it had found and entered every crevice in the fabric of the building and built up inside to such an extent that it had imploded.

'All the windows of the house were shattered and blown out from the inside. It was a terrifying ordeal. We were petrified,' he told her.

At the window of Eric's study she sat with a folder of letters written by Ben Nicholson to various people, while from the balcony, Eric watched the sky for the swallows. She skimmed through pages of hand-written text but, disappointingly, there was nothing connecting Mary Jewels to any of this correspondence. Eric then, miraculously, came up with the name of a nephew of the sisters, Peter Tregurtha, living in Plymouth.

'This could be my best lead so far, Eric. Bless you for that.' Saying goodbye to Eric at the door, she saw that the donkeys had clustered round the gateway and her way out was threatened by their huge bulk. Somehow she couldn't say she was afraid of the animals and reluctantly braved the path towards her freedom.

The donkeys watched and waited as she stepped towards them. Her fear cautioned her. What if they move and come towards me? What if they think I have something for them to eat and search me with their muzzles? What if they crowd me? She would be afraid, whatever innocent behaviour they showed. As she neared, they seemed to grow in size, and beside them she was a mere weed.

She was contemplating returning to the house when suddenly they made off in a lumbering gallop across the field out of her path. Eric had been watching from the house and now operated the gate. It clicked open. She stepped into the lane, closed the gate and heard it lock behind her. She gave a grateful wave in the general direction of the house. Had Eric observed her fear, or merely drawn the donkeys away from the gate so they wouldn't escape into the lane? If they had tried to escape, she couldn't have prevented them.

Rosemary had a hair appointment on Tregenna Hill. She'd known her hairdresser over a number of years. She actually knew more people in St Ives than at home in London.

'Hi Philip.' Their relationship tended to be jokey and teasing. 'Do you realise, I've known you since the time you had hair, and I was beautiful.'

'But I can wear a wig,' he teased.

'I think face masks are in; well certainly in Venice.'

'Anything would be an improvement.'

'Take care, Philip, anymore insults and I cancel Lamorna and Demelza's hair appointments, then you won't be able to tell them about the new concert.'

Philip was producing a show at the KidzRUs theatre, a former Wesley chapel, a huge building they were struggling to buy with fund-raising events and shows performed by the youngsters. It was one of the successes of a successful town and provided a unique opportunity for children to develop their stage craft in singing, dancing, and theatre skills.

'When are you moving down?'

'We'd love to, Philip, but our jobs are in London. We always come to the shows when we're here. The girls would love to be in them.'

'Send them to dance classes, and perhaps by the time you move, they'll be the right age for the chorus.'

'They're doing dance and drama at school because of you.'

'Well, we'll just have to make do with that. Now hair. What are we doing?' He pushed her hair around, finding the natural shape and fall before cutting.

'Listen Rosemary,' he said, 'It's not the professional thing to do, and I can't ask all my customers, but do you mind if I clamp on my earphones and listen to a tape? I have to learn the words for the operatic society's *The Sound of Music*.'

He stepped aside and bowed. 'Captain Von Trapp, no less. I've been so busy rehearsing the kids, and it's first rehearsal for me tonight. I don't want them to feel I'm not up to standard.'

'I know how you feel, Philip. I'm in exactly the same predicament of having to prove myself. Anyway, it's better than having to hear you talk. It's OK, as long as you don't sing out loud.'

He grinned, and clamped on his earphones.

Philip concentrated on the skill of cutting her hair,

127

sometimes mouthing words to the tune, and smiling at her in the mirror. In the next chair, drifts of conversation between a client and stylist came across to Rosemary.

'The car was found at the foot of the cliffs at Hell's Mouth. It was pushed over the edge. It must have been horrifying for her family. Who could do such a thing?'

'She was such a happy person.'

'The police questioned everyone who saw her on that last day. It really brings it home to you when murder happens in your own town.'

'They were asking everyone how she seemed, what her mood was like. Did they know of any strangers who'd suddenly appeared in her life over the last few weeks? Of course with a B&B they're nearly all strangers who knock at your door. First of all they thought it could be suicide.'

'You'd hardly bash yourself over the head to commit suicide. If her body had been washed away, they would never have found out it was murder.'

'Right. Ready for the dryer. Would you like some coffee?' They moved away.

'Philip,' Rosemary said, signalling for him to remove his headphones. 'Who was the murdered person they were talking about?'

'You don t know?. I thought you were quite friendly.'

'Who Philip?' she asked alarmed.

'Oh dear. It was Leah Carmichael.'

'Oh my God! Leah. Surely not. I can't believe it! That's why I haven't heard from her. We were in touch by email, frequently. We were at college together. I knew her before we were married. We often stayed with her.'

Rosemary poured out a stream of memories. Then she paused, thinking about her friend, trying to understand what had happened. Philip put a comforting hand on her shoulder, and signalled to one of the girls to get them both a coffee. He pulled up a chair ready to sit and listen, while she worked through her distress.

'Such a shock. I intended calling on her today; just turning up on her doorstep. I could do that with Leah. Absence made no difference to us. We just started where we'd left off, as though there was no parting or time in between. I told her about my search for a Mary Jewels painting for the cover of my book. She was so excited.'

'I know. She told me a couple of weeks ago. She was really pleased about something she had to tell you. I don't know what it was and foolishly, I never asked. Now, we may never know.'

'Oh poor Leah. Poor love. She always had some sort of surprise for me. It was something she enjoyed doing, treating people, giving them her time, and interest in whatever they were ... I can't believe it.' Unable to continue, Rosemary wept quietly.

Rosemary recalled the many happy meetings with Leah. The last magical moment was over twelve years ago at the Minack theatre, before the twins were born, when Leah was one of Titania's fairies. They sat up late afterwards, reliving their student days and laughing at their college performance in *A Midsummer Night's Dream*.

'Remember how we messed up one time, whispering secrets while resting on our grassy hillock, not noticing the other fairies had gone off stage? Everyone was off stage, and there we were, and the backstage crew waiting to change the scene,' Leah laughed.

'When we finally realised, we did a sort of dance of the sugarplum fairy across the stage to get ourselves off, and the audience applauded our mistake. Can't say the producer was all that pleased with us,' Rosemary said.

The very last morning after Leah's performance at the Minack and after breakfast on the terrace at the Lamorna Hotel, Lewis, Leah and Rosemary walked down to the cove, passing the stream and woods, studios and cottages; recalling the famous names of the Lamorna circle of painters, who lived there at the turn of the century. They drove back to the Minack and stood looking down on the empty stage in the morning light, with its backdrop of the ocean. They bathed in the cool, greeny turquoise sea on Porthcurno beach.

'I believe this is where my spirit is,' Leah said.

Philip touched Rosemary's hand, calling her back to the present.

'There's a memorial service next week. The family are looking for a friend to read her favourite poem in church, but most people can't face it.'

'I know that poem. It's called, *Remember Me*, by Christina Rosetti. I'll read it.'

The news of the murder of such a close friend was distressing and disturbing. Rosemary made contact with the family, sharing their shock and sorrow. 'I want to read the poem at Leah's memorial service,' she said. 'It was one of our favourite poems.' She couldn't concentrate, or write, for many days. Finally, not wanting to be alone with her thoughts in the flat, Rosemary sought the comfort of walking among people in the town and found herself making her way to Talland House. Although other holiday tenants now occupied the flats, she walked round the garden; after all, she could be staying there. Nobody would question her.

She stood on the grassy mound in the garden looking out to the lighthouse. She daren't stand on the terrace; that would be too invasive of the present occupant. The day was heavy and overcast, reflecting her sorrow. A huge cloud hung above St Ives, but over to Hayle Towans, the sun shone.

Vanessa and Virginia, as children, often stood in this spot in the garden. Years later the memory of their mother haunted the women. Virginia wrote, "She was one of the invisible presences who after all play so important a part in every life."

Rosemary had felt herself surrounded by those voices of long-ago children in this house and garden. Or had she just wanted to believe it could happen to her? Whatever the cause, she had enjoyed the experience. How painful, yet cathartic, it must have been for Virginia to write about their mother at Talland House in *To The Lighthouse*. Vanessa had praised the book as the most perfect portrait of the Stephen parents.

'Isn't it lovely,' said a voice, startling Rosemary. A woman opened the doors to the garden and stood on the terrace. 'I've often thought there should be a plaque on the wall in tribute to Virginia Woolf, don't you think?'

'Oh absolutely,' Rosemary agreed, feeling guilty at her trespass.

'I come every year, expecting it to have happened, but nothing. And to think a major writer of English literature is ignored. I can't understand it. Can you?' Rosemary agreed she couldn't understand it either.

Suddenly, the cloud broke and the rain descended in a torrent. 'Come in.' The woman stood aside, allowing Rosemary to enter through the French doors. They watched at the window as the rain quickly soaked the grass and battered down on the terrace. The cloud moved over the sea and settled itself over the lighthouse, allowing through a piercing beam of sunlight to illuminate the white pointing finger, and then it disappeared in the mist.

'Tea or coffee?' the woman asked, not expecting a refusal.

Rosemary replied in like manner. 'Coffee, I think. Lovely.'

They turned with one accord from the window and went into the kitchen. Outside, the rain poured down. The woman put on all the lights to dispel the gloom, which threatened to engulf their spirits. 'My husband and two sons have gone to the Barbara Hepworth garden. Somebody had the good sense to make something of one of our foremost women sculptors, opening her studio and garden to the public, but poor Virginia Woolf is neglected.'

'Sadly, it's true.' Rosemary replied. 'But perhaps some day, someone will realise and pay tribute to her. Along with many other people, I'm ready to support any effort to remedy the situation.'

'Me too. Sit down and tell me who you are,' she said brightly.

'I'm Rosemary Knight. I've taken over a Piazza flat for a month, but a couple of weeks ago my family and I rented flats at Talland House. Strictly, I suppose, I'm trespassing, but as you're a Virginia fan, I expect you'll forgive me. When I was here the sun shone, and I sat in the garden and wrote all day long. It was lovely.'

'I'm sure Virginia approved.'

With a great clap of thunder and brilliant flash of lightning, the lights went out. They made their way back to the living room where more daylight came through the French windows from the garden. They sat on a sofa and stared at that grey illuminated window spot among the dark walls. There must have been times when the young Stephen family sat in this room and experienced such days in their childhood, even though Virginia bathed those memories in magic, likening them to some of the best days in their lives.

Rosemary could quote so much of Virginia Woolf's memories from her book, *Moments of Being*, because she and her family experienced those same pleasures, almost word for word, the same, "In retrospect, probably nothing that we had as children was quite so important to us as our summer in Cornwall. To go away to the end of England; to have our own house, our own garden – to have that bay, that sea, and the Mount: Clodgy and Halsetown bog; Carbis Bay; Lelant; Zennor, Trevail, the Gurnard's Head; to hear the waves breaking that first night behind the yellow blind; to sail in the lugger; to dig in the sand; to scramble over the rocks ..'

In this darkened room she could almost hear the words of Virginia as though they were spoken, and imagine the room with its table in front of the window where her mother would write her letters, or their father his notes for the *Dictionary of National Biography*, much of which had been written in St Ives. She imagined the William Morris wallpaper, the coming and going of the children in and out of the room, and how Virginia and Vanessa would make their plans for one day becoming a writer and a painter. Indeed, Vanessa had written some years later, "I cannot remember a time when Virginia did not mean to be a writer and I a painter."

The gloom of the day encouraged reminiscences. She felt like the ghost of the present merging into the past, recreating that time which had become so special to the lovers of the novels and writings of Virginia, and the paintings of Vanessa. The room seemed to be filled with all the thoughts of those people, who had come to visit this house with their own imaginings about the family who had occupied these rooms, and that garden. It was a place of pilgrimage.

Rosemary was brought back to the present by the

sunlight suddenly entering the room and the voice of the woman sitting next to her. 'I think it's clearing,' she said, walking over to the window. 'The clouds are racing across the bay, and now here comes the lighthouse, back in its old spot. I sometimes think it might move, and am always relieved to see it still there.' She gave a laugh at her ridiculous statement, and Rosemary laughed too.

Walking back into town, in the refreshing aftermath of a heavy rainfall, Rosemary was anxious to return to Piazza and attempt to get on with her writing. It was kind of the woman at Talland House to have sheltered her from the storm, but what was her name, where had she come from? Rosemary was appalled. She must have told her. Had she been asleep? Had the voices of the past overlaid what the woman was saying? It was too embarrassing to contemplate.

As she settled down to writing, the sky filled with sun, the beach with people; the tide rushed in, and a hundred activities took place beneath her window. She wrote without looking up for three hours and sat back with a feeling of satisfaction and pleasure, but the world once more impinged on her day. Her friend Leah was dead. It was much more than the passing of a life. Her friend Leah had been killed. How could she understand such a brutal tragedy? It was time to go out again, and forget.

In taking a walk through Fore Street she decided to have a chat with Robert. He owned a gallery in St Ives. He always liked to give the impression of being well versed in every art deal, and with every art dealer.

Often he was in the know but if he wasn't he could make very good guesses, or pretend to information he did not have. He could never be out-faced.

The gallery was brightly lit and welcoming. The paintings were those of the so called 'middle generation' painters who were in St Ives during the era of the sculptor, Barbara Hepworth, and her second husband the painter, Ben Nicholson. Also on show were Terry Frost, Bryan Wynter, Peter Lanyon, and those of the earlier period, Lindner, Titcomb, Isobel Heath.

Robert was sitting at the desk, hands behind his head, in his most bored attitude, waiting for someone to come into the gallery.

Rosemary opened without ceremony. 'What do you know about Mary Jewels?'

'Ah,' he said, brightening at the possibility of some exchange of banter and getting up to greet her. 'I had some of her work a couple of years ago. Naive painter, wasn't she? Newlyn.'

'Did you really. Where did you get it?' She knew he'd know something of her, or her work.

'Can't remember. Cheap at some auction. Sold it almost immediately. Double the price. Don't know who it was. Don't keep those sort of records. You know me. All up here.' he said, tapping his head.

'Well, it's not up there now, is it? Less than useless.'

'Who wants to know?'

'Me, of course. I'm the one asking you.'

'What's it worth to me?'

'Nothing. You don't know anything.'

'I know she hasn't been written about, so you're not

136

likely to discover anything. I should give up if I were you.'

'I think she's worth pursuing. I'm surprised you don't know more about her.'

'But I've got some slides,' he said, triumphantly, and took a viewer from his desk and searched in a deep drawer among labelled boxes.

Robert handed her a slide of Mary Jewels' work. There was a view of Mousehole harbour with the cottages surrounding the focus of the village, the smallest harbour entrance probably in the country. It was one that could be blocked off to deter the violence of the sea in a storm. The boats rode the choppy seas in and out of the safe haven and gave a glimpse of the life of fishermen, which was often harsh and dangerous.

There were also boats of the bigger fishing port of Newlyn. Mary had watched boats in and out of Newlyn harbour since she was a girl and could capture the feeling of risk in going to sea. Rosemary liked the pictures. They were some of the best she'd seen, but still they weren't right for the cover of her book

'Tell you what,' Robert said on her way out, 'I've got a friend who may be of some help to you. Here, I'll write down her number and you can ring, or not, as you decide. In fact, don't tell her I gave you the number; we were friends, but not quite so much now.' He gave a hearty laugh. He was always falling out with friends, or others with galleries who were in direct competition with him.

6

During all of one week Rosemary had telephoned the number in Plymouth to talk to the nephew of Mary, Peter Tregurtha. So far she'd had no response. She heard the phone ringing in what could have been an empty flat. Finally she got through and introduced herself.

'Hello. Eric Quayle gave me your number. I'm trying to find some paintings by Mary Jewels. I understand you are her nephew. I wondered if you would be so kind and tell me where I can see some of her work?'

'I don't really know. I haven't any myself. I expect they're scattered all over,' he said.

'If I can find a suitable one, I'd like to use one of Mary's paintings for the cover of my book. Do you own the copyright?'

Peter didn't know anything about copyright, but as far as he was concerned, she was welcome to use any of Mary's paintings, as long as the artist was acknowledged.

'I know that aunt Cordelia sold many of Mary's paintings, after she died, to a London dealer, along with drawings and pieces of sculpture made by her husband, Frank Dobson. The aunts were well known in their day and friendly with lots of artists.'

'Augustus John?' she queried.

'Oh yes. I have a postcard which he sent to Mary, telling her to get out of the kitchen and paint.'

Rosemary could hardly conceal her delight. She walked about the flat, phone held to her ear, squeezing herself in the sheer pleasure of hearing some confirmation of Mary's connection with Augustus John.

'When I cleared out Vine cottage, I had to throw things away, papers, letters and stuff. I didn't have a car at the time and could only take what I could carry. I brought home two letters I found from Augustus John to Mary. I'll send you copies when I get back from holiday.'

'Oh, that's wonderful! May I ring you in a couple of weeks?'

'Of course,' he said, 'if I can find them.' The conversation was ended.

'If he can find them!' Rosemary groaned aloud. The possibility of them being lost would mean there was no positive evidence of the connection with Augustus John, and maybe nothing else would turn up as real proof of his association with Mary, only the vague memories of people who knew Mary. Although hearsay was no longer discredited - one only had to look at archive studies of old people relating their experiences to know. It was not absolutely dependable, but a nephew's knowledge should be enough.

There was nothing for it but to wait until Peter returned to Plymouth, meanwhile, she must make plans for the twins. They would be arriving for the second weekend. She must abandon thoughts of Mary Jewels, and her novel, while the girls were staying. They had created a fuss about the delay in coming to St Ives, but Rosemary had to attend the service in the church for Leah, where she would be reading the poem by Christina Rossetti.

The girls didn't know about the murder, and she didn't want them to be part of that trauma. Lewis was very busy tying up his big deal and Sylvia, who worked part time in Swiss Cottage library, had been staying at the Knight's in order that the girls wouldn't arrive home from school to an empty house.

It was the first weekend of Rosemary's 'defection to Cornwall' as Sylvia liked to put it. She had invited the girls to lunch at her flat, having finished work at the library at midday on Saturday. She would take them to Camden Lock market, a place they were not allowed to go on their own. The girls arrived on her doorstep just as she had prepared the table for lunch. They sat at the open window looking onto the lush garden, shared between four tenants, each quarter separated by trellis fencing with a tumble of roses and other climbers. Sylvia's garden was just lawn, with a table and four chairs. She promised them tea in the garden later. They took the 31 bus to Chalk Farm and walked into the crowds at Camden Lock.

Lamorna and Demelza were engaged with jewellery and trinkets and Sylvia with 1930s art deco lamps. They decided to split up and meet two hours later. At the appointed time Sylvia looked anxiously for the girls, who turned up ten minutes late. As they arrived on the scene, a man greeted Sylvia and turned to say hello to the twins.

'Well, look who's here,' exclaimed Sylvia excitedly, 'our friend from Cornwall. Now isn't that a surprise! They look different with all their clothes on, don't they?'

'I hoped I might run into you,' George laughed.

'Yes, I'm sure.' Sylvia laughed too.

The twins didn't laugh. They weren't sure whether George meant Sylvia, or themselves, that he was pleased to 'run into'. Lamorna and Demelza gave one another a sideways glance which meant, Sylvia is behaving like some teenage groupie, all giggles and stupidity, as though this meeting had been deliberately planned. If so, George and Sylvia were over-acting to convince the girls that they were entirely innocent of any collusion in the event.

'We had such a great time on Porthminster beach, didn't we, girls?' George said.

'A lovely time,' Sylvia enthused.

The girls stood by, silent, with bland faces.

'Got some super shots of the twins on video, and wouldn't it be nice if...'

'How exciting,' Sylvia interrupted, jumping up and clapping her hands.

The twins stood a little apart, listening to these two silly adults talking about them, but not directly addressing them. They seemed to be onlookers at this conversation, although they were the subject, or was George really addressing Sylvia? They knew their aunt was keen on George. It was so obvious in Cornwall, and here in London it was even more of an embarrassment. The twins thought again that their aunt was desperately anxious to please George.

'It's far too crowded here. Let's go somewhere we can talk,' George suggested.

'Yes. Yes.' Sylvia began shooing them towards the road.

'Talk about glamour girls,' enthused George, 'my tutor thought the video I took of the twins was perfect.' He turned to address them. 'Would you like to see it?'

The twins were non-committal, but curious, wanting to know how they would look on film. Their inquisitive natures were desperate to agree, but before they could answer for themselves, Sylvia settled it for them.

'Fancy that!' screamed Sylvia, above the noise of traffic on the road. 'We'd love to see your work of art on video.'

'I only live a block away. You could pop in. Won't take a minute to set it up.'

'Well, that would be nice,' Sylvia again answered for them. She and George proceeded ahead, with Lamorna and Demelza having no other course than to follow, feeling both hesitant and intrigued. They didn't like George, but they'd be quite OK with Sylvia around to demand his attention.

They crossed the street and over the canal bridge and took a turning on the left. Somewhere towards the middle of the road George stopped and took out his front door key. 'Barry,' he called, from the hallway. 'We've got some young lady visitors.' They were half-way up the stairs when they had to flatten themselves against the wall as a group of men rushed past them and out the front door. Barry appeared at the top of the stairs.

George addressed him in an angry tone. 'I told you I didn't want anyone here, blast you.' They continued up the stairs, following Barry into a back room. 'Sorry George,' he said, 'couldn't get them to leave.' He smiled a welcome to the girls, hardly looking at Sylvia. 'Well,' he said, rubbing his hands, 'at last, the twins.' They recoiled from him, putting their hands behind their backs so as not to shake his.

'What lovely creatures,' Barry said, advancing on them and stroking their cheeks. 'Such blossoms. Oh George, don't they make your mouth water. Come, you fresh young things and sit beside me, before you get a day older.'

George was smiling hugely. Sylvia looked slightly dis-comforted, and the twins moved away at Barry's advance. 'We've got to get home Sylvia,' Lamorna said, in a quiet voice. 'Dad will be wondering where we are.'

'We promised we wouldn't be late,' Demelza added desperately.

'Won't take a minute,' George assured them. 'I'll set up the video in the next room. Sylvia can help.'

Sylvia saw this as a reason for George seeing her alone and followed him out of the room. The twins turned in alarm to Barry, who had backed off slightly. 'Now don't mind me, young ladies,' he said. 'I'm always pleased to see such beauties.' Lamorna and Demelza were somewhat puzzled to hear themselves described as 'beauties'.

Barry sat himself down in the middle of a sofa against the window, where a blind was drawn down, obscuring any view to outside. On the opposite wall was a table and two chairs. The twins sat each side of the table. George smiled at them. 'I can see we've got a lot of work to do with you two,' he said warningly. 'Lovely young innocents. But isn't it wonderful. All fresh and new. And to think that you should come to see us.' As he spoke, he crossed and uncrossed his legs.

The girls were sorting his language in their heads; 'beauties, innocents, fresh and new.' What did he mean? Nobody had ever spoken to them like this before. How should they behave? What should they say? They looked towards the door waiting for Sylvia's return. She would talk to him. She would know what to say.

'There's a book on that table, and a pen. Would you be kind enough to bring them over, save me getting up from this comfy chair. Now which is Lamorna?' She held up her hand. 'You can bring the book. And you Demelza, can bring the pen. That's very kind girls,' he continued encouragingly, as they did his bidding. They held the things in outstretched hands. George did not take them, so they crept a little closer. He darted forward and clasped their hands. 'I'm a little deaf, my dears, so if you could sit beside me, it would greatly help.' He still held their hands but looked pleadingly at them, and they, not knowing how to refuse, sat each side of him.

'Age twelve; that's right twins?' He looked from one to the other, though he made no mark upon the paper.

The girls nodded. He placed the pad and pen on his lap and moving his hands swiftly, grabbed the top of the thigh of each girl, rubbing his hands from thigh to knee, and rocking slightly.

'Don't!' Lamorna said forcefully, and attempted to get up but George's fingers held tight. 'Leave us alone,' Demelza said, pulling at George's fingers.

'Sylvia, we're going home!' Lamorna shouted, struggling. The girls, realising they were strong as a twosome, punched Barry in the chest. 'Help, George,' he called, 'I'm being assaulted by two virgins.' He laughed as he said this, releasing the girls and seemingly enjoying the battering the twins were giving him. They gave up immediately and ran out of the room to find Sylvia.

'Come and look girls,' she said, emerging from a door along the passage. They went inside. Barry was coming along the passage after them. The room was fairly dark and kitchen chairs were arranged in rows facing a screen. The room smelt musty and unpleasant. They slid onto a seat each side of Sylvia. A video of the twins was already showing. They were lying on the beach, twisting and turning, as they smiled and posed, with George directing their actions. The twins watched fascinated, temporarily forgetting their unpleasant experiences with Barry.

At first they were happy complying with George's demands for their video shots, and then everything changed. The camera panned in and shots of the lower half of their bodies were shown. They remembered George bending down to film closer; that's when they had begun to feel uncomfortable and unwilling to perform, but still George urged their cooperation. They briefly obeyed. Then Joan's voice, calling from the terrace, ended the whole sequence of filming.

'Come up here. I've got a message for your mother and I'll treat you to a coffee. Make it quick girls. Come on!'

Barry was standing near the door. 'We'll have to take a longer film than that George, if we're to please our clients.'

'Our tutor,' George corrected. 'He said he'd like some conversation with the girls so we have audio and pictures.'

'Sylvia, we've got to go.' Lamorna and Demelza stood up, walking ahead of Sylvia to the door, while she remained sitting. Barry barred the way. George moved to stand beside him. As the girls attempted to pass they stroked their heads and pulled the girls to their chests, running their hands over their bodies, and squeezing them. The twins shivered at their touch, nervously tearing at the hands that were molesting them.

'Two ripe plums,' George said.

'Just ripe for plucking,' Barry laughed.

Sylvia watched the twins being fondled and was torn between rescuing the twins from this unwanted attention and snatching the video. But she realised it could be dangerous to warn the men that she was aware of their behaviour. She made a decision not to antagonise them, to remain friendly, which meant the girls had to suffer the mauling. Sylvia unobserved, retrieved the video and tucked it into her jacket. She quickly followed the girls, pushing them between the men and towards the stairs, desperate to get them out of the house. She passed between them unmolested.

Barry protested, 'Hey, don't leave us so soon. We've got a camera set up.'

Sylvia looked at her watch and said gaily. 'Sorry gentlemen, we've got an appointment we just can't miss.' Barry looked as if he would prevent them leaving. He stood at the top of the stairs, barring the way. Sylvia put her arms around the girls and laughingly joked, 'Next time they can do the dance of the nine veils.' It was this silly remark, accompanied by a saucy wink that convinced the men that there would be a next time. They released them. 'See you shortly, then Sylvia,' George said, meaningfully. They were in the bag. They could wait.

'Thank you, Sylvia,' George said, as he watched them go down the stairs to the front door. 'Perhaps you'll stay for tea another time. It's lovely to see you again. Lovely to see the darling twins too. We've got great things lined up, haven't we Barry?' George sniggered. 'Absolutely bloody great,' Barry said.

In the street outside Sylvia was upset, pale, and shaking. 'I'm sorry girls,' she said quietly. 'I'm so sorry.' To their surprise, they went to Sylvia's flat in a taxi. She settled them down in the garden with teen magazines she'd bought them, and went to make the tea. When she returned, the girls thought she'd been crying. None of them said anything about the afternoon's experience at George's house.

Sitting at her desk in the window Rosemary looked out to the beach. It was a chilly morning and people were slow to arrive and set up their encampments with windbreaks, tents, beach mats and chairs. She watched the braver ones establishing their territory, hoping for the sun to come out. The surfers were already out at sea, word having gone round that the surf was up on Porthmeor. She loved seeing them lying on their boards waiting for the one curling wave that would be worth riding and push them to the shore. Other surfers were running across the beach, boards under their arms, connecting cord trailing behind. They plunged into the water and paddled out with their arms, dipping under the white water of an oncoming wave, emerging at the same spot.

This morning there were forty surfers out there. It was difficult counting them as some would be hidden in a trough of the sea, others skimming over the water on their boards before being thrown off, or dropping off, before reaching the shallows. Most were lying in wait, but ready, and then a group would suddenly rise up and come racing in, dipping and curling, skilfully balancing and thrusting ahead of the wave. It was an exciting and enjoyable sight and Rosemary neglected to do other than sit at the window and watch their skills.

This afternoon she faced the difficult task of reading in the church at the memorial service for Leah. She knew she was the right person to read the poem. Other friends were too close and relations couldn't trust they wouldn't break down. Even so, Rosemary was afraid she might falter, and a sense of the occasion would overwhelm her; to cry would be to let Leah and her family down.

'I have every faith in you, Rosemary,' Leah's voice entered her head.

She listened to the service and in between hymns took deep breaths to steady her nerves. It was difficult not to be moved by the obvious distress of the family. The vicar finished his tribute and, with a barely discernible nod, signalled for her to come to the lectern. Her shoes clattered on the stone floor and echoed into the rafters of the barrel ceiling. She chided herself for noticing this triviality on such a serious occasion. What did it matter? But that was life, wasn't it? Such silly things always intruded in the most dreadful circumstances.

There couldn't be anything more chillingly sinister than murder, yet still Rosemary noticed someone's hat. On another bench were Leah's friends, among them were the library girls, Philip, their hairdresser, and Roger, Leah's boyfriend, with his arm around aunt Esme. They were all wearing bright colours, smiling at each other, and determined now to celebrate her life, as they had mourned her death.

Rosemary was careful not to look at the family and allow their distress to interfere with her reading. She remembered the time when she and Leah had talked about the poem. They read it aloud together, and now Rosemary felt she could hear Leah's voice reading it with her. They had stressed the two end lines, as Rosemary did for this reading, "Better by far you should forget and smile, than that you should remember and be sad."

149

There were kisses and hugs from the family outside the church. Why hadn't they known Leah had such a good friend? Why hadn't they met her before? Rosemary explained her itinerant relationship with St Ives and its locals. She was always passing through, making friends and leaving again for weeks at a time. The family were keen to make a fuss of her and needing her to come to the house for tea, but she declined. Selfishly, she wanted to absent herself from the sadness around her.

At the flat, she sat and stared out of the window. The telephone disturbed her reverie. It was Greta from St Ives library. 'Thought you'd like to know I've turned up an article on Mary Jewels, written by Augustus John. It's from Vogue Magazine, dated April 1928.'

'Oh wonderful. I'll come immediately.'

Glad to have something to divert her thoughts, she flew down Back Road West, through the Digey and Fore Street, up into High Street and to the library on the corner of the cross roads. 'We've photocopied it for you to keep. Got it from the British Library.' Greta said. Rosemary beamed her thanks.

Taking her prize, she crossed the road to Café No.4. Julia poured her a hot chocolate. She sat in the back room so as not to be disturbed by the comings and goings and chat at the 'front of house.'

It was a five page article titled, *The Woman Artist*. She read quickly, and only towards the end discovered a short piece about Mary Jewels. John described her paintings as being, "remarkable in the intensity of their earth-feeling. They blaze in the sight, and are almost menacing in their hint of place-magic. The colour and design convey something of the sensitiveness and wonder of primitive vision, and the luxuriance of barbaric nature. If Mrs Jewels avoids sophistication, her painting will be of a refreshing interest." There were two illustrations of her work noted as, 'Cornish Landscapes.' This must have been the exhibition John had arranged at the London Gallery. Ah well, it was something to add to the file.

Rosemary arrived back at Piazza to the ringing of the telephone.

'Where've you been? I've rung a couple of times today. Lucky girl. Not many of us can have a window full of sea; mine's full of traffic and buildings. You should be working on the novel in such ideal conditions. Have you been down on the beach for a swim? Have you been surfing with the dolphins?'

It was Patsy, making her usual remarks about what she might have been doing other than writing; really she was so annoying at times. Rosemary tried to keep the irritation out of her voice. 'I do have to eat, you know, which means I have to shop and cook, to have enough strength to work.'

'Ah, so it's going well. Good. Thought I'd give you a bell. All my authors seem to be deserting me. There's you in Cornwall, someone else has gone writing in Spain, another in New Zealand – just how far are you all trying to get away from me? And here's me stuck in London doing my best to earn us a living. Perhaps I should become a writer. Whoops, there's the other phone. Love to you.'

As usual, with Patsy's phone calls, Rosemary felt guilty. They made her jittery too. She was spending too much time looking for Mary. She was also still mourning for Leah and this sadness wouldn't leave her. She gathered together writing paper and pencils and, leaving her shoes in the flat, went down the outside staircase to the courtyard and out through the private entrance to the beach. The sun was setting, the sky a blaze of red, and the sea golden. All she could do was sit and stare at the sunset. No writing was done.

Just before the red sun disappeared below the horizon, she walked on the beach to regain her equilibrium. The sand was cool on her feet. Further down, where the tide had washed, she trod on firm wet sand, which squeezed through her toes. She liked the sensation. An hour or two would see her restored and ready to write. She looked up to her window where she could see her writing table, waiting for her, beckoning.

On Friday afternoon the twins arrived at St Ives station and greeted their mother with the cheerful expectation of having a wonderful weekend. It began with coffee at Porthminster beach café, where Joan was pleased to see them. 'We can't get enough of this place, the beach, and surfing.' the girls told her. 'And Mum can't get enough of Talland House and Virginia Woolf.'

Brad came to take their order. 'I didn't know you were triplets,' he said.

'He's a master of flattery,' Joan told Rosemary. 'He could make you believe you're not a day over twenty one.'

They laughed heartily. 'This is our mum, Rosemary.'

Brad shook Rosemary's hand, smiling his broad smile.

'You've got a coupla surfers here. You ready to start training girls? You coming Rosemary? The girls love it. Pretty good they are too.'

'It's a surprise to me,' Rosemary said. 'I thought they were as scared of the water as I am, so you won't see me down there.'

'Mum,' Lamorna began tentatively.

'I know what's coming,' Rosemary said, 'You want your own wetsuits.'

'Could we, please?' Demelza pleaded, 'We'll help pay for them.'

Another couple of hours were spent trying on wetsuits and then the twins burst into the flat, delighted with the view to the beach, scattered their things around in their bedroom, and went dashing out to try out their new body boards. Rosemary had not acceded to their requests for proper surfboards. She watched their slim young bodies thrust themselves upon the waves in their pink and green wetsuits, and turn to wave at the window.

Rosemary watched endlessly as the girls enjoyed their activity. Soon, she would begin writing. How lucky she was to have a computer. D H Lawrence, in his cottage at Zennor, had to type his manuscript *Women In Love* onto a huge, clunky, typewriter, unable to correct his mistakes at the touch of a button. What a trial it must have been. Could he touch type, she wondered, or did he have to keep turning his head from page to keyboard. With all her luck, she still couldn't begin. Lawrence, with his difficulties, his ill health, his lack of money, managed to write. He made the best of it.

If only Mary Jewels didn't keep obstructing her progress. What she would do was complete the novel, then go back to searching for paintings. That was the most sensible way to deal with the problem of Mary's interruptions.

The next interruption was the arrival of the twins from the beach, covered in sand and oozing water from their wetsuits. She hosed them both down in the shower, telling them to hang up the suits to continue dripping, and leave the body boards in the shower tray. By the time Rosemary returned with Pizzas from Caffe Pasta, the girls had showered, set the table, and were eagerly awaiting their meal.

How young they were, sitting there with their wet hair straggling around their shoulders, forgetting their sulks and enjoying their lives. It was a change from some of the behaviour, which took them into their teenage phase, when nothing seemed to please them. Tomorrow and Sunday they would be engaged in their lessons, proud of themselves in their slinky wetsuits, with Brad to teach them the art of surfing.

'Well, and how did you get on with Sylvia?' Rosemary opened the conversation, knowing they wouldn't accuse her of being too nosey, or neglectful in their euphoric moods.

'You went to Camden Lock, didn't you? You never told me about it.'

'You wouldn't believe it Mum, but we met that creep, George, there.'

'Don't call him a creep, he's your aunt's boy friend, isn't he?'

They shook their heads solemnly, looking at Rosemary and shyly wondering what to tell her. Should they mention the video he'd taken of them; could they say it wasn't quite proper? But they had posed for it, thinking themselves models and behaving in a sexy way, quite beyond their years. Really it was shaming.

'He's not really her boy friend,' Demelza told her, 'She was crying. He doesn't really like her.'

'He always seemed to be with her. Why wouldn't he like her?'

'He likes us, Mum,' the girls said quietly, and together.

Rosemary experienced a chill as they told her this. What did they mean? What was going on? She must talk to Sylvia. 'I'll ask your aunt about him.'

'No Mum, please don't,' Lamorna said.

'She's upset. Anyway, we're never going to see him again and Sylvia's finished with him,' Demelza said, forcefully.

The girls pleaded with their mother not to mention it to Sylvia. What good would it do? They knew their aunt had understood George's interest in them, and though she hadn't seen his behaviour with them, realised she had possibly exposed the girls to some danger. They were careful not to mention that they had gone to George's flat and had watched the video. There had been a tacit understanding between Sylvia and the two of them that no mention should be made to the parents. They rapidly diverted their mother's attention away from that dangerous ground. It was all in the past and best forgotten.

During the weekend Rosemary was pleased with her progress. She had now dismissed Mary Jewels to some future time and telephoned Patsy to tell her to expect a couple of chapters during the week. 'I'm really enjoying it. This is a great place to work. I walk on the beach and think through my next scene and come to my writing table, over-looking the sea, and there it spills out,' she told Patsy and Lewis. She bathed in a glow of pride and self-congratulation.

On Sunday afternoon she saw the twins on to the main line train at St Erth, and travelled back on the branch line to St Ives. Robert had got off the London train and was returning to his gallery, having bought several paintings by St Ives artists in various salerooms. 'I was going to ring you,' he said. 'The woman whose telephone number I gave you will be visiting Tate St Ives tomorrow afternoon. She'll see you at two o'clock on the roof terrace. She told me that Mary and the artist, Dod Procter, were once very good friends – and now I'm pleased to say, that she and I are friends again.'

That telephone number Robert had given her had been arousing her curiosity, but in her present mood she had valiantly put it aside in favour of working on her novel, and now she was confronted with Mary again. She thanked Robert and said she was rather too busy to meet the woman at the moment. He looked surprised, never having known her turn down an invitation to chase some elusive artist.

Monday morning Rosemary worked hard, and enjoyed writing, but by lunch time she thought she'd done enough to warrant meeting Robert's friend after all. She walked to the Tate along the beach, entering the building and saying a quiet hello to Patrick Heron's stained glass window. She meandered through gallery one, enjoying the exhibition of new works, especially concentrating on the painting by Alfred Wallis *Wreck of the Alba*, now belonging to the Tate collection. It was one of five pictures the old man had painted of this subject after the ship, the Alba, went aground on Porthmeor beach in 1938, and the lifeboat, coming to the rescue, had overturned. The whole town turned out that night, wading into the sea on ropes to pull survivors from the boiling ocean.

There was just time to see the exhibition of Leach pottery in the large Tate showcase and look out to the sea and beach, and marvel at the reflected scenes of the outside world in the huge curving windows, then Rosemary mounted the stairs to the restaurant. On the roof terrace she saw an elegant looking woman sitting alone. The woman rose and held out her hand. They said together, 'You must be Robert's friend.'

Rosemary ordered more coffee and they chatted amiably, until on a natural pause the woman remarked. 'I knew a relative of the Newlyn painter Dod Procter. She said Dod and Mary had been great friends, but they had a terrific argument, and never spoke to each other again. They were both very stubborn people and self opinionated, you know, so neither would give in on a point.'

'What do you think the argument was about?'

'I really don't know, and I think quite honestly they had forgotten too. But feuds tend to go on getting bitter when the whole point for the rift was probably something quite trivial.'

'So it was nothing major?'

'Not at all, but I do know there was some jealousy, or objection, on Mary's part when Dod won so much acclaim with her painting *Morning* which was hung in the Royal Academy. Then it was bought for the nation, and that's a great honour in itself.'

'Perhaps it was not the fame, or the painting that Mary objected to, but the way the model was portrayed,' Rosemary suggested. 'The painting showed a young local girl lying on a couch in a figure-hugging dress, which was perhaps provocative for that time. It would have offended the native sensibility. Newlyners may not have objected to models brought down from London, but someone from their own village would bring the censure of the Methodists on their heads. Maybe she objected to the pose. Perhaps she thought it brought disrepute to a Cornish village?'

'Well maybe. Mary was always getting on her high

horse about something she considered an infringement of the place of her birth by those who moved into Cornwall. But they were always arguing about the other's technique. Dod said Mary didn't know how to draw - which was true. Mary said Dod didn't know how use paint. Why they bothered to argue about it, I don't know'

Rosemary recalled Dod Procter's tonal colouring, almost scraping away the paint she had applied, and Mary used a full palette, liberally, perhaps rather naively, compared to Dod's practised ability. Dod had studied with Stanhope and Elizabeth Forbes, and in Paris.

'Dod was a dedicated painter.'

'Absolutely,' Rosemary agreed.

'And Mary painted when she felt like it. Or when she felt 'inspired', is probably how she would put it. That was another reason for them to argue, and not being able to convert to the other's point of view, they would go off in a huff.'

'I suppose,' Rosemary said tentatively, 'the argument wouldn't have been about some man, would it?'

'Certainly not,' her new found friend replied, turning into her new found enemy. She stood up and fluttered her fingers in Rosemary's direction. 'There's someone I must see,' she said, 'nice to meet you.' She hurried off.

'Oh well,' Rosemary consoled herself, 'I suppose I had to try, even to the point of offending someone.' There was still that link with Augustus John she wanted to know more about. Then a thought struck her. Perhaps Mary and Dod were even older enemies. When Alfred Munnings first arrived in Newlyn in the first decade of the twentieth century, he was a much sought after young man. Were Mary and Dod rivals for his affection?

The artist Laura Knight had adored Munnings' fair good looks, his jokes, his parties and his flamboyant behaviour, much to the annoyance of her husband, Harold. Mrs Tregurtha knew him because he taught her to ride a horse. Probably Mary and Cordelia admired him too.

Dod Procter had accompanied Munnings to the Queen's Hotel on Penzance promenade, where they marched boldly into the hotel and, daring the disapproval of the management, displayed their paintings to some wealthy patrons, hoping for and achieving, sales of their pictures. They also showed the work of other artists who happened to be particularly needy at that time. Did Mary think he should have chosen her for his partner in this art crime? Art and love were funny things, and couldn't be fathomed. Mary and Dod's long feud must have involved art or love, possibly both.

Rosemary's curiosity was now completely aroused. She needed to contact Mary's nephew. Over a week had passed and Peter Tregurtha should have returned from his holiday. She walked back along Porthmeor beach, threading her way through holiday makers, who stripped off their clothing, determined to achieve a sun tan. Rosemary sat on the terrace of Porthmeor beach cafe with a pot of tea, enjoying people-watching. There was an exceptionally low tide. She noted the boiler of the wrecked ship, the Alba, protruding out of the water, surrounded by the rocks that had caused its doom.

From her mobile she rang the number in Plymouth. Sometimes it was an embarrassment to bother people with questions they were not prepared to answer, or were evasive in their replies, or guarded, or indeed something they had forgotten about. She became adept at listening to tones of voice, which told her which of these she was dealing with. Peter was back from holiday and prepared to talk.

'What was the dark secret that Mary and Cordelia didn't want to talk about? I understand it was something to do with the family.'

His answer was without restraint or concealment. 'Of course, at that time, it was a sin, and something to be ashamed of, but these days, who cares?'

Rosemary waited expectantly. Was this going to be something about Augustus John and Mary? Was a love affair about to unfold?

'Thomas Tregurtha, their father, emigrated to South Africa.'

Oh dear, she thought, disappointed, this wasn't the line she was expecting.

'He went there in 1915 to seek his fortune. I think it had something to do with prospecting for gold. The elder son followed him out there, but it wasn't a success. There was some trouble over money and they got into difficulties. The father shot himself.'

'Oh dear!' she said, jolted into the only response she was capable of making. So that was the dark secret that none of the friends of Mary and Cordelia were ever privy to; a suicide. Modern day tell all and shame the devil, had never really caught up with them and they had carried their secret to the end, leaving the younger generation to disclose their history.

'I haven't been able to find out any more about my aunts from letters. I think aunt Delia threw an awful lot away after Aunt Mary died, and she sold off most of Mary's pictures too, and her husband's drawings. Cordelia was married to the artist, Frank Dobson. I never knew where the paintings went. There were only a few left in the cottage. I kept a couple and gave one to Mrs Fox who had been a good friend to my aunts. If anything else turns up I'll give you a ring.'

'Thank you,' Rosemary replied. She was still coming to terms with the father's suicide and what this would have meant to the family. He had died in debt and left his wife and two daughters without means of support. In 1915, when women of their class did not work, it was indeed a serious situation. They probably had a little family money, but a weekly income was still essential. Mary and Cordelia in their late twenties could hardly go to Newlyn fish market and take to gutting fish with the local girls. No wonder Mrs Tregurtha let rooms to 'gentlemen' and these happened to be artists.

Cedric Morris had stayed there, and there were others, especially students studying with Stanhope and Elizabeth Forbes. There would be friends of artists, too, who would come to Cornwall for sketching and painting holidays. So this was one of their links with so many of the artists, and of course with Cordelia marrying Frank Dobson, the connections grew even wider.

Dobson had started as a painter but became interested in sculpture through his friendship with the son of a local monumental stonemason who had shown him the stonemason's tools and instructed him in their use. The firm had provided head stones for many of the artists who had adopted Newlyn and nearby Lamorna cove as their spiritual homes.

Peter Tregurtha had also mentioned a student who studied with Dobson when he was making his reputation as a sculptor. Elizabeth Muntz, from Canada, assisted Dobson in his workshop. Peter remembered her staying at Vine Cottage, when the family came home to Newlyn. She gave him a hammer, on which she had carved his name, so he could try his hand at shaping stone.

'I wasn't really interested. But I remember there was a piece of sculpture in the garden, carved by Dobson. It was a gigantic head in granite. I don't know what happened to it. I remember being frightened as a child. It looked very gruesome in the garden in the moonlight. All the bedrooms overlooked the garden and it used to fascinate me. I used to stare at it, until it grew legs and I could make it move. Then I would yell for aunt Mary. She was my favourite, although she had a fearsome temper. Oh, look. I'll have to go, there's someone at the door.'

'What about the letters from Augustus John?' she insisted.

'Ring me next week. I haven't found them yet.' The phone was hastily replaced. She had to content herself with waiting and there was a weekend in between. She must concentrate on her writing.

Mrs Fox, the woman who had outbid Rosemary for

the Jewels painting at the auction, expressed her thanks when Rosemary rang to tell her about the shameful and closely guarded secret that Mary and Cordelia kept to their graves.

'Well the old devils,' she said, 'I expect they did that purposely, always hinting at secrets to keep people intrigued. They had all those years to get used to a suicide in the family.'

Rosemary offered another explanation. 'Perhaps Mrs Tregurtha made them keep silent. She was very religious, and suicide was a sin in the eyes of the church.'

'Maybe. Maybe.' Mrs Fox sounded unconvinced.

7

As often, when Rosemary was troubled by her inability to write, and her lack of confidence in what she had written, she turned to Virginia Woolf, for comfort, for inspiration, for solace; she did not know. She randomly opened a page of her published letters; Virginia was struggling with the final reworking and retyping of a novel, which she considered, "no good at all." She was also anxious to get on with her biography of Roger Fry, the artist and art critic, and she was dealing with her feelings on relationships, on motherhood, on refusing to go to an International Congress of Writers Conference in Paris, and turning down the offer of a Companion of Honour from the Prime Minister.

Even genius had its complications and self-doubt. Rosemary considered herself lucky by comparison and, feeling humbled, started to write the next chapter. But she was, she confessed to herself, rather more inclined to write up her notes on Mary Jewels.

She was so deeply into her writing that when the telephone rang, she was startled.

'Lewis, how lovely. How're things going with your clients? Are the twins OK?'

'Everything's absolutely fine here. We've managed to sign up our contact, who has recommended us to other people, so we're more or less taking a breather, and I'm taking a couple of days off. Sylvia's at home with the girls and I'm on the train at Paddington, so I'll see you this afternoon.'

Rosemary had been writing for a couple of hours. She had neglected to wash up after breakfast and the flat needed a general tidying up before Lewis arrived. She was excited and looking forward to seeing him. They had always found that taking days off work midweek was like doing something quite daring and risky. They had often stolen days from work when they were younger and taken themselves off on a train to the sea-side or country and now, being in Cornwall, away from home, and without the twins and their usual responsi-bilities, they could expect a good time.

They met on the balcony of the Ocean Grill restau-rant, overlooking the harbour, where their table was booked for late lunch. Lewis was carrying a small overnight bag. He was without his briefcase and some-how it made him look younger and carefree not to have that particular item. It had become an object of serious intention, but this was a holiday. They could put away their thoughts about work and concentrate on each other.

'The girls were furious about me coming here with-out them. They accused us of wanting to get rid of them. I pointed out that they'd had a weekend here, were bought expensive gear for surfing, and that their mother and I were going to enjoy being two again. You'll be pleased to know they're going to leave school as soon as possible so they can leave home. They may even go as far away as Australia, so we don't have to see them often.'

Rosemary laughed, but it made her realise suddenly that this place both brought the family together, and separated them. 'We should have bought a place in St Ives years ago Lewis. We were always here when the girls were younger. They think its just as much home as London. Maybe we should consider it now?'

'Yes. We should think seriously about it. We'll get the local papers and see what's available, and what we can view in two days, while I'm here.'

At the flat they spread the papers around, alighting on any property that appeared interesting and desirable. The problem was that most were out of their price range. If they were affordable, they were outside the town. The initial excitement turned to disappointment.

'What if we asked my sisters whether they would be interested in sharing the cost? Sylvia said she was considering moving here.'

'I knew those sisters would come in useful some day. We'll each have shares, as long as they leave the school holidays to us and the twins.'

'Oh yes. Take their money and tell them when they can have the place!'

Instead of the two days Lewis had taken off to be with Rosemary for a nice relaxing time, they had now provided themselves with a problem, which niggled at them. They walked on the beach and discussed when they should approach the sisters. It was hardly a subject to be talked about over the phone. Meanwhile, they would look at some of the likely properties on the market, just to get an idea.

'The place I'm going to show you is new in this week. It has two bedrooms, ample storage space, a terrace, and a view over the harbour,' the estate agent explained, as they followed him to the Warren. 'I can recommend it. It's one of the nicest cottages we have on our books.'

It was indeed a very good property. Everything was of a high standard. New bathroom and kitchen, good views, but the rooms were extremely small, and in two rooms were great chunks of elvin rock, and though painted white to minimise the effect, were part of the wall and stuck out in uneven lumps. This was a common feature in many St Ives older houses where this very hard rock face was too difficult to cut away.

They reluctantly turned down that property and were taken to another 'in need of renovation.' It was a substantial house on one of the terraces overlooking the harbour, and in turning this one down explained they had no time to wait while heating, rewiring and plumbing were installed. It had to be a house that could be lived in with no major alterations. On that evening of viewing properties, they walked on the pier, their minds on the financial difficulties of owning a house in St Ives.

There were a number of small boats fishing in the bay. While they stood idly watching, two larger boats tied up on the pier and brought in a catch of mackerel. People were crowding round watching the fish being sluiced with sea water and tipped into baskets, which were hauled by rope onto the quay, emptied into fish boxes, and whisked away to Newlyn for the morning fish market.

Young Boy Stevens was one of the crew. He mostly worked out of Newlyn with the bigger boats, but here he was with his father and uncle, working out of St Ives for the summer season. The Knights remembered him as a boy leaning on the rail on the quay, looking on while the men unloaded dog fish, ray, monkfish, turbot, and other fish found in local waters. 'I want to leave school and go fishing with my Dad,' he told them. Now here he was in his yellow oilskins doing exactly that, but he landed only the common mackerel on handlines, and even they were less common. These days he didn't talk to visitors, but took on the dour, hard faced attitude of men who were finding it impossible to make a living at something they were born to, and loved. It was hard being deprived of their Cornish heritage.

Even the old grey seal found it hard to beg for a portion, as he nosed around the boat, waiting for a fish to be thrown, snuffling through his whiskers to gain attention. Having hung around to no avail, he made off to a line of smaller boats and, heaving his great bulk up, flopped onto the boat's side, tipping it so that it filled with water and sank. There were no fish. He swam on, sniffing around and sinking several small boats, amusing the onlookers, before coming back for a final try at coaxing a fish from the boat unloading its catch.

The Knights went to bed early, sitting up in bed drinking wine, being dazzled by the light coming off the sea and sand and watching the endless waves rolling onto the shore, smoothing down footprints, flattening sand castles, filling moats, and moving inexorably to its tidal limit; its unstoppable force, reshaping the imprints of man.

Tonight they were philosophically sad, made love almost sadly, like a comfort, holding, and softly caressing each other, lying quietly. There was nothing of the former madness, when they felt released by not having the twins around, and made love in the most awkward places, laughing and chasing each other like a couple of crazed teenagers.

Two hours later they awoke to the sound of the surf in an ugly mood, booming and crashing; the rain slashing against the windows. The call of the lifeboat rockets rent the sky. They got up and dressed in all the weather proof gear they could lay their hands on and made for the harbour. Something sinister was happening.

Already on West Pier cars were shining their lights on the waters in the harbour. The inshore boat was cruising, up and down, round and round, in a frantic search of the seas. The lifeboat was launched and directed its huge spotlight on a broader area outside the inshore boat. On Smeaton's Pier an ambulance arrived. A helicopter hovered close over the lifeboat, circling and circling, its powerful light raking the ocean.

In all this activity was a feeling of desperation. It was palpable to the watchers on the slipway, who conveyed their views to each other on the happenings. A few fishermen from the Sloop were gathered and drifts of their conversation reached them through the raging wind.

'Had a meal, a few drinks, nothing to speak of.'
'They were in the dingy.'

'Three of them.'

'There's their boat, just off the pier.'

'They'll pick them up.'

And they did pick them up. The inshore boat raced to the steps and the boatmen carried up a man between them, laying him down on the quay, where the ambulance men started resuscitation, one breathing into his mouth, the other giving rhythmic thumps to the chest, pressing down with both hands. The inshore boat raced away to continue its search.

The lifeboat and helicopter began a concerted activity, the copter hanging over it, until the watchers could see a man lifted from the boat on a line. Moving away, the helicopter made for Smeaton's Pier. The man remained dangling. It was the quickest way, rather than haul him into the copter. By the beams of several lights they saw him, body taut, arms outstretched, head back, like Christ on the cross. The helicopter handed him, twisting on the winch, into the arms of several men, who took him into the ambulance. The watchers knew he was dead. The crew were still working on the first man, but little response came from the victim.

It was a sobering sight. The helicopter renewed the search in a wider area, the two lifeboats continued their up and down routes closer to shore. The third man was not found. The ambulance drove its sad cargo of two dead men to the hospital. Rosemary and Lewis were considerably shaken by the sight, and by the valiant efforts made by the rescuing team.

They made their way up the Digey, intending to look over the wall at the surf on Porthmeor beach pounding up the shore. They struggled past The Tides café, where they often had coffee and lunch in that sheltered spot, but this evening the Digey's narrow lane acted as a funnel for the westerly gale roaring in from the Atlantic. They were stopped in their tracks by the force of the wind and clung to each other to remain upright. The wind snatched their voices from their mouths. They turned off at Rose Lane and made their way to Back Road West, where they were more sheltered by the cottages lining the beach, though the wind whipped through the gaps furiously.

In the double glazed safety of the Piazza flat, they made tea, and crept into bed, pulling the blinds and curtains over the windows to shut out the brute force raging outside. It had caused the deaths of two men, and probably a third. They could now see the dual attraction of the sea that both provided and took life. Those who knew it respected its power. They now understood what this meant to those brought up to live and work by the sea.

Next morning, the town already knew of the accident. A marine biologist had died; a man serving as spokesman for the fishermen's co-operative; and a fisherman. They had come over from Hayle in a boat, rowed ashore in their dingy, met some friends and celebrated by having a meal and a drink in the Sloop. All were experienced men of the sea, but in seating themselves in the dingy on the return trip, it had somehow capsized. The men, though swimmers, had been hampered by their full bellies and the rough seas. It had happened only yards from the harbour. It was unbelievable.

The experience of the drowning rather dampened the idea of Rosemary and Lewis owning a cottage in St Ives. They wouldn't want to see many such awful sights, and know the sorrows of the local folk, or hear the prayers and mourning in the chapels and churches.

Lewis was going home next morning. They decided to have an early breakfast at the Alba, next to the lifeboat house before he caught the train. At their window on the world, they watched the tired, silent crew hosing down the boat, before they were released home. They had been out all night and had not recovered the third body. According to some, it was probably rocking in the bays around Godrevy lighthouse. Everywhere, as they walked along the Wharf to the train station, little clusters of residents were talking about the night's event.

Rosemary had thought of going home with Lewis on the train, rather than remain with the sorrow in the town. There was just a week left of the time at Piazza, but Lewis insisted she stay and work on her book.

Rosemary couldn't settle to work. The sun shone, the storm had blown itself out. Only the people were left to pick up the pieces. On Porthmeor beach the holiday-makers were setting up their encampments ready for a day of pleasure, most of them unaware of the drama that had taken place off the now peaceful harbour the night before. She would walk to Clodgy, along the coastpath and look out on its topmost point to the five bays. This path also led to Zennor, and beyond to Land's End.

The coastpath was largely devoid of houses almost its whole length. It would skirt round the only town on the way, which was St Just, even then it was only a small defunct mining town. At Sennen Cove it followed the road along the beach, then up to its final destination, Land's End. When they were younger the Knights had intended to walk to Land's End, but the farthest they managed to trek to was Zennor, where the target was the Tinners Arms, and lunch.

Rosemary made her way along the beach but on a sudden impulse found herself taking the footpath to the artist, Isobel Heath's house, thinking that as she had been involved with so many painters, both in St Ives and Newlyn, she may well have known Mary Jewels. She remembered that Robert had asked her to 'take a look at the paintings,' if ever she ventured into Isobel's house. He had been sent packing when he arrived at Isobel's door and asked if she had paintings she wanted to sell, hers and other artists' works she had collected.

Robert had gained a reputation for sharp practice. He bought at auctions, or from artists' studios and sold them at a profit in his gallery. Artists were wary of him. It was for this reason Rosemary had kept away. She didn't want Isobel to think she was interested only in her paintings for commercial gain, even though she was thinking of trading in her own painting by Isobel should a Mary Jewels come up for auction. Nor did she want to be linked with a dealer who had only profit on his mind.

She arrived at this solitary house set in fields, near the quarry, with a splendid view over to the cliffs at Man's Head. Isobel had fought fierce battles to prevent the footpath being taken over for the building of houses, and the right of way had remained open to the public. At the garden gate Rosemary saw a huge flat stone lying on the ground, painted on it in white was a message. 'Knock loudly and wait a long time.' She knocked loudly and waited. No one came. She pushed open the gate, forcing it against grass and weeds, which had grown behind it. The door to the kitchen was unlocked and, having tried unsuccessfully to make Isobel hear, she entered and stood waiting, in case she should suddenly appear.

The sink was filled with greasy dishes and on the cooker used saucepans were piled high. There was congealed fat in a frying pan and sharp teeth marks where it had been gnawed by mice. The floor was muddy with dirt, and everywhere neglect was obvious. Only the cat came to greet her. The only evidence of food was in its dish on a stool.

'Hello! hello,' came a cry from another room. 'Hello,' Rosemary called, hoping she hadn't alarmed Isobel. She made her way towards the voice and came upon Isobel sitting in a chair by an unlit fire with a grate full of cold ashes. There were piles of old newspapers in every corner, and the table was littered with magazines, articles, letters and bills. The curtains were drawn, keeping the light from entering, and the room dim.

'I'm sorry to come barging in like this, but I wondered if you were all right.'

'I'm better now. Had flu, but I've got up today. Still a bit groggy, but I managed to ring the doctor. He's coming this afternoon and I thought it would be better to be downstairs and on my feet. Could you bring over that electric heater and plug it in. I haven't got round to lighting the fire.'

'Have you had anything to eat?' Rosemary said, plugging in a two-pin socket on the heater and noting the frayed cabling. There seemed no point in saying that the connection was dangerous, she had lived with this condition for some time and obviously, the whole house needed rewiring.

'Have you got some soup in the cupboard I could heat up for you?'

'That would be nice, dear. Have a look and see what there is, will you?'

Rosemary went into the kitchen and shuddered. There was plenty of tinned food in the cupboard but no hot water. She would have to clean a saucepan and wash some dishes. She boiled several kettles of water and filled up the sink, finding only soda to break up the grease. She washed all the dishes and saucepans, cleaned down the surfaces and was doubtfully eyeing the floor.

While Isobel was sipping her soup the doctor appeared at the kitchen door.

'Ah, Mrs Heath has got some help,' he said, obviously pleased.

'No, not really. I happened to be passing and popped

in. I've given her some food and tidied up the kitchen. It doesn't look as if anyone has cleaned the house for some time.'

He raised his eyebrows by way of agreeing and went through to Isobel. She heard his voice calling, 'Let's have some light on the matter, and shame the devil, shall we?' He pulled back the dusty curtains. The doctor dealt with his patient and then began rummaging in the over-full desk, looking for a telephone number. 'I'll ring them when I get to the surgery,' he informed Isobel. He walked over the washed but still muddy kitchen floor on his way out.

'Don't bother yourself too much,' he said to Rosemary, 'I don't think she'll be staying here very long.'

'Phew!' she replied, all hot and bothered. 'I don't think I'll go prying in to people's houses often. Serves me right.' She straightened her aching back and went through to Isobel.

'That doctor's a nice man. My husband left me in the clutches of a Trust. He used to do everything in the house. He knew how useless I was at cooking and housework. The doctor's going to ring them for me. I have to admit to defeat at last. It comes to us all.' Isobel sighed, but wasn't unhappy.

Now that the curtains were drawn Rosemary could see many of Isobel's paintings on the walls, and those of other artists, but she didn't pause to look. Somehow it didn't seem right to be bothering an ill woman with questions, or asking to look at the paintings in the house. Rosemary lit the fire and made Isobel comfortable, with everything to hand as far as she was able, and left, thinking to return to ask questions about Mary Jewels when she was better.

However, that was the last time she entered the house and saw Isobel. A few days later the house was boarded up and some time after that a 'for sale' notice appeared. The Trust had been forcefully reminded of their responsibilities by the doctor and had whisked her away and taken her into their care.

Tired and dirty after her work in the house, Rosemary returned to Piazza and showered. She fell asleep and dreamed of washing a towering pile of saucepans and never reaching the end of her task. Rosemary never found out if Isobel had known Mary Jewels, and regretted her missed opportunity.

That evening the twins rang. Lewis had mentioned the possibility of buying a cottage with the assistance of the aunts. 'It's a great idea,' they enthused, 'we can make the most of our wetsuits. You know how you like to have value for money on your investments.' The girls were in a giggling and teasing mood. 'And we could leave the wetsuits in our cottage, and not clutter up your wardrobe here. But they don't smell too bad.'

'What do you mean they don't smell too bad? My wardrobe? You can remove them immediately. Put them in the attic. I don't want my clothes smelling of stale sea water.'

'Only joking, Mum. Dad's already put them in the

attic. We've been telling Sylvia how much better off she'll be in Cornwall with all that sea and sky. She won't have to turn the druggies and drunks out of the library there. And maybe she could drive the mobile library van to all those country places and villages. She can buy her own property, and a share in our cottage, then she'll be there to look after the place.'

It was the first born twin, Demelza, who was the spokesman, but one hundred percent backed up by Lamorna, who added, 'We said if she hadn't enough money she could talk to Auntie Penelope and Miranda and get them to buy a share. It's no good asking Dad to talk to them, they always think he's joking.'

'Very tactical of you girls. You don't need any advice from me. Let me know how the plan is working.'

'Mum.' It was Demelza again. 'Can we come down for the final weekend? Then we can travel with you. Help carry all your stuff.'

'Is that your main objective?'

'No, not really,' the girls laughed. 'We want to have another surfing lesson. Brad said we're really good. Please.'

'All right, but this time you really will pay for your own lessons. You're beginning to cost a fortune.' The girls were screaming with excitement in the background as they handed the phone over to Lewis.

'Sylvia's really taking this seriously. I'm negotiating with her through the twins, as you've already heard. And she is going to contact the others if her finances aren't adequate. I think we might have something going for us, especially with the pressure our girls are putting on Sylvia. She seems to fall in line with everything they say – practically eating out of their hands. Don't know where they get their diplomacy from.'

'Craftiness, more like. They can really pull out all the stops when it's something for their benefit – haven't you noticed?'

'Apparently, we're going to see the other aunts this evening. No. No. Correction. I've been told I'm not allowed to talk to your sisters, in case I turn everything into a circus, and annoy Miranda and Penelope before Sylvia and the girls have tuned them in to the idea.'

'I think that's wise, Lewis. Anyway, put the girls on the train on Friday after school and I'll meet them at St Ives. They'll probably arrive with a sack full of their aunts' money and we'll buy something suitable. Bye for now. Love you all.'

Rosemary knew she had to make up for lost time and rose early next morning with a determined effort to work solidly for a few hours. Two hours into the session and she was having breakfast, with no thought of continuing. She packed a picnic, a flask, a book and writing paper and pen, 'just in case.'

The Land's End open top bus left the Malakoff around ten o'clock. It travelled the winding coastal road past scattered farmhouses, and green pastures with few cattle. The sea was constantly in view on the right. The road climbed to Eagle's Nest, then dropped down to Zennor. It rose again out of the village and forty minutes later Rosemary alighted at the Gurnard's Head hotel, where she had coffee, before taking the path over the fields to the headland. The field path was somewhat overgrown, but still visible. It had been closed for over a year during one whole season of the BSE outbreak. Even the coastal route at many points had been affected when fields of grazing cattle touched the paths.

Ahead was the Gurnard's headland, sticking up large and spiky, and named for its likeness to the fish, the Gurnard. The path began to get tricky and Rosemary decided to sit on the sheltered side of a grassy bank out of the wind, rather than proceed to the more difficult terrain on the headland. This was a spot beloved of Virginia Woolf.

Nothing would have changed since Virginia had tramped around here and stayed at Porthmeor farm, complaining about the noise of the geese in the farm-yard. She and her companion had walked to St Just some few miles further on. Rosemary gazed around before opening her book and reading Virginia's words.

"By looking over my left shoulder I see gorse yellow against the Atlantic blue, running up, a little ruffled, to the sky, today hazy blue. And we've been lying on the Gurnard's Head, on beds of samphire among grey rocks with buttons of yellow lichen on them."

All afternoon Rosemary sat and dreamed, composing scenes in her head, making a few notes on paper, watching the sea for the small boats that would drift past, and the flotilla of gulls sometimes accompanying them, meaning they had fish aboard. They were cutting and preparing them for a local shop, or restaurant, the heads and innards making tasty morsels for the marauding gulls. She enjoyed her picnic lunch, there in the quietness, pinned to the earth by the sun and the wind, unable to resist the dominating forces that seemed to engulf her.

Sometimes a few figures would appear on the path below, braving the dangerous rocks and climbing to the summit. Often she would lift her head and someone would see her. They waved. She waved back. It was one of those things about walkers, always to acknowledge a fellow hiker. She liked that brief recognition. It was like a release from the power that held her. But still, she could not get up and walk away. It was the urgency of the bus timetable that eventually freed her. If she missed the bus, she would have to take a taxi.

The murmur of voices on the bus to St Ives didn't engage her curiosity. They were only background noises to her solitary mood. The evening journey along the coast road was as pleasurable as the morning ride. At Piazza, she immediately set to work, typing her notes onto the computer, hardly looking up from her table to see the activities of people on the beach, or the relentless sea making its mark upon the shore. She wrote until the light faded, the last of the sun's brilliant golden glow, yielding sufficient shine to finish the last sentence. When she looked up she saw the huge red ball half drowned in the sea on the far horizon. It hovered, and then sank.

The telephone rang. It was Patsy. Rosemary in her soporific mood merely said, 'Patsy I'm busy writing. Ring me tomorrow,' and put the phone down. It was a painless way of answering the unasked question. She knew Patsy would be pleased, rather than offended by

Rosemary's curt response. She could imagine her satisfied grin, 'Oh good, she's working,' she'd say.

Rosemary dragged herself to bed, missing dinner, and slept a dreamless sleep until seven the next morning when, feeling energetic, she realised she hadn't swum all summer and went through the private courtyard onto the beach. There was a faint chill in the air and she walked on the edge of the tide wrapped in a huge bath towel, daring herself to enter the freezing water. When she did, it was exhilarating. It took her breath away. The water was clear and fresh and the waves plunged over her.

Back in the flat, she showered, and felt extraordinarily lively and bright. It was a wonderful feeling. She was released from the quiet confinement of yesterday. With her hair still wet she made her way along Back Road East to Porthgwidden beach cafe for breakfast. The balcony was a great place to sit in the morning. The sun rose higher and it was sufficiently warm to dry her hair. Never was coffee more eagerly drunk, or breakfast more enjoyable, or her long stint of writing more satisfying.

Still in a lively mood and needing to be away from her desk Rosemary walked round to St Ives Museum. There was just a chance, that in their odd collection of paintings from the early period, there might be a Mary Jewels. From Rosemary's experience, things turned up in the unlikeliest of places. The main room was hung with various flags, painted murals, show cases, photographs and a great deal of interesting material about the history of fishing and mining in St Ives, but there was no Mary Jewels among the paintings.

Hovering by one of the show cases she was interested to see several swatches of material in silks and linens. The patterns and colours were various and named for the local scenes they represented, Zennor Hill, Cornish Farm, Flowers of Lelant, Ding Dong Mine, Godrevy. A very interesting collection.

Rosemary's sixth sense was still operating. Something was going to 'turn up' she was sure. She walked along the harbour, turned up Lifeboat Hill, past the Church to the Archive Study Centre, above the Parish Rooms. While she waited for the centre to open, she booked a table for her evening meal at The Wave restaurant in St Andrew's Street.

'Ah, Rosemary,' said a voice at her side. 'I've been meaning to get in touch'. Janet, the Study Centre co-ordinator, invited her inside. 'We've got a whole collection of photographs, just donated. Perhaps you'd like to come up and look through. They're so new we haven't even catalogued them yet.'

'I'm feeling lucky,' Rosemary replied, following Janet upstairs. She sat her in front of three boxes of assorted photos and brought her a cup of coffee. During the morning she looked through hundreds of photos of boats, the fishing industry and the old town; all very interesting, but there were no photos of artists or paintings. She was about to abandon the third box, but plunged her hand into the centre of the collection and pulled out various postcards. There among them was a card with a photograph of two women, very well dressed in fashionable clothes of the twenties. She turned it over and read –

"Mrs Cordelia Dobson and Mrs Mary Jewels, model-ling the silk dresses designed by Mr Alec Walker of Crysede. These exclusive garments were made in his factory in Newlyn. You are cordially invited to attend the opening of the shop in New Road, Newlyn, on 10 July, 1921."

'Wow!' Rosemary exclaimed. 'I've found something wonderful!'

Half the staff of the centre gathered round to see this discovery.

'My grandmother had one of those Crysede dresses, but it was in linen. I remember the design, it was called Lobster Supper. I remember it because she told me a story about it,' Clare, one of the young work experi-ence girls, said.

'Well, come on, let's hear it,' a few voices urged.

Clare had everyone's attention. 'Now, let me get this straight,' she began. 'My grandmother's sister was the manageress of the Newlyn shop, and there was a din-ner party given by Alec Walker, and his wife Kay, to cel-ebrate the opening. The table was laid with large plates of lobsters. There were coral shells holding salads and dressings, and silver cutlery, and coral candles. Apparently, Alec Walker was so enchanted with the table setting that he made everyone wait to eat while he sketched this new design for the fabric, Lobster Supper.'

'That is fantastic Clare,' Rosemary said. 'A wonder-ful story. I wonder if Mary and Cordelia were at that party. They must have been friends if the sisters were

185

wearing those dresses. I wouldn't think they were employees. But this photograph is lovely. Really shows how gorgeous Mary and Cordelia were as young women.'

'I think we've got some information on the firm of Crysede,' Janet said, bringing a file of newspaper cuttings and a book on the subject. 'I'll photocopy some of these articles in case they're of interest.'

'Yes. I've found something,' Janet said, 'Listen to this. In April 1926 Crysede took over the old pilchard cellar on the island. The firm will provide much needed jobs for the local workforce in St Ives, who will be trained in dyeing and printing on linen, crepe-de-chine and silk, and the make-up of these materials into fashionable garments.'

'So this firm of Crysede is where Mary and Cordelia bought their beautiful clothes,' Rosemary said. 'And I've been looking at these designs in the museum. I knew I'd find something extraordinary today.'

She ordered a copy of the photograph from Janet and arrived back at Piazza delighted with her find and her new knowledge of the designs of Alec Walker. She rang David at the Book Gallery, a splendid repository of second hand books, articles and ephemera on the art colony of St Ives, and put in a request for information on Crysede and Mary Jewels.

'You're welcome to come and browse,' he said, 'meanwhile I'll put a search on the computer for anything we might have.'

The girls were ecstatic, as always, as Rosemary met them off the train. They rushed ahead of her down to the Porthminster beach café to find out what was available for them at the weekend. By the time Rosemary arrived dragging along half the luggage, they had ordered drinks and were signing up for membership of the St Ives Surf Life Saving Club, and arranging to join in their fund raising activities on the Porthmeor surfing beach the next day.

Rosemary had collected her photograph of Mary and Cordelia in their splendid dresses, and showed it to Joan at the café.

'I used to have a Crysede silk scarf in three different blues.' Joan said. 'The design was called Newlyn Harbour. I might still have it if I look hard enough. It was a twenty first birthday present, but I'd forgotten it was connected with this part of the world.'

'I'd love to see it Joan, because there is some connection with Mary Jewels.'

Over dinner at the Piazza flat the girls reported on their visit to the aunts in their bid to secure some money for the partnership of buying a cottage, or flat, in St Ives. It worked out that Penelope would need to have a properly drawn-up agreement, so she didn't miss out on all the best summer months. Miranda had to discuss it with her husband, who was not keen on holidays, because he spent too much time working away from home. He was away at the moment.

'So that doesn't look too hopeful,' Rosemary said.

'Sylvia was the only one who was really keen, Mum, and she said she hasn't counted her pennies yet. So we're still waiting for her decision.'

'There's nothing more to be done, than just wait and see what happens.'

Nothing could dim the enjoyment of the following day when the girls looked out of the window and watched the young lifesavers arriving on the beach, with parents in tow. They gathered around their St Ives pennant and when Lamorna and Demelza saw Brad and Dave arrive, they raced off to join the company. Rosemary watched out of the window as she saw the girls being introduced to other youngsters, and begin running between flags for a warm up.

There were various activities, with learning beach safety skills, lessons in basic surf skills and techniques, with competitive races intermingled, and a great number of fun events for the entertainment of the crowd on the beach, to encourage them to put money in the Air Ambulance collection boxes.

The girls were happy to have Rosemary watch out of the window and wave every now and then, rather than have her on the beach with them. Brad also gave her a wave. Eventually, they were so engrossed in their games they forgot to look up and Rosemary, sitting at her desk, also forgot, except when loud cheers called her attention to the winners of the team races. The visitors and other youngsters were fascinated by this display from the children of the town, envying their living so close to the sea.

An hour into the event and things were still lively. The next time Rosemary raised her head, everyone seemed to be standing still, gazing in one direction. Brad was on a beach telephone, and two lifeguards were racing towards him. The other youngsters were drawn away from the scene and encouraged to sit down. They were listening intently to what they were told, and seemed concerned. One of the children was lying on the beach and being attended to by the lifeguards. It was a child without an accompanying parent. She watched as they knelt down either side of the child, not encouraging her to rise. It was obviously a girl, with the pink flashes on her wetsuit.

Now one of the lifeguards stood and telephoned. Brad moved towards the little group of youngsters and began explaining something to them. They sat huddled together, nodding and compliant. The parents were instructed in some activity and, together with the available lifeguards, began clearing the beach. People were hastily picking up their belongings and moving further up the western end. The tide was now sufficiently on the retreat to leave a large area of flat sand.

In the distance could be heard the sound of a helicopter, and suddenly it appeared large, blustery and ear-splitting, over the island chapel. It hovered momentarily, and then noisily but gently, lowered vertically on the beach. A stretcher was brought out and with the assistance of the lifeguard, the child was carefully lifted and carried to the impatient helicopter. The door slammed shut and the craft lifted off, with a good deal of noise and down draft. Now the mood of the youngsters was triumphant. They rose to their feet and waved until the helicopter was out of sight. It disappeared over the island to the cheers of the crowd.

'Mum, did you see that!' exclaimed the girls, as they rushed in, showering sand and a liberal sprinkling of water everywhere. Rosemary was too anxious to know what had happened to scold them.

'It was a real live rescue.' They tumbled over each other's words in the telling.

'It was Sally. Her mum wasn't there.'

'She fell over and hit a rock or something.'

'They've taken her to Treliske hospital.'

'They collected heaps of money afterwards.'

'Brad said she's not too badly hurt, but she needs to see a doctor. She'll be OK.'

'Well, that's good. Now go and shower, and get changed. Then clean up the mess you've made of this floor.'

'We made loads of friends. They're really nice.'

'But they're lucky because they live in the town.'

'Go,' Rosemary said, pointing to the bathroom.

While the twins were showering, there was a knock on the door. It was Brad.

'Hi Rosemary. I wondered if the twins were OK. They got here safely, did they? I didn't see the creepy guy anywhere. You saw the drama on the beach? That's gonna be OK too. One of the girls fell and broke her collarbone, at least that's what we think it is. But she's not worried. She couldn't wait to get taken up in the air and away.'

'Brad,' said Rosemary, putting on the kettle for coffee. 'About the creepy guy. What do you mean?'

'Ah, well, that's the whole point. Joan asked me to tell you about him. You know, George somebody or other …'

'George Tatum. My sister's friend. Well at least, I

think he is. But why...?

'Working on the beach, you get to know these bums who try to chat up young girls. And when he started making a video, Joan called the girls up to the café. We didn't like that one bit and advised them to stay away from him, or call me if they were worried. But, hey, I'm sorry. I didn't know he was your sister's friend.' He paused. 'Then again, I still wouldn't trust him.'

'Video! They didn't tell me he had taken a video of them.'

'A video's always suspect.'

'He was supposed to come and meet us, to ask our permission to interview the girls, but he didn't turn up.'

Taking his coffee from Rosemary, Brad raised his eyebrows questioningly.

'Looks as if I've put my big foot in it. I guess I thought the twins had told you about him, but Joan insisted I mention it, in case the girls hadn't talked to you about this chap.'

'They've told us a lot about you and Dave and only said that they didn't like George. I suppose you should listen to children when they have such a strong aversion to someone. According to my sister, George was most polite, never made a pass at her, and wasn't angry when the girls were rude to him.'

Brad raised his eyebrows again, and pursed his lips at the idea that there was something good about him not making a pass, or not being angry. Rosemary mirrored Brad's facial expressions.

'What do I do about this? I'm especially alarmed that the girls haven't told me. And I'm angry with my sister for her insistence that they be nice to him. Is she mad? Oh for goodness sake, I've even told them to be nice to him.'

'I haven't seen him around for some time, so obviously he's no longer a threat, but perhaps a quiet word with your sister. Though the girls should be warned. According to Joan, it's better to scare the socks off them, than become victims by thinking that nobody could wish them any harm.'

'Yes. I'll have to tread carefully on this one. All we have is a feeling that George Tatum is up to no good, in spite of his angle about making a study of twins. It's difficult to trust anybody these days.'

'Yeah. Difficult not to set alarm bells ringing. Thanks for the coffee. I'll leave before the twins realise I'm here. Tell them to rinse their wetsuits thoroughly. They can get a bit smelly if sea water dries on them. Hey look, don't worry. I'm sure nothing nasty happened.'

Rosemary did just that. She worried. The words 'nothing nasty happened,' played over and over in her head. Why hadn't she questioned Brad more closely, asked precisely what he meant by those words. What did he suspect? If there was something to uncover, she would have to tease it gently out of the girls, since they hadn't confided anything to her. They may have chosen Sylvia as their confidante, and if her sister was hiding anything, she wanted to know why. But, in order to get to the whole story, she must wait for the right moment. The train journey home would provide her with a captive audience. There was nowhere for her girls to escape to while she questioned them. Yes; the train journey would provide the answers.

8

There was so much to do before the weekend was over. There was the phone call to Mary's nephew, Peter Tregurtha. There was also the members' viewing of the new Tate gallery exhibition. Rosemary waited for the girls to finish showering to try and persuade them to come along. Their horrified faces told the story

'Mum, we've arranged to have a barbecue on the beach with some of our friends. In fact, you've got a choice,' Demelza informed her. 'Kate and Simon's mother said to ask if you would like to join them.'

'We're ready to go. We've got to meet them in ten minutes. We've already said, yes, so really it's up to you, Mum.' Lamorna said.

Rosemary's plans were upset. Her girls had given her an ultimatum. They had challenged her, and were now facing her, expressions hopeful. She realised that if she didn't rise to this occasion, it would be another mark against her.

'Well, I wasn't expecting suddenly to go to a beach picnic, but you seem to have made the decision for me, though I'm not exactly dressed for it.'

She watched their faces, which turned from expectation to triumph. They had won.

'But, I'll probably only stay an hour. I want to see the Tate exhibition. You can come if you want.'

'No Mum. We'll stay with Kate and Simon. Their mum will be there, so she'll look after us. We're having a barbecue. She's bringing all the stuff with her.'

'So what am I supposed to bring, at this late hour? You should have told me sooner.'

Why had they put her in this position?, she thought angrily.

Lamorna took her hand and led her to the window. 'Look Mum, that's where we are. We'll go down and tell them you're coming, shall we?'

Rosemary nodded her head in resigned agreement. They were already going through the door. Now she had to decide what to take. She hastened to Woolworths and bought the ready prepared barbecue kit for use on the beaches. Opposite, the Deli provided sausages, bacon, rolls, salad and drinks. She hoped it would be appropriate.

When the girls saw her struggling through the sand with the shopping bags, they raced to her aid. 'Cool, Mum. Cool.' They were delighted with her, and Kate and Simon's mother greeted her in friendly manner.

'Hello. Rosemary, isn't it? Sue.' She extended a welcoming hand. 'So glad you've brought something. We have another couple of unexpected guests. I expect we'll have quite a few gatecrashers. When there's a beach party, everybody you know invites themselves.'

Rosemary smiled as if she knew exactly what Sue meant. They were soon surrounded by other mothers and children, also busy unpacking their contributions. The atmosphere was informal and friendly and Rosemary found herself enjoying the occasion, but still in the back of her mind, was the members' invitation to the Tate private view.

'I have to leave you shortly,' she told Sue. 'I have previously arranged to meet a friend. I should be gone about an hour.'

'Don't worry, we'll be here for hours. I'll make sure Lamorna and Demelza don't go wandering off,' Sue assured her.

The twins, having made all that fuss about her coming, hardly looked up from their activities to wave goodbye.

The gallery was cool. Most people had gravitated to the bar upstairs, the noise filtered down the double staircase. In gallery one, a small celebration of the Nicholson family was featured. A Barbara Hepworth delicate stringed piece of sculpture was mounted on a tall plinth enclosed in a showcase. Sir William Nicholson showed beautifully painted portraits and Ben Nicholson's White Reliefs hung next to his first wife Winifred's evocative painting *The Gate to the Isle*. Their daughter Kate was represented by *Carbis Bay and Godrevy*.

It was cheering to see these works, but even so, both Winifred and Kate were largely forgotten in art circles. It proved again, the inability of the art establishment to recognise women painters. Winifred especially, Rosemary thought, was as dedicated and interesting a painter as Ben, but was not given the same status; was it largely because Ben had experimented with more abstract forms? However, in that case, why wasn't Vanessa Bell celebrated as an innovative artist? She had produced radical works of art twelve years before Nicholson. Opinion was decidedly against women artists.

Rosemary walked back along the beach. The time to tackle the problem of this man George, Rosemary decided, was when they were in London. Let the girls remain untroubled and enjoy their few days in St Ives. She would tie up a few missing links on seeking information on Mary Jewels. It was time to ring Peter Tregurtha, Mary's nephew.

The large party of children was still on the beach. The girls were playing below the window of the flat. She was glad to see them playing ball, like the children they were, instead of apeing the older girls. She watched the group as they stopped their play, to look at four young women sauntering along in sarongs, laughing, and generally attracting attention. Rosemary despaired as she saw the envy and admiration on the twins' faces, then a group of girls followed behind the women, copying and exaggerating their walks, swinging their hips and showing off. They turned and ran screaming with laughter as one of the women caught them at it. The twins glimpsed Rosemary at the window, grinned and waved.

Rosemary waved, turned from the window and picked up the 'phone.

'Hello, Peter. It's Rosemary Knight. I rang about your aunts and ....'

'Yes. I've found the letters from Augustus John, I told you about. I'll read them out, then I'll send you copies.'

Rosemary couldn't believe things had started so well. She rather thought Peter, being quite elderly, would have forgotten all about her request for the letters, and she'd have to explain all over again. Then he'd have to search, and so it would go on until he would finally say he'd lost them. This was indeed a windfall. She listened, smiling as he read the letter, and wrote down the words in shorthand.

"Dear Mary. Do forgive me being so long in replying. I would greatly like to see your recent work. Are you coming up to London with it, or sending it? I will do my best to get a show arranged somewhere. I shall want some of your things myself, I am sure. Let me know when I shall be able to see them. AJ"

'That one was from Chelsea, dated 1929.'

Rosemary drew in a breath of delight, but didn't interrupt for fear of diverting Peter's attention away from reading the letter.

'There were other letters from Augustus John and different artists, but I'm afraid there was so much to deal with that I threw almost everything away. These two survived by chance.'

Rosemary wanted to scream at him. It made her so angry when the evidence of people's lives was destroyed but, she reasoned, you couldn't expect everyone to regard old letters as important, so she calmed down. To encourage him to continue, she said mildly, 'Thank you for that. I'm so pleased you managed to save these letters. What's the date of the next one?'

'Ah, that's dated 1932, so there must have been quite a few others in between, and many afterwards. It says,'

"Dear Mary. Here's the cheque. I am delighted with the additions to my collection. *The Village, Paul, The Mill*, all excellent. I think I could have one of your things for a theatre drop-curtain. I much enjoyed seeing you and Cordelia again and meeting your excellent mother. I look forward to another visit. Remember my parting words. AJ"

So, he did arrange the exhibition for her. 'How intriguing,' Rosemary said, "remember my parting words." Does he say what they were? Have you any idea what he meant?'

'Maybe it was about getting out of the kitchen and into the studio to paint. I did find a postcard which told Mary exactly that, but I've since lost it, I'm afraid.'

Rosemary was hoping for something a little more salacious, but Peter could give no other explanation. John was involved in many intriguing infatuations, love affairs, and was so frequently in and out of love, or lust, that it was difficult to believe that both Mary and Cordelia could have escaped his clutches. Had the 'excellent mother' who had been described by Mrs Fox 'as a paragon of virtue' managed to thwart his designs on the two sisters? Had she herself fallen for his charms?

Augustus John had certainly bought Mary's paintings. This was a wonderful discovery. Proof at last. Were they still in his family? Why did Michael Holroyd make no mention of Mary or Cordelia in his biography of John. Were they of so little consequence, or did the writer not find out about the sisters? John was in Lamorna in 1914 and noted 'some very attractive young girls among the people.' Did that include Mary and Cordelia?

Were the women rivals for his affection? Judging by his reputation, he would certainly not have hesitated in making love to both of them. However, no amount of speculation could solve the problem. But whatever the circumstances, the friendship lasted for many years according to Peter's recollection of John's first meeting with them and the dates on the letters.

Peter interrupted her train of thought. 'Cordelia was the dominant one. She made the decisions about where Mary's paintings should be exhibited, what price to charge, who should handle the work, and if the right approach wasn't made to Delia, then the gallery owner, or private buyer, didn't get the picture; whatever Mary might have to say about it.'

'I remember the Newlyn Gallery arranging an exhibition, somewhere up country, of naïve artists from Cornwall. Mary was told the exhibition wouldn't be truly representative without one of her paintings. The others exhibiting were William George, a fisherman from Mousehole, Bryan Pearce and Alfred Wallis, both from St Ives.'

'And did the exhibition ever take place?'

'Probably with the artists I've just mentioned, but it did not include Mary. Both aunts objected; Mary because she wouldn't exhibit in any show which labelled her a naïve or primitive artist, and Cordelia because of Alfred Wallis who, she said, wasn't even

Cornish and was an ignorant old fisherman posing as an artist. They were quite snobbish in that respect. William George, on the other hand, was well read and therefore acceptable. Bryan Pearce was truly Cornish and a genuinely naïve painter. Mary objected to being connected with any school of painting and, according to Cordelia, only Mary's paintings represented the true Cornwall.'

Although Rosemary had seethed with anger at Peter's destruction of so many letters, she was also grateful to him for revealing more of the character of his aunts and for leading her to other sources. Being of an obsessive nature, as Rosemary's family and Patsy constantly reminded her, she knew she couldn't let the trail to Mary Jewels go cold. She must continue her search, wherever it led and however trivial the connection.

As usual, when looking for Mary, Rosemary was too disturbed by her latest findings to get back to her novel. She made copious notes on her discussion with Peter. Also, she was still haunted by the death of Leah, and that tragedy had some impact on her writing and changed it in an irreversible way; how much these alterations mattered, remained to be seen. She put her script firmly aside and went through the courtyard to collect the girls from the beach.

Sue and her children were packing up to leave. When she saw Rosemary coming, she waved a goodbye, indicating that the twins were now in her care.

'Demelza, Lamorna. We're going for a walk.'

'Oh Mum, we're still playing rounders,' Demelza complained.

'We're going up to Talland House.'

'Why can't we stay here on our own?' Lamorna said.

'Because I want you with me. Your father wants to be sure you're safe.'

'Safe!' the girls exploded, indignantly. 'Who's going to kidnap us from the beach with all these people around?'

But Rosemary was haunted by the spectre of George, and no amount of pleading could persuade her to leave the girls, so they tramped slowly after their mother up the beach, turning round to shout frequent goodbyes to their new friends.

On the way Rosemary bought a bunch of flowers as a thank you to the person who had invited her into Talland house out of the rain, and whose name she didn't know. The woman was delighted to see them, and provided tea, and while the twins wandered round the familiar garden, she talked.

'In the sixties, I was a young student studying art history and fine art at college. During the summer break I came to St Ives to model, and study, at the St Ives School of Painting. The modelling helped pay my fees. Leonard and Margery Fuller, both painters, ran it. They would take us to different parts of town where we set up our easels and worked. Later we would go to the studio for criticism from our tutors, and a cup of tea. I remember there was a young naïve painter there, who they left to develop on his own. He has since become famous. I believe it was Bryan Pearce.'

'Yes. I know Bryan's work. He's still living in St Ives and, as you say, has since become well known as a painter in the arts colony. His paintings have travelled the world into private and public collections.'

'Good for Bryan. I'm still a naïve painter, in spite of my efforts to learn, but I'll never be famous, and must be satisfied with enjoying the process of painting.'

Rosemary looked at some of the paintings the woman had been working on and noticed their similarity to the heavy impasto work of Mary Jewels, with their bright, untoned colours. It was very strange, but she was also like Mary to look at, with thick black hair, dark eyes, and heavy features. She was tall, a very striking looking woman, but Rosemary wasn't going to point out those resemblances.

'Your work reminds me of Mary Jewels paintings,' Rosemary said thoughtfully, 'the way her cottages tumble on a hillside, the trees, the boats, the colours, the figures. Quite remarkable.'

'It's funny you should say that. I haven't copied her style; didn't know of her until I saw a couple of Mary Jewels' paintings at the Tate Gallery in London, then I thought the same thing.'

'Of course, the retrospective exhibition of St Ives and Newlyn painters in 1985. I had completely forgotten. Stupid of me. I must get out the catalogue and take a look.'

While her host put away her paintings, Rosemary walked through the garden for the last time, to find the twins. They were hiding. She could hear their voices, and following, expected to come upon them, then giggling, they would be elsewhere, behind the trees, or round a bush. They would come up behind her and touch her shoulder. When she turned, they were gone.

She called quietly, searching in the dark part of the garden among the trees. They did not come out of their hiding place. She could hear them talking over the stream rushing down the stone steps. Then they were behind the fence in the garden next door. 'Come along, we're going home,' she said. They made no answer. Frustrated, and cross, she went back to the house. As she walked in through the French doors she saw the twins sitting on the sofa.

'Where've you been Mum? We've been waiting for you for ages.'

'Vanessa, Virginia, you shouldn't tease me like that,' Rosemary scolded. The twins looked at her, wide eyed. Their mother appeared not to notice she had called them by different names. She was thanking the woman, and then they were down the path and on their way to Piazza. 'Mum,' Demelza said, breaking the silence that engulfed them. 'What was that woman's name?'

Rosemary jerked to attention. 'I've no idea,' she laughed. 'I meant to ask her, and forgot. How strange.'

'Yes Mum, you are strange,' the girls said. Rosemary caught a knowing look, which passed between them. 'Sometimes you don't even know our names.'

The weekend was over at last and they were on the train journey to London. Now was the opportunity to question the girls. Rosemary tentatively asked if anything was worrying them. They could tell her whatever was on their minds; or if they were having trouble with anyone. The girls turned the inquisition on its head.

'Chiefly, Mum. We're worried about you. Bit crazy,' Demelza said.

'You are a bit weird when you're writing, you know,' Lamorna said, trying to soften the blow to their mother's self-respect. They didn't want to worry her. Once she'd finished writing they were sure she'd return to normal. 'You'll be ok when you've got all that stuff out of your head.'

'Yes, all those imaginary people talking to you. I'm never going to be a writer and forget my own children's names,' admonished Demelza, always her sternest critic.

Lamorna and Demelza looked at one another and began to laugh at the memory of being called Virginia and Vanessa. Their mother hadn't realised what she'd done, and the girls hadn't told her. It was such a joke.

Rosemary was reluctant to be outfaced by their derisive laughter. She tried again. 'I'm sorry, girls. But don't worry about me. I want to know if there's anything I can do for you. Some little problem your Dad and I can solve. Hmm?'

The girls shrugged, and shook their heads. It was typical of their mum to try and stave off any criticism of her, and then turn the tables. There was nothing they could tell her that she would understand. As for

George, well that was over. They would never get caught up with him again. They would tell him to piss off. They had rehearsed saying it to one another, and shouting, 'Piss off. Piss off!' to get the right angry tone. Even Sylvia had been disillusioned, they thought, and if not, they'd tell her to piss off too if she tried to take them to his house again. They laughed at the idea of it and gave a reassuring smile to their mother.

Rosemary relaxed in her seat. There was nothing to tell after all. Nothing to worry about, except perhaps the harsh, though just, criticism of her behaviour when she was writing. But wasn't it the same for any working mother? At least she was at home most of the time, even if her head was somewhere else.

Refusing to feel guilty, she turned her attention to her own interests. She had a couple more chapters of the novel to show Patsy. It had been a tussle, trying to occupy the twins, dealing with Lewis's upset at her constantly going away, grieving for Leah, and fighting against her thoughts on Mary Jewels, but she was well on target. She had managed to begin writing on arriving back from Talland house, and the twins had offered to make supper as long as they could stay out late on their last evening.

'You can watch us from the window,' Lamorna said.

'We won't leave the beach and we'll wave every ten minutes,' Demelza offered.

It was a very reasonable suggestion, and Rosemary settled down to work. The writing was going so well that it was dusk when she realised the lack of light was causing difficulties. She would often continue to struggle because if she got up to put on the light, the flow of words would cease. The sound of the door slamming brought her back to consciousness. The twins arrived at the flat, rather disgruntled.

'Well mum, we waved, we tried throwing stones at the windows, we lit a fire and had a firework display, built a huge sand castle ...'

'We wrote 'help' on the sand, we swam naked, we drifted out to sea in a dinghy – and still you didn't see us. We could have been kidnapped, and be miles away by now in a gypsy caravan, and you wouldn't know.'

'Oh dear,' said Rosemary, bleary eyed from her concentrated writing, 'I'm sure I must have waved a couple of times.'

The girls mutely shook their heads, and giving their aggrieved, disapproving looks, took themselves off to bed.

Remembering that last evening and the wounded attitude of the girls, Rosemary wanted to repair the damage she had done by forgetting them, and abandoning them on the beach, having that very afternoon told them they were not to be left alone. She offered to play Scrabble with them on the train. They gave her a withering look, shared out two files of letters and ignored her.

Well, they had dismissed her so she was now at liberty to dwell once more on Mary. She realised that the sisters were so close that Mary couldn't be written about without regard for Cordelia. Why had Mary never remarried? Why had Cordelia never remarried?

Were they such good companions that neither could part from the other? Perhaps they were jealous of one another, and managed to see off any passing admirers, so they had no successful or lasting love affairs. But Mary and Cordelia were probably victims of the First World War when, as well as Mary's husband, so many other young men were killed. Because of a shortage of men, women were deprived of a husband and children.

Rosemary looked at her notes on the conversation she had with Peter. She recalled him telling her about Cordelia's husband and providing more detailed knowledge.

'Aunt Cordelia married Frank Dobson in Marylebone, London, in 1918. He studied stone carving in Newlyn. Some of the tomb stones in Paul churchyard are his; then of course he began wood carving, and turned the whole thing into fine art and called it sculpture. Why are stone-masons workmen, and sculptors artists? I've never under-stood it.'

Peter laughed at the idea of the transformation of the career, which took Cordelia and her husband away from a craftsman's workshop in Newlyn to a studio in Chelsea, where they mixed with a Bohemian society of artists, writers, musicians and dancers.

'Aunt Mary lived with Cordelia and Frank in London, and they divided their time between Chelsea and Newlyn. Unfortunately, Dobson got involved with somebody else, and the marriage broke up. Aunt Delia was heart broken. She didn't even get to keep the sketches and paintings he did of her and Mary. I do remember he was commissioned to produce a

207

sculpture of a famous ballet dancer, but I can't remember her name.'

'Thank you so much, Peter. I'll see if I can track down the dancer. It's very hard for a piece of sculpture to disappear. There must be a record of where it was exhibited, or it may be in a private collection somewhere.'

That must be her next quest; to see if a book had been published on Frank Dobson and find out the name of the dancer and see the portraits of Mary. Thank goodness for libraries and telephones.

'Greta, have you got a book on a sculptor called Frank Dobson.'

'Yes. Funny you should ask; I've just put it on the shelf. Shall I reserve it for you?'

'Thanks. I'll come and collect it shortly. It'll make interesting reading on the train.'

At home in London, waiting for her, was Roger Goodwood's catalogue announcing an auction in a few weeks time, of the studio paintings of 'Isobel Heath and friends.' She regretted she would not be in Cornwall for the viewing and the auction. There were several small paintings for sale, not illustrated. She couldn't possibly pop down again just for the auction. She thought to ask Robert to buy one for her, but he was self-interested and would buy them for himself, and sell to Rosemary at a higher price. She decided to leave a telephone bid and chose a painting for its title and size, just above the estimated price.

In West Hampstead life resumed its normal pace, and although the girls had assured Rosemary that there was nothing to worry about, she remembered Brad's words of warning with regard to George and his behaviour towards the twins, which had aroused Joan and Brad's suspicions. Rosemary determined to visit her sister at Swiss Cottage. She would meet Sylvia at the library and take her out to lunch. The conversation would naturally turn to what happened in Cornwall, and the practicalities of owning a joint property.

Rosemary had intended taking a subtle approach, instead she blurted out in her usual blunt manner. 'Have you seen anything of George since you've been back?'

Sylvia put down her knife and fork. 'It seems,' she said slowly, 'that I was mistaken in that man. I'm ashamed to say it, but he was not in the least interested in me.' She hurriedly resumed eating.

'But you were with him quite often – with the twins, weren't you?' Rosemary gently probed.

Sylvia finished her wine in one gulp, and pushed the rest of her food around the plate. She couldn't think how she was going to give an explanation to having put the girls in some danger, because she had been foolishly led by a man she thought was interested in her.

'Look Rosemary. I don't know how to say this. And believe me, I didn't know. But it was only when we went to George's house that I realised ...'

'You went to his house! The girls never said. You never told me. Why did you go to his house?' Rosemary's gentle approach was now over. She was seriously alarmed.

Sylvia's face blazed with conscience and embarrassment.

'Because he said he wanted to do a questionnaire with the twins, and show the video he took of them on the beach.'

'The video. Yes, Brad told me about the video.'

'I didn't know about the video. He took that before I got to know him. Believe me Rosemary; I thought he was genuine. He said he was working on a college project, studying twins.'

'What happened in the house?'

'Nothing, as far as I know.'

'As far as you know!' exploded Rosemary, leaping to her feet. 'We'd better get home immediately. I must get to the bottom of this. They say children don't tell their parents about being molested. I can't believe it. Were they alone with him in the house?'

'No. But they were alone with his friend.'

'Alone with ...'

'Look, sit down Rosemary, I'm trying to tell you about it. Don't worry.'

In a state of agitation, Rosemary plonked herself down in the chair.

'Don't worry! This gets worse and worse. I can't believe it. I can't believe it,' Rosemary repeated.

'I meant to tell you. In fact I was going to tell you today, except you brought it up first. I've put paid to that bastard's activities, and his mates, and his so-called clients. It's over. Look, read this.'

'You've kept us completely in the dark. How could

you be so bloody stupid, Sylvia!'

'For God's sake Rosemary, read the bloody paper!'

When Sylvia took the twins to Camden Lock, it was already arranged with George that they would meet accidentally. He had telephoned her and explained that they were running short of time on their project, the questionnaire had to be filled in and they were anxious to take some photos of the girls. 'And of course, I'd like to see you again Sylvia. Been missing you.' Sylvia had thrilled to those words and replied in like manner.

When they got to George's house, Sylvia experienced the first sign of alarm when a group of men had come running down the stairs. His friend Barry seemed an odd character and she hadn't liked the way he leered at the twins. However, she was diverted in this thought when George took her hand. It was the first physical contact he had made towards her and she was excited at the prospect.

'We'll let Barry get to know the two flowers,' George said, leading her along a passage. 'He'll make a few notes for their profile.' He grinned, and holding her hand tightly, took her into a room. Sylvia looked around the dim interior. The blinds were drawn and they were in semi-darkness. A video was coming to an end, which showed a group of six scantily clad young girls waving their goodbyes at the camera.

George released her hand. He sorted through a few videos. 'Sit down,' he said. It was only in this unsavoury room that she began to suspect George and Barry of some ill intent towards the girls. She heard the girls call, and they came running to her. 'Just in time,' George remarked. The video had started. Sylvia was shocked to see Demelza and Lamorna flaunting and flirting with the camera. George's voice was heard directing their actions and was now relishing the film he'd made, and actually licking his lips. Barry was watching with a permanent grin on his face. The girls were shamefaced and embarrassed.

Rosemary opened the local newspaper. 'Raid on paedophile house in north London,' ran the headline. 'A number of videos, photographs and computers, were taken from a house in London when police raided it after a tip-off. Two men were arrested and taken in for questioning. It is believed that members of a paedophile ring were using the premises for viewing pornographic videos of children. Other arrests are expected to be made shortly.'

'Oh my God,' moaned Rosemary.

'It's all right. Don't worry,' Sylvia said. 'I took the video. I've destroyed it. It was me phoned the police and reported those two bastards. The twins are not involved in any way, I assure you.'

'But what happened in that house, when you weren't with them?' Rosemary demanded.

'I don't know, but nothing serious, I'm sure. We all watched the video. They were only alone for five minutes.'

Rosemary groaned aloud. The sisters sat quietly thinking over the situation, then Sylvia continued, 'I can't tell you how ashamed and sorry I am that I didn't know what was happening. It was so stupidly naïve. I haven't questioned the girls, and they haven't told me anything. I thought I'd leave that to you, so you'd know the whole story, after I'd reported them to the police.'

'I hope it doesn't mean the girls will be involved in a court case, as witnesses. It would be so awful for them.'

'I told you Rosemary. I took the video. Those two bastards aren't likely to complain that I stole a video. It would mean even more evidence against them. There's no possible connection with the twins, don't you see?'

'Thank God for that Sylvia. Thank God you had your wits about you and there's no evidence to show that the girls were involved in those sordid activities. But I don't understand how you could have left them alone with strange men!'

'You leave them alone all the time, Rosemary. A beach in a small seaside town is no safer than a London street. You should have thought about their safety yourself before blaming me. If you'd been with them, the video wouldn't have happened.'

It was an awkward parting. Both sisters were feeling angry, aggrieved and guilty. They would need some distance before meeting again.

Things weren't going right for Rosemary at the moment. At home she was further upset when she rang the auction house to see if her bid for a Mary Jewels painting was successful. It had gone for £20 over her offer. And now she had another ordeal before her. She had to confront Demelza and Lamorna about George Tatum and his friend. Then when Lewis came home, he would have to be told the whole episode. She prepared tea and took it into the garden. Anxiously, she awaited the girls' return home from school. She'd try to make it as relaxed as possible, though she didn't feel that way herself.

'Lamorna. Demelza,' she called, as the front door slammed.

'What?' They said rudely, and stood impatiently at the door to the garden, ready to disappear to their room as soon as they answered their mother's query. It was bound to be something about where they'd hidden some item of clothing, or school books, or anything else just as boring.

'Put your school bags down and come out for tea.'

'Oh Mum,' they complained, 'We've got to ring Pat and find out …'

'I want you out here now; what ever plans you have made can wait.'

There was something in their mother's voice that couldn't be ignored, and throwing down their bags, they came into the garden and sat sprawled on the garden chairs. Rosemary split open hot freshly-made scones, and gave them jam and cream to spread. They were impressed with their tea. It was soon devoured and they were relaxed.

'Now. I'll come straight to the point.' Rosemary

began. 'What happened in George's house when you went to see the video he took of you?'

The girls were open mouthed with surprise that their mother knew, but instead of the expected evasive answers, they acted as though released from sitting on some explosive material. They blurted out a stream of swear words in angry tones, which she wisely ignored, and then they began to be frank about the whole episode.

'That bastard. I'm going to kick his arse if I ever see him again,' Lamorna shouted.

'And I'll bloody well push him down the stairs. Those sort of men should be locked up,' Demelza added.

'But what happened?' Rosemary persisted, pleased they were at last telling their tale.

'Nothing, Mum. The two of them just leered at us. The other one, Barry, tried to put his arm round us, pretending he wanted to ask questions. Yuk. He was putrid.'

'Bloody vile and putrid. Sylvia was disgusted with us. We watched our video and we hated it. We hate George.'

'We were stupid little kids, Mum. Honestly. Brad told us to tell him to bugger off, or he would do it for us. But we didn't want to make a fuss.' The twins were now near to tears with the relief of confession.

'Look girls. I only want to know that you are OK, and nothing; promise me; nothing more than that happened to you. It's important for me to know.'

'Really Mum. Nothing. We nearly pushed George off the bench in the hide when we went bird watching, and he tried to cuddle us.' The girls laughed. 'Stupid man. He knew nothing about birds.'

Rosemary felt momentarily sick at the words, 'he tried to cuddle us,' and then she was angry and wanted to shout at the girls, but she calmed herself with an effort, and gently said, 'Anything else Lamorna? Demelza?'

'Mum,' Lamorna said shamefaced, 'there's that video.'

'That's all right.' Rosemary said, clenching her fists and still trying to control her outrage. 'Sylvia took it away with her when you left the house.'

'You won't show it to Dad, will you, Mum. Please' they begged.

'I haven't even seen it. Sylvia destroyed it.'

The girls collapsed with relief. Rosemary didn't tell them that the men were now in jail. There was no point since there was no evidence to implicate them in the affair. She didn't want to make a bigger drama than that which concerned the girls. Instead she said, if anything like that ever happened again, would they promise to tell her. And they were quite entitled to be as nasty as they liked to any man who made similar approaches.

'In fact, forget all our teaching about being polite; shout, scream, kick, scratch, and make the biggest fuss you can to bring people's attention to what is happening.'

'Yes, we will mum. We've learnt to recognise creepy guys; we think.'

Rosemary made sure the girls were out at their

friend's house, while she told Lewis. He had taken the matter very badly, blaming Sylvia for the part she had unwittingly played; blaming Rosemary, blaming himself, blaming the girls, and storming around the kitchen saying he was going to kill the bastards and where did they live. Why hadn't the girls told their mother about it? Why hadn't they told him, so he could've cut their balls off.

'Lewis. As far as the girls are concerned, it's all over. The police have the matter in hand. I'm sure they've told me the whole story. Don't start questioning them and making it worse. Let them know from that experience that these men don't have to be tolerated. They can kick and scream and make a fuss to draw attention to any incident they don't like. I've told them that, and when you've quietened down, you can tell them too.'

Rosemary knew how hard it was for Lewis to contain his frustration and anger, to be inactive when he wanted to lash out at the perpetrators of an assault on his daughters.

'OK. Yes. OK,' he said.

Unfortunately, the whole episode soured Lewis's relationship with Sylvia, in spite of her gallant attempt to fool the men, to steal and destroy the video, and to inform the police. He hardly spoke to her, so she didn't come visiting the house. Penelope and Miranda were also distant, because of Lewis's attitude, though they were not privy to the circumstances of the estrangement. The question of buying a house in Cornwall between them, was forgotten. The twins daren't men-

217

tion it, and Rosemary got used to the idea that it wasn't going to happen.

In Hampstead High Street Rosemary wandered into Waterstones and browsed among the books, alighting on the biography section. She was in a quandary. Her life was disjointed. Her time was spent travelling between London and Cornwall. She had an obsession about where she could write. Lewis, still angry about the near miss of his girls being involved with a paedophile, lashed out at Rosemary.

'Get a grip on yourself. Stop thinking you are a reincarnation of Virginia Woolf.'

'Don't be stupid Lewis. It has nothing to do with Virginia Woolf, I thought I could write at Talland House, because that's where I had the inspiration for my first novel.'

'Try writing at home Rosemary. It's very disturbing having you go away all the time, leaving the girls, or disrupting their lives for a brief weekend in Cornwall.'

'But the girls love it!'

'They need some order in their lives in view of all that's happened over the last few weeks. Think of them. Think of me. I agree with their opinion of you – you are weird. And you are selfish.'

Rosemary left the house in a bad temper, knowing there was truth in what Lewis said; but how could she change her nature? She blamed the book she was trying to write; she blamed her agent for persuading her that she could write a novel as easily and as eagerly, as she approached her non-fiction work on art and artists.

'You won't have all that trouble with research, letter writing, photocopying, and travelling to see people, taking photos ...'

'I know. I know. All right I'll try it, Patsy.'

And Rosemary had tried, and as far as she was concerned, it wasn't a success. She skipped through the autobiographies of novelists at Waterstones. It seemed that she hadn't had enough traumatic life experiences. Their drug addiction, drinking problems, abuse in childhood, the battering by a partner, had made them into writers. Rosemary, on the other hand, obviously had too sheltered a life. It was positively a drawback. It was something to be thought about, but not something she could resolve. Even the murder of Leah and the alarming and worrying incident with the twins, hadn't softened her nature, or turned her into a wise and learned woman.

Over lunch at Burgh House, sitting in the garden among the plants and flowers, she questioned her need to put her writing above other necessities. Why did she not consider her husband and her children's needs first? Was she deliberately avoiding her responsibilities? The question hadn't arisen before, at least not before the possible danger to the twins.

She rang Lewis. 'I've been thinking,' she said, 'When this book is finished, and I seriously have my doubts that it will be, we'll talk about me finding a job. I think sitting down at a desk in an office will ground me. Knowing that my world revolves around that small area might be a good discipline for sitting still. What do you think?

'Rosemary love. I hadn't intended you should whip yourself for my sudden outburst. I just wanted you to think a bit.'

'Well, I have Lewis, and that's my solution.'

'Leave the future to sort itself out, but for the moment, I know you have to complete this novel. If you don't, you will blame yourself for failing, and blame me for making you come to a decision to give it up.'

'Well, it has been a struggle, and I've come this far, but without much joy. OK, I'll carry on and make it happen. Thanks Lewis. See you tonight.'

9

Rosemary hadn't been in touch with Sylvia for some time, and was surprised when she received a letter and, on opening it, to see an address at The Terrace, St Ives. 'Dear Rose, Here I am at last. I wasn't going to let my stupid misjudgement put me off St Ives. It happened so quickly. I sold my flat in Swiss Cottage, gave up the library, and have already got part-time work at St Ives library. I'm enclosing details of the house. You'll love it. It's on the terrace, looking over Porthminster beach and the bay. It's rather bigger than I intended, but it means you can come and stay with the twins (even if Lewis doesn't want to). It also means that I've no money left to invest in a cottage with you (though Lewis wouldn't want me to anyway). Come any time. The twins will love it. Please give me a call, or write (even if Lewis doesn't want you to). Love Sylvia.'

She couldn't help but sigh in sympathy at Sylvia's bracketed remarks. At the same time she experienced a tinge of jealousy that her sister had managed to buy a house in St Ives and they had not. Ever since the episode with George and the twins, Lewis had regarded Sylvia as largely responsible for the whole sorry story. Rosemary had been caught between the two of them, seeing justification in both arguments. According to Lewis, Sylvia shouldn't have got into a situation, which put the twins at risk. Sylvia acknowledged some blame, 'I know I've been a fool,' she said, but defended herself. 'How was I to know? Would you have known? He seemed genuine enough and he pretended to be interested in me, though when I think about it, it wasn't a lively chase, just a mild jog.' She couldn't help a wry grin at her willingness to believe that the man had been attracted to her.

The twins had to account to their father for every move they made. He had to know who they were meeting, and where and when. Their mother ferried them around to friends' houses, and picked them up afterwards, so that her presence became an embarrassment, and they would rather stay home than accept invitations to meet anywhere. It was all their mother's fault, why couldn't she object to their father's rules. Couldn't she make up her own mind?

'We could get one of those factory clocking on and off machines,' Lamorna said cheekily to her mother.

'I advise you not to say that to your father,' she said, 'He's only concerned for you and trying to protect you. In any case, I agree with him.'

'But it's been ages since then, and nothing happened, Mum. We keep telling you.'

'The potential for something happening was there. You were in danger, whether you like to believe it or not.'

'We wish we hadn't told you.'

'You didn't tell me. That's what's worrying us. It was Joan and Brad who first alerted me to what was going on. I think Sylvia intended to, but whether she would have got round to it, knowing she had practically col-luded in it, I don't know.'

The twins were quite happy to heap more blame on Sylvia for trying to persuade them to like 'the creep,' and their mother for paying more attention to what was in her head, than what the twins were doing. Their father was generally dismissed. He had never asked where they were, or who they met. Now all that had changed. The twins kept out of his way as much as possible, thinking they were going to be in trouble, whatever they did, and were never going to be forgiven. It wasn't their fault that a man on the beach was a pervert and interested in young girls. How were they supposed to know? They kept up a tirade of complaints to their mother about their unfair treatment.

'Perhaps we should have worn a burka,' Demelza suggested. They daren't make the same remark to their father, even though he kept stressing to them that it wasn't their fault. It felt like their fault, the way he never forgot the episode, and was constantly reminding them to take care.

'He has a lot on his mind with his business at the moment, so for goodness sake don't give him any cause to worry about you.'

The girls groaned. They complained about their fate in their room, hardly daring to venture out of doors except to go to school, and having little to say at meal times, in case they risked saying the wrong thing. Their mother was therefore happy to break the tension of the household by telling them the news of Sylvia's swift exit to the West Country.

The girls were at last pleased about something and wanted to know when they could visit and longing to surf. 'You ought to go and finish your writing Mum, and we'll come with you - that's if old misery guts Dad, doesn't object. Honestly, we don't know what poor Auntie Sylvia's done. Dad was always teasing the aunts, and now he hates them.'

The twins, now that their interests were being served, were championing Sylvia.

'You don't have to ask Dad whether we can go, surely Mum. It's up to you, isn't it?' Demelza looked at her mother with a challenging grin.

'I think we'll take the car and have a quick weekend trip. Friday, I want you home from school without delay. OK?' Rosemary decided, meeting the challenge.

The girls were cheering as their father came through the front door, looking harassed and tired. When they saw him, they raced upstairs, and left their mother to do the explaining. It wasn't as difficult as Rosemary expected having regard to the row they had about her constantly on the move to Cornwall, and leaving him to fend for himself.

'As long as the girls are happy and they stick with you. Don't let them out of your sight, and don't leave them with that irresponsible sister of yours, ' Lewis advised. 'I shall probably be working at home all weekend so I could do with the house to myself.'

Rosemary had wanted to say that the restrictions on the girls' freedom had gone on long enough but, seeing his weary face, she resisted. She would try and get back to some normality. The effect on the girls was to exaggerate the whole episode. They had suffered enough. If only Lewis would let go, it would give them all a release from his anxieties. And it was time to stop blaming Sylvia. But she would bring this to his attention when they returned from Cornwall.

It was a happy trio which set off from West Hampstead with the blessing of Lewis. The weekend was going to be fun. Rosemary would work, the twins would surf, and Sylvia was looking forward to showing them her house. She had already bought some of the famous John Miller prints of blue sea and yellow sand, so calming. The setting of his house and studio on the edge of the beach, looking across to the Hayle estuary and the towans, had inspired these minimal and evocative paintings, and the images were popular as prints.

Sylvia had also bought some Bryan Pearce and Alfred Wallis prints. How different were their portrayals of St Ives, Bryan with his flat, bright colours, calm seas and toy-like boats, showing a quality of serenity. Alfred was all emotion and turmoil in his tumbling seas and skies, and the threat to his working boats. How well the pictures looked in her St Ives house.

On her terrace at the back of the house Sylvia had tubs with a variety of palms from 'Hardy Exotics,' at White Cross, on the way to Penzance. Her windows did not need net curtains. They looked out over the bay and down onto Porthminster beach. She could see the train when it came through the bridge and round the bend to arrive at the station. Godrevy lighthouse winked nightly in the bay, and far away on the horizon, Trevose Head lighthouse winked back. It was the reality of her dream come true, to be in Cornwall, and have the pleasure of welcoming her family to her wonderful house in St Ives.

Rosemary, Sylvia and the twins, stood in the hall embracing. It was a reconciliation without words. Sylvia's anxiety to please was obvious.

'Lamorna, Demelza, I've sorted out the nicest room for you. It's at the front and overlooks the bay. I thought you'd like that. Mum can have the room looking down to the courtyard and over the garden. I've bought new linen, and had all the rooms freshly decorated. And I hope you'll love it here.' Sylvia choked back a tear. They were overcome with the pleasure of the occasion.

Their first port of call in the morning was to Porthminster beach café. It was still warm enough to sit on the terrace, though the holiday season was over and they were counting down to closure for the winter. There were people walking on the tide line and a few scattered families on the beach, but visitors to the town were an all year round feature since the opening of the Tate Gallery in its spectacular setting on the surfing beach at Porthmeor.

'Nearly time for your holiday, Joan,' Rosemary said.

'Can't wait. Just can't wait. It's been such a hectic summer. I think we're all suffering from the stress of success. But who could complain about that?'

'Where's Brad?' Lamorna asked.

'Gone to Australia.'

'And we didn't even say goodbye,' Demelza said.

'He'll be here again next year. Actually, he won't be in Australia till December. He's touring around Europe at the moment, but promised his mum he'll be home at Christmas. I had a card today. It read, 'Dear Joan, my mum said thanks for looking after me.' I seem to be a surrogate mother for these young lads and lassies from Australia. I think my name goes round on the bush telegraph.'

'Now the Australians have gone, the surfing school's closed.' Lamorna grumbled. 'We'll have to go out on our own Demelza.'

'You can leave the surfboards in my yard when you go home. I've a perfectly good shed in the courtyard,' Sylvia offered, 'And it'll make sure you come back again.'

'Of course we're coming back. Just try keeping us away. And Sylvia, you should see the heads turn when our surfboards are riding on the roof of the car. You'd be surprised how many people look at them and know we're going to Cornwall and surfing.'

'You're a couple of show-offs,' Joan told them.

'Never mind the image girls, think of the convenience of having them here,' Rosemary said. 'And you can leave those smelly wet-suits in the shed too, or our attic will soon smell like the ocean gone sour.'

In the afternoon Sylvia went to her part-time job at the library. Rosemary called at the St Ives Bookseller, to pick up the latest signed copy of a novel by Helen

Dunmore. Reading was so much more enjoyable than trying to write. She relished the pleasure of opening the page and Helen's first paragraph of magical words taking her into another enchanting world. The girls lazed around on their boards in the gentle sea at Porthminster. Rosemary sat beneath an umbrella on the beach, watching the girls and enjoying the freedom of not having to worry about her novel and wonder where the next sentence, or the next paragraph would come from.

It had been hard work, but during these last months Rosemary had blocked off her empathy with art and artists, and gradually worked her way into the story line and finally knew where she was going. She only had the last chapter to complete. She had posted off the bulk of the manuscript with a great sigh of relief. If she ever held the book in her hands, she would open the printed and bound pages and read it as though it was entirely new, and someone else had written it. Only in manuscript form did it seem to have anything to do with her. But, the publication of the novel was by no means certain. The editor could still reject it, in spite of Patsy's threats, whips and encouragement to keep up the pace, and all that agonising would be for nothing. She could only wait and see.

At four o'clock the girls went to the house to change and shower and Rosemary made her way into town. She met Sylvia as the library closed. She came out thrusting some photocopies at her. 'Greta said to give you these. She found two articles about Mary Jewels, one by Sven Berlin, the sculptor, who lived in St Ives at one time, and another by a Cornish journalist.'

Over tea at the house Rosemary read the articles. The Cornish writer, Francis Tremain, described Mary as 'unchanging as a slab of Cornish granite.' Sven Berlin wrote, 'she understands the beautiful proportions of cottages, and little fields bordered by stone hedges. She is a west country artist in the true sense.'

That evening Rosemary and Sylvia had been invited to a private view of the members' exhibition at the Penwith Gallery. The girls didn't want to accompany them and trail around looking at paintings, pottery and sculpture.

'Honestly Mum, we'll be fine on our own. No need of a baby sitter. Next birthday we'll be in our teens.' Lamorna said.

'Look, we promise not to open the door to anyone, unless someone shouts 'fire' and we have to escape,' Demelza added.

'If there's anything worrying you, give me a ring and we'll be home straight away,' Rosemary said, ignoring the girls' sarcastic remarks.

'What do you think, Sylvia?' Rosemary asked.

Sylvia was amazed to even think of giving an opinion on such a delicate matter.

'Look Rosemary, it's up to you to leave them on their own. I daren't have any view on the matter. I don't want to get myself in trouble with Lewis.'

The girls stood, arms folded, expressions painfully

critical of a parent who was tiresome and tedious, and for whom they had little belief in her ability to make a sensible decision, and trust to the girls' commonsense. Rosemary gave in under their cold scrutiny, wondering if there would ever be a time when she would get it completely right with her two girls, who were either accusing her of neglect, or condemning her for curtailing their freedom.

Recently, they had been even more truculent. There had been a brief period, after their sudden blurting out of the episode with George, when they had seemed relieved to have told Rosemary. Things were more relaxed between them. Then just as suddenly, they had reverted to their sullen moods and secretive behaviour, not allowing conversations above what there was for dinner, or school work. They positively clammed up at any mention of St Ives. It was so very odd. They were often lost in thought, and were easily startled. They whispered together constantly, until both Rosemary and Lewis wanted to shout at them. As a consequence of the obvious irritation felt by their parents, they spent much of their time in their room.

'It'll be nice if they come back with a smile on their faces,' Lewis whispered, kissing Rosemary goodbye on their trip to Cornwall.

Sylvia and Rosemary returned late from the Penwith Gallery, having been persuaded by friends to have a drink at the Sloop afterwards. They had wandered along the Wharf, enjoying the evening, watching small boats rounding Smeatons Pier to unload their catch of mackerel. They stood on the Malakoff overlooking the harbour, watching the lights in cottage windows, many now dark from the loss of holiday makers having gone up north, to London, America, Japan and Europe. The whole world seemed to turn up in St Ives. When they got to the house the twins met them at the door.

'Dad wants you to ring him immediately. He sounded upset. He said it doesn't matter how late it is. He wouldn't even leave a message. He didn't want to ring your mobile, and we tried to ring, but you probably didn't hear,' Demelza said accusingly.

Rosemary went to her room to find out what Lewis's urgent news was.

'Rosemary; an awful discovery,' Lewis began. 'That chap George they had in custody in London, was also wanted for questioning in St Ives, because he had stayed at Leah Carmichael's house.'

'No. Really!'

'It's very bad news, I'm afraid.'

'What Lewis?'

'Under pressure, he confessed to her murder. It's all over the London papers.'

'What! Oh my God, Lewis, him? The same man who was chasing our girls?'

Rosemary choked back tears of shock, disbelief, and terror. She had difficulty assimilating this information, and collapsed onto a chair, her breathing shallow and rasping. Her mind racing to scenes of horror.

Lewis continued, 'Apparently Leah caught him molesting a young girl. She was coming out of the shower, in her robe. Her parents were out. Only George and this poor kid were in the house, and

Leah came in, just in time. Rosemary, are you still there?'

'Yes. Yes. I'm trying to take it in. I can't really believe it. Poor Leah. Poor Leah. Oh dear, our girls Lewis.'

'Yes. It seems the girl he was abusing didn't tell her parents. Apparently, Leah told him to get out of her house and warned him she would tell the parents, and report him to the police. They argued. He hit her, dragged her into the car, drove to Hell's Mouth and pushed it over the edge.'

'Oh God. How awful!'

'The girls are not overhearing this, are they?'

'No, of course not. I'm on my own. I shan't say anything to them, but I'll have to tell Sylvia. It'll be an awful shock to her. A shock to all of us.'

'Oh Lord. I've treated that woman like a pariah these last few months, partly blaming her. Now I realise, she could possibly have stood between him and the girls; the very fact that she was around, if you see what I mean.' Lewis said.

'Yes. The girls could have gone to the house on their own, because they wanted to see the video, and then ... It could have been different. And Sylvia too may have been in danger. She said she had to pretend to go along with their plans for the twins, to get them safely out of the house.'

Rosemary was quiet for a moment, holding the phone to her ears shuddering, and thinking of all the implications and possibilities of how things could have turned out. She couldn't put the phone down. She had to be connected, even in silence, to share this ghastly tragedy, and averted disaster to her own family. At last, Lewis said.

'I realise now that it was probably a very risky business. Look, Rosemary, I'd like to apologise to Sylvia. Tell her I said she was right. Nobody could do anything about a man like that, who preys on young girls. They're well practised at it. But would you break the ice. Tell her I'm sorry.'

'Yes, Lewis. That at least will be something to come out of this. And can you release the girls from your anger and disapproval? We'll have to tread very carefully with them.'

'It's only concern for their safety, Rosemary. Surely you can see that?'

'It looks, and feels, more like punishment, believe me. And they've got to feel you are in sympathy with them, especially now with this terrible news. If they don't hear anything about the murder in St Ives first, then we'll have to sit down quietly with them at home, and tell them.'

'OK. But keep it from them if you can. They're bound to find out sometime, and it'd better be from us. Look Rosie, I'm sorry to burden you with this, and upset you. I should have waited until you got home but ...'

'No Lewis. It's OK. I couldn't have kept it from you either. Let's say goodnight now, or they'll wonder what secrets we're talking about.'

Rosemary, pleading tiredness, went straight to bed. She couldn't sit around with Sylvia and the girls with her face as distraught as she felt, and not blurt out the whole thing. She had to bide her time. And she didn't want to spoil the lovely feeling in the house with her sordid news.

In the hallway of her house Leah was confronting George, holding a note from her guests, who explained that they had gone home early because their daughter had said she was feeling ill. 'She wasn't ill. She was terrified,' Leah shouted. 'That child may not have told her parents, but you're not getting away with it; as soon as I can I'll give them a ring and tell them what ...'

The sentence remained unfinished as George struck a blow to Leah's head. Leah took the punch on the side of her face and promptly kicked out at him.

'Get out of my house,' she yelled.

'Nothing happened to the stupid girl, you silly bitch,' he shouted, delivering another glancing blow.

'That's because I prevented it.' Unafraid by the attack on her, Leah pushed past him towards the garden door, and her car. 'I'm going to the police.'

'Do you think the police are going to believe a girl who roams the house with practically nothing on? She's a menace,' he shouted. 'You're not going to the police.'

George did not back off, but followed after Leah. He picked up a garden spade, and as Leah reached out to close the car door, he smashed it onto the top of her head. 'I warned you. No one goes to the police.' As she slumped to fall out of the car, he pushed her in, struggling to hoist her inert body over to the passenger side. The keys and the car were his.

It was late evening as he drove the car out of St Ives. By the time he reached Hayle and drove up the road towards Gwithian village, it was twilight. People had left the Towans and beaches, and the lonely landscape and roads. He drove past the clusters of chalets on the sandhills. He caught glimpses of the lights of St Ives twinkling across the sea and over the low windswept hedges of the road.

In his fear, George seemed totally conscious of everything around him, even the wind was soft and murmuring. The only thing that disturbed him was the body of the woman, slumped forward and wedged between the dashboard and the seat. Her dark hair cascaded around her and moved with the rocking of the car. He was glad he couldn't see her face. No car passed him on the road.

At last, he lurched off the road onto the field. He drove unseen, over the rough turf towards the edge of the cliff, bumping over the ground, and pushing away Leah's limp body, which had released itself and continually gravitated towards him, her head resting against his shoulder. 'Get away from me, you bitch,' he shouted.

He shuddered at the touch, and got out of the car. He dare not close the door for fear he couldn't push it over the cliff and he would have to drive closer. Slowly, and with a huge effort, he edged the car closer until the weight took it over the cliff. He fell down as it did so and watched the vehicle bounce and roll. It landed upside down in a huge splash into a high tide. What a thrilling sight it was. He laughed, in sheer relief that he

235

was free of the woman's body. He was no longer responsible for it.

George was exhilarated and exhausted, but triumphant. 'I've done it!' He lay there a long time on the turf, looking up into the sky, watching the night sky as it slid over to the west, and covered the last blue tinge of the day. Tomorrow, he would leave St Ives. He didn't look again over the cliff to see the car. It was all over. He could forget about it.

He wandered from the field to the road, watching for cars. He didn't want to risk calling a cab and having the driver report having picked up a lone male around the time the car was first sighted smashed on the rocks at Hell's Mouth. It was a long lonely road that took him into Hayle, and houses, and people. He walked nearly all night stopping to flatten himself against a hedge, or turn into a gateway, should a car's headlights threaten to pick him out, and worst of all, offer him a lift. He arrived back in the early hours of the morning.

George entered Leah's house through the garden door, which was still open after he'd followed her to the car. He was now the only occupant of the house and there was nobody to question her absence. He slept for a few hours, packed his rucksack, and wandered down to Porthminster beach for one last look at the twins.

George sat huddled into himself and was surprised and angry when Sylvia lay a hand on his shoulder. He almost screamed at her touch. He was so edgy and highly-strung. He leapt to his feet, and made off along the beach, almost running, then checked himself. She was following, slowly, but determined to catch up. He would have to be careful not to arouse her suspicions. They were supposed to be friends. He sat down at the end of the beach and composed himself, ready for her approach. His forced smile was like a snarl.

On leaving Sylvia, gaining her sympathy, and giving an adequate reason for his odd reaction to her, he caught the train out of St Ives. There was no one he knew, or even recognised on the train, only holiday makers, who stared out of the windows, taking their last look at paradise. He had no friends in the town. He left a note on the hall table, dated two days previously, so it would seem he left the house the day before her death. 'Dear Leah, Thank you for your hospitality. I've had a wonderful time. Hope to see you again. George.' He couldn't help a demonic chuckle.

The opportunity for telling Sylvia the tragic news came the next day as they walked on Porthmeor beach. The girls had found their courage and were out at sea in their wet suits, lying on their body boards, waiting for the huge waves that would sweep them screaming with delight to the shore.

It was Sylvia who raised the subject. 'Something's wrong, isn't it? Something Lewis said last night. I knew from your face. It's something to do with me. He still hasn't forgiven me. He doesn't want the twins anywhere near me. He wants you to go home.'

'No Sylvia. Nothing like that. He wants me to apologise to you.'

'Apologise. Really?'

'Yes. Really. He will do so himself when we get home and we've sorted things out with the girls, but for the moment, he wants me to tell you he's sorry he blamed you for getting mixed up with those men. It wasn't your fault.'

Sylvia's face lightened with relief. 'Sorry? What's changed his mind? I thought I was an outcast forever. I thought it would always be my fault.'

'Give a wave to the girls, in case we forget in the next few moments. In fact we'd better sit down.'

Rosemary realised how difficult it must have been for Lewis to tell her over the phone. But there was no easy way to tell Sylvia. She was still in shock herself. Her eyes filled with tears as she began to tell the terrible news.

'Rosemary, what is it?' Sylvia said, alarmed at her sister's tears.

'Do you remember my friend Leah who had a guest house in St Ives?'

'The one who was murdered?' Sylvia said, with a shudder.

'They've found out who did it.' She paused. 'It was George.'

The girls came screaming in on a huge wave and were flung onto the beach. They picked themselves up, waved, and clutching their boards, went plunging into the surf to be thrown screaming to shore again.

Sylvia's terrified scream matched the girls'.

'Oh God. A murderer! I nearly fell in love with that man. Oh my. Oh dear!' Sylvia was distraught. 'I took

238

the twins to see him, a murderer. I tried to persuade them to like him. It could have been ...' She broke down in tears.

'But you put him behind bars Sylvia,' Rosemary reminded her, putting a comforting arm around her heaving shoulders.

'The twins don't know yet. We mustn't let them see us crying.'

'I'm OK. It's the shock. Such a shock for you too.' Sylvia rocked to and fro in distress. 'Oh poor you.'

'I'll get us a drink,' Rosemary said, trying to control her tears. She clambered up the beach to get a take-away coffee. They sat staring out to sea, automatically drinking their coffee, lost in awful thoughts of what might have been, but remembering to give the occasional forced, cheerful, wave to the twins.

'I've just realised something,' Sylvia said. 'That time when he was so strange on the beach – it must have been the day after he murdered your friend. He kept running away from me, and had such a haunted, menacing look on his face. He was really weird, and to think I tried to cheer him up, to comfort him. I put my arm around him, and I gave him a kiss. A bloody murderer!'

'If you hadn't reported him to the police, he would still be out there as a danger to other young girls. Maybe a threat to another life. Who knows!'

After lunch Sylvia went to bed, shuddering quite uncontrollably and with a fearful headache, trying to sleep to ward off the intrusive thoughts of the murder. The girls were off to the KidsRUs theatre to see the last performance of the youngsters' latest show and were invited to their party afterwards.

Rosemary, still in shock and unable to settle her nerves, decided to walk along the coastpath out to Clodgy and the five bays. It was a footpath that required keeping your head down and watching your step over rocky terrain. The concentration helped ease her burden of fearful thoughts. She thought that the pain of Leah's murder, although it would never leave her, had subsided a little over the last few weeks. Now the agony of it had returned and redoubled. Nevertheless, the sun was shining, the sky was cloudless, the sea was blue, the little boats fished for mackerel, the gulls formed themselves in squadrons for beautiful flights out to nesting sites on the cliffs, and the air was soft and warm. It was a perfect afternoon. All those clichés of a perfect day couldn't sooth her aching heart.

The walk was over too soon, and still she couldn't face being with the twins and acting as though nothing was wrong. They knew her too well, and would start asking questions, which she couldn't face answering. In this unsettled state of mind Rosemary decided to call in the gallery to see Robert for a chat. He hadn't known Leah so she could be sure there would be no talk about her.

'Ah!' he said, as she stepped through the door, 'Just the woman I want to see. I've found some Mary Jewels. I've taken photos for you. A woman came into the gallery telling me about her collection of paintings. She invited me for coffee to see the pictures. And there among them were two Mary Jewels.'

'I might have known you'd come up with something,' Rosemary said. 'You've never failed any of my requests, and it's the best delightful diversion I need to cheer me up at the moment.'

Robert didn't question her need to be uplifted; instead he searched in the drawer of his desk and brought out a viewer and a box of slides. Rosemary looked into the aperture. It revealed a strange painting, rather like Botticelli's *Birth of Venus*, much cruder, but charming all the same. In this painting a young woman was lying in a shell, with her hands in the same position as the Venus. Her hair, wound with flowers, cascaded down to one side. The setting was a stream, or lake, surrounded with trees and flowers. A swan glided by.

'It's beautiful,' Rosemary exclaimed. 'How did she come by it?'

'It seems to have two names, one *The Little Mermaid*, the other *Leda and the Swan*. I knew you'd love it. The woman was visiting Newlyn. It was some time in the fifties, she was leaning over Newlyn Bridge, looking down at the water. A woman stopped to talk to her. It was Mary Jewels. She was invited to the cottage for tea and bought two paintings direct from the artist. The other's called *The Lady of Shallot*, which I've bought. It's being framed.'

'Oh, that's wonderful.'

'And take a look at this. I bought it in a house sale a couple of days ago.'

'Why do you have all the luck?'

'Because I deal in pictures, you only dally with them.'

He offered another slide.

'Wow!'

A large figure of a woman stood in the sea, naked to her waist. Her red skirt swirled around her. She dominated the sea and small Cornish fishing boats. The oil paints used were vibrant blues and reds. It was called *The Cornish Siren*.

'It looks very much like a self-portrait. Well, so Mary thought of herself as the Cornish Siren, did she?. I think she fits very nicely into that category,' Rosemary said.

'You can read into it what you like. I've managed to find a few of her paintings. Others are bound to turn up.'

Rosemary was getting more excited at what else she might come across in her mission. Mary was becoming a real character.

'Tell you what. If we find enough pictures between us, I'll have an exhibition of her work. There'd have to be some for sale, of course. I'll set up a search through other galleries, and on the internet,' Robert said.

'Brilliant. Meanwhile, I have an idea of my own. Thanks Robert.'

The weekend visit to Sylvia was over. It was a great success in spite of the shared sorrow. 'You know I'll always want you here,' she said. 'In fact I've willed this house to Lamorna and Demelza, but don't tell them.'

The twins were reunited in their affection for their aunt, though she felt they were rather subdued, quieter than usual, but they hugged and kissed her to show their love. They left their surfboards in her courtyard and their wetsuits hanging in her garden shed to prove it.

At home in London Rosemary tried to put the whole sorry episode of the twins and their involvement with Sylvia and the two men out of her head. And still she shed tears at the thought of her friend Leah, and her tragic death. She tried desperately to get on with her daily routine. She rang her agent, but there was no way she would tell her of the incident with the girls; that had to be kept a closely guarded secret. She hoped her anxieties wouldn't reveal themselves in her writing, or in her voice on the telephone. Patsy was pretty sharp, and knew when her authors were in trouble. She took a deep breath, determined to sound in control, and confident.

'Patsy. Hello, it's me. We're back from Cornwall. I sent you a couple of chapters. I'm quite pleased with them. I hope you approve.'

. 'I hope I approve, too. I'll have a read through and give you a call. Perhaps you can come into the office and we'll go over them together. I notice from the first few pages that your character is a bit feistier from when she started out. I quite like her. It's a good development; as long as she doesn't change again. Anyway, we'll see. One of my authors changed his character's name twice, and didn't even notice. Another changed countries, would you believe, and another wants to change his own name. I said unless he is writing in a different genre then he should stick to his God-given name.'

'I'm sure you're right.'

'Of course I'm right. Why wouldn't I be right? What's happened to you?'

'Nothing. Don't be so nosey and suspicious Patsy. You know I'm always upset coming home from Cornwall.'

'All right. I forgive you. I look forward to the final chapter. Be in touch.'

Really the woman was impossible. There was never anyone more right than her agent, Patsy. It was so exasperating.

Next day at breakfast, Rosemary was surprised to have another call from Patsy. She rather suspected she was in for a lecture to keep her deadline date in mind; not let the thread of inspiration desert her; carry on writing and keep the momentum going. She was rather taken aback at the cheery and friendly tone of her tormentor.

'I find this Cornwall, you keep writing about, fascinating.' Patsy said, 'I've never actually been there. How about a couple of days at St Ives? A hotel, I think. My treat. Don't fancy shopping and cooking. I'll stay for the weekend, and leave you to write for the rest of the week. You've always said it's the best place to work.'

'Well I ...'

'Come on. Nobody'll miss you at home, and I deserve a break.'

'I was going to say that the twins have already booked their half term holiday at St Ives with their aunt Sylvia. She doesn't know how to say no to the girls.'

'Perhaps she doesn't want to say no. I'm sure your girls are charming.'

'Hhmm. Actually, I was going to put them on the train, and stay in London. But, my sister would have room for all of us, if you fancied staying there. Of course there'd be a bit of washing up, but Sylvia's a keen cook, so no cooking. And you might find that the girls, at close quarters, are not as charming as you might think.'

'This puts a different complexion on the matter. In fact, I'm not the easiest person to live with either. Can I think about it and get back to you?'

'Fine. Meanwhile I'll have to sound out Lewis. It'll mean deserting him again. Bye Patsy.'

'Now what's Patsy got up her sleeve?' said Lewis, entering the kitchen just in time to catch a piece of toast as it flew out of the toaster.

'Self-catering for you again Lewis. Patsy wants me to show her St Ives. I volunteered Sylvia's place. She suggested a hotel for the weekend.'

'As the terrible twins are staying for the week, you might as well stay too. I'm used to taking second place to St Ives. I'll just have to run around the house naked, with my pants on my head, on my own,' Lewis said, laughing.

This sounded so hilariously funny to Rosemary that she burst into laughter. She and Lewis were still laughing as the twins came to say they were leaving for school. They looked askance at one another. Both parents were obviously mad. All their friends parents were crazy too, none of them behaved like sensible, proper adults. They waved languid and sombre goodbyes at the gate, and rolled their eyes as they watched Lewis and Rosemary, curl up with laughter, on the doorstep.

'I don't know what we're laughing about,' Lewis said, trying to straighten his face and not succeeding.

'It's not that funny thinking about you running around the house naked, on your own.'

They both burst into fits again, closing the door on their bewildered children, and staggering back to the kitchen, to roll around the table, clutching their aching stomachs. Rosemary, especially, was hysterical. Her eyes were streaming, and every time she looked at Lewis, she set off laughing until she had to take herself out of his sight. Unfortunately, he followed her into the hallway. Rosemary collapsed helplessly at the turn of the stair, and Lewis sat on the bottom step, trying to take deep breaths to restore his normal self.

'Stop Rose. Stop,' he pleaded.

'Can't stop. Go away,' she hiccupped, and then she was crying; crying with hard painful, rasping sobs.

Suddenly, it was over. Both of them tired out with emotion. They looked at one another, Rosemary from the top of the stairs, Lewis from the bottom. They were exhausted. They knew instantly the cause of their odd behaviour, and were glad the twins had not seen the worst of their seizures.

'Shock,' Lewis said.

'Delayed shock,' Rosemary agreed.

Lewis toiled up the stairs and helped Rosemary to her feet. They made their way to the bedroom, got into bed and held and comforted one another. Rosemary shivered, and tried to stem her tears. Lewis rubbed her back soothingly.

'They're safe,' he said. 'The girls are safe. Close your eyes. I'll stay. Work can wait.'

They heard the telephone ringing downstairs and ignored it. The answer machine kicked into play. It surprised them both when they awoke an hour later, feeling refreshed and cleansed. They showered together, holding, rocking and soothing one another, letting the water flow over them until they felt healed and relaxed.

They dressed and walked out of the house holding hands. They strolled up to Hampstead and had lunch in the secluded garden at Burgh House. They ate silently and did not refer to their extraordinary behaviour. It was something they had to go through. They did not talk about anything, but experienced a quiet and comforting enjoyment in one another's company. Lewis took a cab to work and Rosemary went home. She turned on the answer machine.

'Hi Rosemary. I've thought about Sylvia's place, and knowing my faults, I think I'd better stay in a hotel, but I'd love to come to dinner some time, and meet your sister. I expect you'll probably want to stay with her. Let me know of a hotel by the sea, if possible.'

Rosemary dialled Sylvia's number and was pleased to find her at home. She meant to ask how she was, how the house and job were shaping up, what sort of weather was promised for half term, instead she blurted out.

'Lewis and I have had the most frightening experience. It sounds silly, but we laughed until we cried. It was like a terrible storm. I feel washed out and exhausted. Delayed shock I think.'

'Oh Rose. I know what you mean, but with me it's been different. I think I've cried nearly every day. I hope I'm coming to the end of this session of tears. It's been awful and ...'

'You should have told me. No one could understand your problem better than me.'

'I know Rose. I wish I could have talked to you, but I thought it would remind you of an awful time, and oh dear, I'm starting to cry again.'

'Hush dear. Look, I'm coming to St Ives with the twins, and we'll have a long talk, and get through this together.'

'Thanks Rose. I very much look forward to you coming. I'll put the phone down now and have my little weep. Goodbye.'

10

Patsy deposited Rosemary and the girls at Paddington Station to catch their train to St Ives, while she set off on her lone car journey to the same destination. They would meet that afternoon at Sylvia's house on the Terrace. At the station the girls stocked up with magazines, puzzles, crisps, sweets, drinks, baguettes, chocolate, fruit, nuts and all manner of comfort foods to help them through the five hour journey. They also had their CD players, and games. They spread themselves out on a table for four, littering every space with their baggage.

'You can go and have lunch in the dining car, Mum. You'll enjoy that, and then you won't have to object to everything we're eating,' Lamorna said.

'And you won't have to disapprove of our magazines and music, and all the stuff you don't like us looking at and listening to,' added Demelza.

'Well, thank you ladies,' Rosemary said, and was glad to take advantage of their generous disposal of her company. She would take a long leisurely meal, linger over coffee, read, look out of the window at the delightful countryside, and talk to Lewis on the phone.

All went according to plan, except that she was on the point of ringing Lewis, when she noticed the man sitting opposite her. He took from his briefcase a book titled, *The Innocent Eye*. On the front cover, featuring a bright green sea, and white waves, was an Alfred Wallis painting with a boat climbing a tumultuous wave. Below that were two smaller paintings, one by Bryan Pearce, and the other by Mary Jewels. Rosemary put aside the phone and waited an opportunity to speak to her fellow diner. They had not approached one another to talk during their meal, being absorbed with their own occupations and thoughts. As they simultaneously raised their coffee cups, their eyes met. They smiled. This was the opportunity Rosemary had been waiting for.

'I'm very interested in the book you're reading. I know the work of all the painters and am especially fascinated by the artist, Mary Jewels.'

'I'm glad to hear it,' he said with some surprise. 'I'm writing a review of this new book on primitive and naïve artists. Many people know the two men and their paintings, but few have heard of Mary Jewels.'

'I know. I know. It's so exciting to see her name.'

'I'm Cornish, you see, born in Newlyn. That's how I know about her. Mary too, was born in Newlyn.' He chuckled at his recollections.

'Are you by any chance, Francis Tremain?'

'That's me.'

'I've got the article you wrote about her when she had an exhibition at Newlyn Gallery in 1977, the year she died.'

'Ah, yes,' he said. 'I had a hard time with Mary. She refused to talk to other reporters. If they weren't Cornish they were turned away at the door with insults and a fierce disapproval of what she termed, their 'journalistic turns of phrase.' Even I, as a privileged Cornishman, was often dismissed with my tail between my legs.' He gave a wry smile, remembering his battles with Mary.

'I don't know why I bothered sometimes. She was such a tartar. She told me no other painter influenced her. Her knowledge came from being Cornish, having a direct link with the sea, and boats, and harbours of her native land. She was just a painter, she said, neither impressionist, nor traditionalist, or any of those other isms or ists, that label artists. "Neither am I a naïve painter, which makes me sound like an illiterate peasant, nor a primitive painter, which turns me into a savage," Mary tartly informed me, and then practically threw me out of the cottage.'

'I've heard of some of her mistreatments of people.'

'I remember both Mary and Cordelia standing at the door in a rage, and I was an admirer, intending to write a very sympathetic and praiseworthy article on her work at the Newlyn exhibition.'

'In spite of her faults, you're so lucky to have actually known Mary,' Rosemary enthused. 'I'm intrigued with her paintings and want to choose one for the cover of the novel I'm writing. I like her loose style, and her application of paint. I love her cottages tumbling down hillsides, and her harbour scenes and boats.'

'I agree. I don't own a painting, I'm afraid, so can't help you.'

Rosemary listened, intrigued, by her companion's tales. She learned that Vine Cottage was the communications centre for information on what was happening in the two art colonies of St Ives and Newlyn. The gossip was all about artists. The sisters had talked of conversations they'd had with their visitors, such as Stanhope Forbes, Alfred Munnings, Ben Nicholson, Christopher Wood and Augustus John.

'Memories of a life in Chelsea were also recalled, from what Henry Moore was wearing at a 1920s arts ball to what the Sitwells said to the butler.' Francis said, but he had now forgotten many of the details of these tales. 'Some thought Mary's conversation more interesting than her paintings.'

Francis hurriedly gathered his things together as the train pulled into Truro. Rosemary said a reluctant goodbye, hoping she would meet up with him again, but had failed to ask for his address, or telephone number, or give him hers at St Ives. She came down to earth when the twins, noting her long absence, finally came to find her, and guide her back to their seats.

It was three o'clock when Patsy knocked on the door of the Terrace. Sylvia welcomed her in, and the twins met her for the first time. Rosemary felt strange meeting her agent in the company of her family and, much to her surprise, the twins and Sylvia seemed to hit it off with Patsy right away, while Rosemary's association with her was guarded and defensive. She supposed it was because theirs was a business arrangement.

'I like the Pedn-Olva hotel, with its balconies and spectacular beach. And is that Virginia's lighthouse out there in the bay that I can see from my window?'

The girls were anxious to pass on their knowledge of Virginia Woolf, and promised to show her Talland House. They took her for a tour of Sylvia's house and garden, showing off their wet suits and surfboards, inviting her to join them on Porthminster beach. They would take her to the café for a drink. Patsy said she'd like nothing better. Sylvia and Rosemary were able to prepare dinner and talk without interruption. They sat in the window drinking tea, watching the three making their way across the beach to the café.

'Have you and Lewis managed to tell the whole story of George Tatum to the girls?' Sylvia was anxious to know.

'No. If it has affected us three so much, it must surely trouble the girls. They may have nightmares. They could be emotionally upset. It could affect their school work, or their behaviour. We really don't know how to manage it. It's very cowardly, and remiss of us not to bring the subject up, but they seem to have forgotten about George. In fact, when I think about it, opportunities have arisen, but the girls have somehow steered us away from the matter.'

'If you think it'll help, we could sit down with them some time during the week, but maybe you and Lewis want to tell them.'

'I think Lewis is rather shying away from talking to them about it, or about anything, for that matter, so perhaps I'll take advantage of your offer Sylvia.'

'Just say the word.'

Three hours later the three of them returned for dinner. The girls, with never a word, rushed up to shower and Patsy accepted a glass of wine and sat at the kitchen table, looking rather troubled.

'I'm to warn you that your lovely daughters have something important to tell you. I must say I was shocked when they told me. The little loves have had no one to talk to.'

'Really,' Sylvia said, pausing in stirring something in a saucepan.

'I'm sure I make a point of talking to them every day,' Rosemary said in her defence, ruffled at this virtual strangers' criticism. She had certainly not found her agent someone to confide in, sympathetic, or understanding, but more of a task master. It was odd that her daughters obviously saw her in a different light.

'It's not talk in a way that matters,' Patsy said.

Sylvia continued stirring with her wooden spoon.

'It is not something trivial,' Patsy continued.

Rosemary was irritated, pressing her lips together for fear of saying something she'd regret later. She felt undermined by her daughters' disloyalty to her and the family, and imagined it was another of their punishments for her supposed neglects. However, she must wait to hear what the girls had to say. Sylvia put down her wooden spoon and tasted with a metal one, looking thoughtful, then continued stirring.

Lamorna and Demelza came into the kitchen, their long hair still wet from the shower. Their mother took two towels from a cupboard and draped them round their shoulders, lifting up the dripping hair. Her action said, don't accuse me of disregarding my children.

Sylvia stopped stirring, did a final tasting, and poured

the ingredients from the saucepan into a bowl and put it in the oven. All eyes were quietly watching her activities rather than broach the subject soon to be talked about. Everybody waited.

'Mum,' Demelza blurted out. 'Me and Lamorna have been wanting to tell you something for a long time, but we didn't want to upset you.'

Cold fingers clutched at Rosemary's heart. She looked at each girl in turn. There was only sympathy in their eyes. What could it be if it wasn't her neglect of their needs? She could only wait for Demelza to continue.

'Well, that bloke, George. He murdered your friend Leah.'

'Don't be upset, Mum.' Lamorna said. 'We know he meant a lot to you aunt Sylvia, so we couldn't tell either of you.'

'We read it in the paper a few weeks ago,' Demelza said.

'Oh my darlings.' Rosemary cried, 'you've kept this to yourselves for such a long time, with no help from us. I'm afraid we did know about it. We kept putting off telling you, hoping for an opportunity, because you needed to know. Oh dear!'

'We didn't want to upset you either. We've all had a terrible time.' Sylvia said.

'Well, so much for family unity.' Patsy broke in. 'I'm glad I haven't any children. It must be very hard for you, trying to protect each other all the time, and yet being so misguided; and so stupid, I might add. I'm pouring us all another glass of wine.'

The family were stunned by the revelations, but

Patsy's down-to-earth approach was a relief to them all. They could do with a dressing down they felt. Tears trickled down the faces of both Lamorna and Demelza.

'Sorry Mum. Sorry auntie Sylvia.'

'No. It's entirely our fault. We're the ones to be sorry.'

Rosemary and Sylvia comforted each child and ended up drying their wet hair, and brushing it soothingly, while Patsy got through a bottle of wine on her own.

Dinner was a quiet affair. The twins were exceptionally considerate and washed up while Sylvia made coffee. They were grateful for the chatter, which Patsy kept up at a fast pace. There were no replies needed to her stories about her deviant, distinguished, dilatory, depressed, dysfunctional and downright damned disaster-prone authors. 'They all fit nicely into a 'd' description,' she said. 'Even Rosemary, who is a darling.'

Sylvia escorted a none too sober Patsy to her hotel and to her room, helping her into bed, and turning out the light. 'Come up to the house after breakfast tomorrow. Goodnight.'

'Goodnight lighthouse,' she said, and fell asleep.

The twins were still in a subdued mood the next day and Rosemary knew they needed something to help ward off the effects of revealing their long held secret. She and Sylvia were too closely involved to be positive in rallying their spirits, but Rosemary had the answer. They could go and stay with their godparents, near Penzance. There was a new foal. She printed out the picture she had received by email that morning from Rachel and Desmond with a note saying, 'If you're coming down for half-term, we'd love to have the girls and show them the new foal.' Lamorna and Demelza's faces lit up with joy at the prospect of staying with their Godparents and the horses; they would forget about surfing.

'I think we'd better have no more secrets,' Rosemary said, as she saw the girls on the train at St Ives station.

'No Mum,' they agreed, contrite.

'So I've told the Penhaligans what's been troubling you. They said they know about it, and you can either talk to them, or not, just as you like. They're picking you up from the train at Penzance.'

Later that morning, with Patsy and Sylvia, Rosemary was fortunate to meet the Cornish writer at the St Ives Society of Artists private view, making notes for his review of the exhibition. Rosemary touched his arm.

'Hello,' she said, 'Remember me. The Mary Jewels fan?' He turned and gave her a friendly kiss on the cheek. This seemed to be the general practice at private views. 'Tell me,' Rosemary whispered, 'Is there anyone as good as Mary Jewels here?'

'No. But don't tell anyone I said so.'

It was a useful meeting, and Francis introduced her to other people who had known Mary, while he continued his note taking. On talking to a woman who had worked at the Newlyn Art Gallery, Rosemary discovered that at Mary's exhibition in the year of her death, Cordelia had brought Mary along and left her sitting downstairs, surrounded by her paintings, while she went off shopping.

'I like the paintings,' Mary told the curator, 'They are so colourful,' obviously forgetting they were her own, though a few days previously at the private view, she had accepted congratulations on her work, had chatted to other artists, discussed the work with friends, and given advice to people on which paintings to buy.

Mary, at times bright and sparkling, was becoming more forgetful and eccentric. That morning, after touring the gallery, admiring the work, and talking volubly, her mood changed. She became distant and vacant, not knowing where she was. The curator brought her a cup of tea, and led her to a chair. She sat silently waiting for her sister's return. From her bag she took out a bright pair of yellow gloves and drew them on. When one of the gallery staff went to assist Mary up the stairs, it was discovered that the gloves were plastic washing-up gloves.

During the afternoon, Patsy drove to Newlyn. Rosemary wished to renew her acquaintance with Vine Cottage, and take photos from the road outside. Then, judging there was no one occupying the house, they walked around the garden, and peered in through the windows. All this told them nothing more about Mary. There was no residue of Mary and Cordelia clinging to the place, in spite of the family's long presence as occupants for over one hundred years. 'Should there be?' the practical Patsy queried.

Rosemary explained that artists had congregated here, meetings had happened, tea had been taken, Augustus John had visited; Ben Nicholson had driven over from St Ives on his motor cycle; Alfred Munnings had arrived on his horse and taught Mrs Tregurtha to ride; Frank Dobson had lived here with Cordelia. Stanhope Forbes had sat in their garden painting a picture for the Royal Academy, and oh, there were so many others. This cottage had retained none of that magic. The visit was a disappointment.

'You have a romantic nature, Rosemary; a sentimental attachment to places. I don't see or feel anything about the cottage. It is merely a charming home.'

In the centre of Newlyn they came upon the war memorial. They walked around it, reading the names and there was the name of Mary's husband, A.O Jewels. Rosemary had forgotten about it. The nephew, Peter, hadn't thought to remember it either. Here was a young man, who had probably never left his village, except to experience the empty sea in a boat. He had gone abroad for the first time to a war in a strange land, and never returned.

'Now this is something genuinely sad,' Patsy said. 'The loss of a young man from the village of Newlyn, torn away from his wife, deprived of a family, and whose life amounted to nothing in its brief years.'

They returned to the car and continued out of the village to Paul, just outside Newlyn, and found the Tregurtha family grave in the churchyard. 'The family all lived to a ripe old age,' observed Patsy, reading the inscription on the tombstone. 'Mary died at the age of ninety-one and is buried with her ninety-six year old mother, followed by Cordelia in 1989 at the age of one-hundred-and-two.'

'Neither of the sisters, had children,' Rosemary said. 'They ended their lives in a home in a small village near here called Madron, where their fellow Cornishman, and artist, Alfred Wallis, had died in 1942. In his time it was still known as the Poorhouse. They would have hated the idea of dying in the same place as Wallis, 'the illiterate peasant,' as they called him.'

'What happened to Mary's paintings?'

'After Mary died, Cordelia, so I am reliably told, sold most of Mary's work to a London dealer, thirty or forty paintings, as well as drawings and sculpture by her husband Frank Dobson. She was advised by the Newlyn Gallery not to sell them, but ignored the advice and did it anyway.'

Rosemary continued the story as told by Mrs Fox, who witnessed many scenes of Cordelia selling pictures. Even though Mary was dead, if someone came to buy paintings, Cordelia would put her finger to her lips, as though preventing Mary from knowing she was selling her work. In the parlour she would pull out the canvases one by one, naming the title and explaining the circumstance of the picture. 'We were picking bluebells in Lamorna woods, and I told Mary to capture the scene. There's the stream running through the valley, and there's me picking bluebells. Here's Mousehole harbour. We were often there because Mary liked painting the cottages. And here's Newlyn, the boats and harbour. Of course we knew the sea, we had grown up by the harbour.'

With the weekend over, Patsy, said a fond farewell to Rosemary, advising her to keep on with her writing, and perhaps forget about Mary Jewels for the time being, interesting though Patsy was sure she was. She patted her hand, reminded her she had a week of writing in front of her, told her to get back to normal life, and drove off. But normal had again changed perspective. There was the revelation by Lamorna and Demelza, and their weeks of agony in trying to keep the secret of the murder to themselves, and there was the distress of Sylvia's memories. Rosemary's head was full of intruding thoughts.

It was a struggle; not only to search her imagination and experience for the story line, but to push Mary Jewels aside. Memories of the woman at Talland House had resembled Mary so much that her face haunted her. She would have told her of the likeness, but it seemed too weird and odd. The whole thing had been strange, meeting her while she was trespassing at Talland House and being invited in from the rain; meeting a second time, and still not knowing her name.

The memories disturbed her so much that she was forced to stop writing, couldn't get her head round character and plot or fuse them together. She went to St Ives library and found the catalogue for the show at the Tate in 1985. There was the painting, *Cornubia* painted probably in the mid fifties, and exhibited at the Newlyn Gallery in 1977. This was the one. This was the picture she would like to illustrate the cover of her book. She would ring Patsy and tell her.

Cornubia was another name for Cornwall and

according to Rosemary's interpretation of the painting it represented the fertility of the county. There couldn't be anything better. Now she would have to find out where the painting was, and get permission for its reproduction.

On an impulse, she tracked down a former assistant curator of the Tate in London, whom she had met at the opening of Tate St Ives in 1993. He had been largely responsible for organising the Tate exhibition in 1985. She rang his home number, not bothered whether he remembered her or not, but she found him willing to talk about the Cornish exhibition in London.

'I want to know why you included Mary Jewels in that show. Why feature a woman artist who has been overlooked, and almost forgotten?'

He answered her query with his opinion. 'I think she is a very underestimated painter. In researching for that exhibition, which was based on the west country artists, I threw my net very wide and caught Mary.'

'I'm simply amazed. Do you know where the painting *Cornubia* is now? Have you any idea who owns it?'

'Afraid not. I'm well out of art circles now, but I do know who encouraged Mary to start painting. The artist Cedric Morris, from whom I got first hand information, was living in Vine Cottage at that time with Mrs Tregurtha and her daughters. He put a paint brush into Mary's hand and told her to produce a painting by tea-time. This she did. It was successful, and she thought of herself as an artist from that time on.'

Backing up the faith in Mary Jewels as a painter was another friend from Tate Gallery circles who said he knew Mary in the fifties, and encouraged her by supplying her with canvas and paints. He thought her work showed a gentle humour and was delightful in its freshness and charm. It captured the Cornwall that was felt rather than seen. She was truly Cornish. 'A genuine Celt, with Celtic vision,' he affirmed. And still, Rosemary mused; she hasn't really been written about. She was not part of art history.

She thought of another, more important woman painter, Vanessa Bell, sister of Virginia Woolf. That woman was a modernist, innovative, painter in the early twentieth century, when much of Britain's art was stuck in the Victorian era. She had exhibited in London with the Post Impressionists in 1910 and 1912 with Matisse, Cezanne, Van Gogh, Picasso and Gaugaun. When the public came to view, they were either shocked, or enraged, by paintings that were radical and new to their eyes.

Why did so many women artists disappear? Why were they ignored by the art world so that eventually, apart from a few scattered paintings, they no longer existed? Certainly they were sparsely represented in national collections.

It was one of those blustery days, with the wind whipping round corners, catching you unawares; an unsettling day of racing clouds, spattering rain and sudden bright sunlight. The sea was wind driven and curling white horses foamed liberally over the ocean.

263

From a window on the Terrace Rosemary looked over to Hayle where the sun seemed to have settled permanently on the beach and over the sand hills. She remembered how they used to set up camps in a cleft of the dunes when the wind blew too strongly, or the sun beat down too harshly. The children had loved that lunar landscape and the wooden chalet they rented with a direct view to the sea and St Ives.

On an impulse, Rosemary decided to visit the area and walk on the deserted beach. There was an easterly wind blowing and it would be sheltered on that side, while the harbour in St Ives would be taking a battering.

Sylvia had taken the train over to Penzance to see Lamorna and Demelza ride their horses and look at the new foal. It was developing fast and seemed to grow every day. The girls were engrossed in writing lists of names but hadn't decided yet what they would call it.

'We're having a great time mum, so we'll leave you in peace to write,' they said.

Rosemary wished they could all have gone to the Towans, and spent the day there, but she had to be content that the girls were happy with their god parents. She got into Sylvia's car and drove through showers and sunshine. The sandy paths she remembered were still there, the maram grass clung to hillocks, helping to stabilise the shifting sands. Wild flowers grew undisturbed. She slipped and slithered down great mountains of loose sand to the beach, where she sat and emptied her shoes and walked barefoot along the foaming tide's edge.

Coming to the community house, where games, a big

screen for watching sports, and meals and snacks could be obtained, she clambered up from the shore and sat on the benches overlooking the beach, enjoying a cold drink. She and the girls would be going home shortly. They had been coming to the St Ives area for ever, Rosemary thought, and hadn't managed to buy themselves a house. It was wonderful to have Sylvia to stay with, but it still wasn't the same as their own little place, with their own key.

'Hello,' a voice said at her side. 'Do you mind if I sit here?'

Rosemary turned, and greeted a woman standing beside her. 'Hello. I'm sorry,' she said, 'I was so occupied with thinking about having a house here, that I was quite lost.'

'Having a chalet here has been lovely for my family. The boys are growing up and wanting to travel abroad, so my husband and I are selling our chalet. I've come to say goodbye. I'm a bit sad about it and wanted to talk to someone. I thought as you were on your own, you wouldn't mind.'

'No certainly,' Rosemary said, shuffling up on the bench to make room. 'You have a chalet here, on the Towans?'

'It's one of the original 1930s wooden chalets, full of light and sea views, and yet cosily tucked into the sand dunes. The evening sunsets are magical here. We shall certainly miss it.'

'I'm sure you will. I never considered a chalet,' Rosemary said, thoughtfully, 'but it's such a great idea, and affordable, compared to a house.'

'Would you like to see ours? I'd love to show it to you. We're selling it fully furnished.'

Rosemary followed the woman up and down the lumpy terrain, along sandy paths until they came upon a blue painted chalet tucked into a hollow, yet with a full view of the sea over to St Ives. There was a veranda, with a fence picked out in white. Two large windows and a half-glazed door were curtained in blue and white striped material. Inside, the décor was blue and white, with white wood panelling in every room, and blue painted wooden floors.

'It sleeps four comfortably. A double and two singles.'

'It's charming. Really charming,' Rosemary enthused, noting the fairly well equipped kitchen, the shower room, and the handmade patchwork quilts in the two bedrooms. The living room was adequate, with a good sized sofa, a wood burning stove, a window seat, and extra large cushions for sitting on.

'Well, I hope someone will buy it with a couple of children, and get as much enjoyment from it as we did. I'll make a cup of tea. We can sit out on the veranda. It'll be my last day and I'd like to share it with you, if you have the time.'

'I'd be delighted,' Rosemary assured her. 'And please do tell me something more about the chalet, and how you came to own it.'

When Rosemary arrived back in St Ives she rang Lewis. However, he didn't pick up the phone, although by now he should have been home and cooking his evening meal. Where was he? Rosemary worried. Was he stuck in traffic? Suppose he'd had an accident and was in hospital. She'd forgotten to take her mobile, and been out all day. The answer machine in the hall was flashing. 'Hello Rosemary. Rachel has invited me to stay for supper, so I'll be back later. Bye.' It was Sylvia. Now she would have to spend the evening alone. As Rosemary put down the phone the front door opened, and there was Lewis.

'Darling, it's only me,' he cried, seeing her worried face. 'I thought I'd surprise you and come for a long weekend and travel back with you and the girls.'

'Perfect. Absolutely perfect, darling. I love you. I'm so excited. It couldn't be better.'

'Is it me that's perfect, or something else that's perfect?'

'Lewis. We've bought a chalet on Riviera Towans. It's perfect.'

Rosemary and Lewis set out at once for Hayle, Rosemary explaining how she'd met this woman, now her friend, whose chalet had just come on the market. 'When you see it, you'll understand, Lewis. You won't be able to resist it.'

When they arrived at the chalet, the woman had gone, the site office had closed so the key wasn't available. But every room to the chalet had a window and Lewis was able to peer through and see it for its attractive self, and through Rosemary's charmed eyes. She watched anxiously for his reaction.

'Rosemary,' he said, picking her up and twirling her

around on the veranda. 'It's perfect. Just perfect.'

The warm evening sun had settled to a golden glow. The wind had dropped and Rosemary walked on the Towan's beach holding hands with Lewis.

'Maybe we'll come to our chalet at October half term,' Lewis said.

'Even Christmas,' Rosemary said. 'But for now, I agree with Virginia Woolf who thought that all the months of the year were mere experiments, for this one perfect month, September.'

On the train journey home to London Lewis had the pleasure of telling the twins about owning a chalet, describing the furnishings and colours, drawing pictures of it, making plans on how they could decorate their rooms, and answering their myriad questions about how soon they could go and stay.

'We'll hoist up a flag, so Sylvia can look through her binoculars and see whether we're at home. Then she can come over for tea,' the twins decided.

While Lewis and the twins made plans, Rosemary reached into her luggage for the book on Frank Dobson. He had sculpted a bust of the Russian ballerina Lydia Lopokova in 1923. According to the critics he had caught the grace, elegance, and balletic nature of the dance in a study of her hands.

She turned to the back pages and the illustrations. There, to her delight was a photograph of Lydia, standing next to the bust, in the same attitude as the sculpture. She further learnt that a painting of Lydia by Vanessa Bell, was shown along with the bust at a London Group exhibition. It was certain that Mary and Cordelia attended to see Frank Dobson's sculpture on display. It was very likely they met Virginia and Vanessa at that show. Why hadn't Virginia made some cryptic remark about Mary and Cordelia?

Rosemary's thoughts ran away with her. She wondered at the childhood lives of Virginia and Vanessa Stephen at Talland House. For twelve long summers they had looked out over the bay of pure blue green sea to Godrevy lighthouse. Virginia wrote and practised her writing, and years later captured those days, that house, and her parents in her novel *To The Lighthouse*.

Vanessa had been inspired and struggled with the difficulties of paint and canvas, and the study of works of art, and both girls had achieved their aims. Vanessa had written, "I don't remember a time when Virginia did not mean to be a writer and I a painter."

It was intriguing, Rosemary thought, to wonder how the legendary sophisticated beauty of the Vanessa and Virginia Stephen girls would compare with the vibrant beauty of Mary and Cordelia Tregurtha. At some point, their lives touched through knowing the ballerina, Lydia Lopokova.

The two sets of sisters were so different; the Stephen sisters fey, delicate of feature, and tranquil; the Tregurtha sisters, dark, prominent of feature, and fiery. Surely the love of Cornwall would have united them. Did they like each other? In all Virginia's copious journals and diaries, there was no mention of Mary or

Cordelia. She hoped further research would reveal something more.

Through the months when Lydia was in the studio in Chelsea, sitting to Dobson, Mary and Cordelia became friends with the dancer. They found Lydia enchanting. She danced for them in return for their entertaining stories of life in Newlyn and their tales of Cornwall.

Vanessa Bell found Lydia's high spirits irritating, and Virginia Woolf ridiculed her for her naivety and wondered whether she ever had a serious thought in her head. Lydia was light-hearted and carefree. She danced at parties, which must seriously have eclipsed the contribution the Stephen sisters could make.

Although the marriage of Cordelia and Frank Dobson was happy, fate intervened in the form of one of Frank's students, who replaced Cordelia in his affections. Lydia, a friend to both husband and wife, found her loyalties divided and the friendship too difficult to maintain. It ceased to be troublesome when Cordelia, suffering this living bereavement, returned to Newlyn to live quietly at Vine Cottage with her mother and sister.

For a couple of years Cordelia led a reclusive life, but gradually her confidence and courage returned. It was then she took over managing Mary's paintings and her exhibitions. She presided over the tea ceremony where negotiations and prices were determined. She had a tale to tell of each of Mary's pictures, legendary or factual.

On a bright afternoon, in London, with no particular thoughts in her head, Rosemary was carried swiftly along with the idea that had just formed in her head. She must contact Patsy, and forestall any notions she might have of any future books, although with this thought came a worry. She had sent off her final chapters of the novel a week ago, and had received no phone call from her with enthusiasm, or disappointment.

As she reached the house the telephone was ringing.

'Hello,' she said as she picked it up. 'I know it's you Patsy.'

'Yes. I've been meaning to ring, but these last chapters ...'

'Something wrong?'

'I couldn't believe my eyes. I knew you were working well, but these final chapters are inspired. I had to read them twice in case it was the wine talking to me. You've matured over these last few months. It shows in your writing. I think it's a very good book. Congratulations.'

'Does that mean, I really am a novelist?'

'Certainly. And the publishers like the photos of the paintings you sent. They agree with your choice and think the Mary Jewels picture, *Cornubia* would be excellent for the cover of the book; the back view of the woman, head turned slightly, with either side of the figure the cottages and scenes of Cornwall. Excellent.'

'Good. I'm glad everyone approves of *Cornubia*. All I have to do is find the painting. It seems it was sold and bought by a private buyer after the Tate show. And do you approve of Mary Jewels?'

'Of course. I have some personal knowledge of her

and Cornwall now. Why?' Patsy asked suspiciously.

'Because that's my next book.'

'But the publisher wants to sign you up for another three novels. I've been urgently negotiating an advance. It's a most attractive offer.'

'I need refreshing, and I'll be ready to make a decision on whether I want to sign up for even one novel, when I've discovered all there is to Mary and completed a book on her. I shall dig a little deeper, find some more paintings, and have a book launch and exhibition in a St Ives gallery.'

'Well, I was going to argue with you, but it seems pointless. You've obviously made up your mind. Send me the first chapter as soon as you can, so I can gauge the style and tone and find the right publisher.'

'Brilliant. I'm coming to see you tomorrow, so I'll bring it with me.'

'You're probably half way to finishing the book. I might have known.'

That evening, on opening her email, she found a message from Leah's family. It jumped up and shocked her. The twins noticed her flinch and wondered if her imagination was turning her funny again.

'Dear Rosemary,' it read. 'We found an unsent email to you on Leah's computer, saying she had a surprise for you. We also read Leah's notes on her desk and it seems she intended giving you a painting. We think it must be the surprise she planned for you. We very much want to carry out her wishes and will be despatching a large picture to your London home. Please expect it in a day or two. We, that's the family, are grateful for the beautiful reading of Leah's favourite poem in the church. We are pleased she had such a lovely friend in you. With many thanks. Leah's family.'

'How extraordinary,' Rosemary said aloud.

'Oh no,' said the twins in unison, rolling their eyes. 'What now, Mum?' but they were smiling, indulgently.

Rosemary couldn't possibly explain the full extent of the unsent email, which would take them back to the day of the murder, but fobbed off the girls by saying a friend was sending her a painting for the cover of her novel. Next morning the large parcel arrived. She left it standing, still wrapped, in the hall.

The twins rushed past her on their way to school, kissing and hugging her briefly. In their happier state, they were much more tolerant of her, less critical, more affectionate, now they were free of their secret burden, which they had tried to conceal from her. Rosemary, likewise, found herself more considerate of their needs, and less selfishly inclined to go her own way without a family consultation.

Lewis, in his hurry, entirely missed seeing the parcel, but kissed Rosemary lingeringly. She waved the three of them on their way, then she knelt and carefully removed the packaging. The head of the painting appeared first, the head turned to show a profile, a scarf flying out in the wind, then a hand and arm were revealed, and Cornubia's bare back, and Cornish cottages ranging down the side of the figure. In the corner of the painting was the signature, Mary Jewels.

'Oh bless your heart Leah,' Rosemary sighed. She knew that the inscription in her book on Mary Jewels would read, 'Dedicated to the memory of my dear friend Leah.'

Now Rosemary was free from writing the novel, and was officially engaged in research, she was eagerly in pursuit of further information on Mary Jewels, but knew she would be forever in the shadow that had spoilt their summer. However, next summer there would be holidays in their chalet, and in Sylvia's house in St Ives.

Sylvia had her job at the library to contend with, and her new house. She also knew that over her lifetime, she would be forever in debt to the twins, escaping her conscience by granting them all their particular whims and fancies; the ever biddable aunt; the twins benefactor.

Rosemary, determined to pursue her course. There were a few ends to tie up and add to her files, before she began gathering her notes and writing the book on Mary Jewels. She contacted Sven Berlin, now in his eighties, to follow up the article he'd written about Mary. She'd first met this wild, handsome, outcast St Ives artist at a retrospective show in the town ten years ago.

The exhibition of his paintings and sculpture was held at Will's Lane Gallery. Many years earlier he and his wife had left St Ives, driving a horse-drawn gypsy wagon. He was humiliated and disgusted because the council was erecting a public toilet next to his sculpture studio at Porthgwidden beach. The indignity was too much to bear.

The studio was a one-up one-down unprepossessing building, with few windows, and Sven had used the outdoor space as much as possible to carve and shape his sculptures. His strength was legendary. He was a figure to be admired, as he wielded a hammer, or chisel to shape stone. Downstairs the room was littered with tools and shavings, and half grown shapes. Upstairs the room was often crammed with artists come for a drinking party, which then spilled down to the beach frequently breaking out into arguments on some question of art.

Sven Berlin, like Augustus John, was a supporter of the gypsy way of life, and he too, was enchanted by Mary's Romany appearance. On leaving St Ives he chose to live in a caravan in the New Forest, but always remembered the wild horse rides across the Penwith moors with his beautiful wife, Juanita, and the stir they caused in the town as they rode into St Ives. The couple galloped across Porthmeor beach, through the cobbled lanes to the harbour beach, where they tied their horses to the railings opposite the Sloop Inn and made a rowdy entrance to the bar. Sven was a magnificent man, with a lion's head of hair, and a wonderful physique; a romantic, tempestuous, but tender man.

It was Sven who answered the telephone to Rosemary's call. After the preliminaries of his long remembered bitterness about St Ives and the philistine councillors who had turned him out of his studio, and Rosemary's sympathetic response, he softened his tone and asked how he could help.

'How well did you know Mary Jewels?' Rosemary asked.

'Mary? Loved her. I used to visit her in Newlyn. Quite often, actually.' He chuckled, as though remembering such times. 'I had one or two of Mary's paintings at one time, but had to sell them to meet expenses. One was called, *Cornish Cottages*, Newlyn. Can't recall the other one. I got on well with Mary. Yes, very well with Mary.'

'Not everybody did. You must have been a special friend.'

'Pretty special, I should think.' Rosemary heard the smile in his voice.

'What about Cordelia?'

'Well.' He paused. 'Let's just say, she wasn't all that keen on me.'

'Ah! But as you were a special friend of Mary's. Can I ask you an important question? It's something I've been trying to find the answer to for some time.'

'Ask away. If I know the answer, you shall know it too.'

Rosemary came straight to the point, 'Tell me Sven. Do you think Mary Jewels escaped the clutches of Augustus John?'

He understood precisely what she meant, and without pause, he immediately came up with a firm answer, 'No.' There was a long silence. 'There were not many women who did.' There was another prolonged silence, then Sven said, 'Both sisters thought the world of Augustus John.'

'Intriguing,' Rosemary said.

At first, this seemed to Rosemary to be the last word on the subject, and then she began to think again. These two handsome men were a kind of brotherhood of attractive predatory males, who admired the dark gypsy type of woman, and who probably shared each other's secrets. Sven Berlin had told her that it was Augustus John who had taken him to meet Mary Jewels.

Was there another story here?